Anshaw, Carol.

Seven moves.

$21.95   WITHDRAWN

SEVEN

MOVES

S E V E N
M O V E S

CAROL ANSHAW

HOUGHTON MIFFLIN COMPANY

BOSTON   NEW YORK

1996

For information about permission to reproduce selections from this
book, write to Permissions, Houghton Mifflin Company,
215 Park Avenue South, New York, New York 10003.

For information about this and other Houghton Mifflin trade and
reference books and multimedia products, visit The Bookstore at
Houghton Mifflin on the World Wide Web at
http://www.hmco.com/trade/.

Library of Congress Cataloging-in-Publication Data

Anshaw, Carol.
Seven moves / Carol Anshaw
p. cm.
ISBN 0-395-69131-1
1. Women psychiatrists — Illinois — Chicago — Fiction.
2. Lesbians — Illinois — Chicago — Fiction.   3. Women —
Psychology — Fiction.   4. Missing persons — Fiction.   I. Title.
PS3551.N7147S4   1996   813'54 — dc20   96-16134   CIP

Book design by Anne Chalmers; type is Electra.

Printed in the United States of America

QUM   10 9 8 7 6 5 4 3 2 1

FOR MARY KAY KAMMER

ACKNOWLEDGMENTS

I'd like to thank:

Janet Silver, my editor; Jayne Yaffe, my manuscript editor; and Jean Naggar, my agent

Mary Beth Shaffer, for helping me think like a therapist

Mohammed Jebbour, for illuminating Morocco for me

Lyn DelliQuadri, Denise DeClue, Stacey D'Erasmo, Diane Lefer, Sydney Lewis, Peggy McNally, Barbara Mulvanny, Sharon Sheehe Stark, Eliot Wald, and, most especially, Jessie Ewing for their support, suggestions, and criticism

My parents for their generosity

The National Endowment for the Arts, the Illinois Arts Council, the Ragdale Foundation, and the Ucross Foundation for — variously — time, space, and financial support during the writing of this book.

Love has no mind.

It can't spell unkind.

It's never seen a heart shaped like a valentine.

— John Prine

SEVEN

MOVES

CHRISTINE SNOW tries to ignore the simmering pain at the small of her back. A little commercial flashes up in her imagination. Dancing ibuprofen in top hats. She won't be able to get relief until the end of the session, though. For the moment, her own minor sacral troubles will have to yield to the more significant suffering of her client, Rosario Delacruz, who, at the moment, is experiencing a difficulty common to the situation: bringing matters essentially nocturnal into the less accommodating light of day. Chris leans forward in her chair, trying simultaneously to help and to stretch.

"You always describe him as either Satan or Svengali," Chris says. "Maybe both images come out of the same fascination. Fascination has a way of obscuring things. What I'm saying is, if you could get a little distance, you might not find him all that interesting or original, only a thug. Like other thugs."

Rosario lowers her lids, a fan of spidery, mascaraed lashes, and nods deeply, as though she is taking this under advisement. At the same time, soundless tears begin making their way through her eye makeup, washing muddily down the steep Incan planes of her face.

Chris doesn't know whether the crying means she's getting her point across, or not. She is often completely over her head in the drama of Rosario, who is Mexican-American. This hyphen is the rope in a tug of war between the bold self she has created and the subjugated one designed for her in the cultures of her birth — mainly Mexican, but with a Haitian element on her mother's side, a Peruvian branch in her father's tree.

Professionally Rosario is the most well assembled person of Chris's acquaintance. She took a business degree and, with money she made waitressing during semester breaks, living lean, investing her tips, she bought a piece of a trendy restaurant on Armitage. Her personal life, on the other hand, is a disaster. She is attracted to cold, punitive men. The latest of these is the IRS auditor who came to look over the restaurant's books. Tony has a twitch high in his left cheek and suffers from TMJ. He wears an appliance in his mouth at night to prevent him from grinding his teeth to nubs as he sleeps.

The relationship Rosario has with him, as she tells it, is a rush from high to low, then back up again. The highs are mostly about the sex, which is, according to her, sensually religious, approaching on its knees the meaning of life. "I weep the tears of angels," she has told Chris, then adds, dabbing at the air with her Kleenex, "You wouldn't understand." In Rosario's belief structure, gringas do it with the lights off, shower after, leave their lovers' backs unmarked.

It is Tony who does most of the marking, though. A few weeks ago, Rosario came in with fingerprints on her forearm, mottled in blackish purples and deep maroons. Today the left side of her face has the color and stretched shine of a plum buffed with a sleeve, ready to eat. From this epicenter, the color tints down to pointillist magenta, made up of thousands of burst capillaries.

"It is a terrible shame I feel," she whispers. "As if I am the one who did this to myself."

In spite of the wash of nausea flooding her, Chris has trouble pulling her gaze off Rosario. People think that shrinks are dispassionate, detached from the misery of their clients, concerned but in a measured way that also allows them to surreptitiously check their watches, hum a catchy tune inside their heads. But for Chris the problem is of an opposite cast. She has great difficulty putting aside the concerns of her clients even between sessions, placing their cares on some recessed shelf of benign neglect, in some cool, damp keeper bin. From having gone through troubled periods of her own, she is only too aware that for the sufferer, the days between therapy sessions are often just so much treading away from the last one, toward the shore of the next, with a great fear of sinking in between.

And so this between time is occupied for her, too, with strategies for prodding or guiding or simply allowing the client to move forward, trying to figure out whether a tentative step is in order, or an abandoned leap. And beyond this direct, professional analysis, their continuing dramas invade her thoughts, sometimes her dreams, and often her supposedly free hours with their messages on her voice mail, tearful or tight, nagging at her until she can return the calls, get things at least a little calmed down or smoothed out, then return to wherever she left off in making a risotto, running a bath, spending time with friends, or with her lover.

In the middle of some mildly interesting social conversation at, say, a gallery opening, holding a plastic cup of cheap chardonnay and a breadstick wrapped in prosciutto — some situation in the supposed smack middle of a hip urban good life — she will be missing a large portion of the experience for worrying that, say, Jocelyn Egan will not make it through her job interview without a panic attack. In this same way Chris is terribly vague on the plot lines of many movies.

This relentless distraction, she hopes, is worth something. She knows she does worlds of good for a few patients, is at least adequate to the task of most. Inevitably, she fails entirely with some, and this always chafes inside her like heartburn. Often her greatest challenge is fighting the impulse to be expedient, to go for the immediate over the long haul, giving in to a longing to fluff up these anxious sufferers, straighten their ties, check their breath. Get them focused and peppy enough to enjoy the here and now of their lives, which have been rushing by while they sit on their own sidelines, unable to participate fully. Rosario, for instance — wasting her prime on guys who bleed off the confidence she has built up within herself.

A particular problem in counseling Rosario, aside from the cultural moat between the two of them, is that Chris's strategies meet with tricky resistance as Rosario finds an infinite number of ways to take charge of her own therapy. A couple of weeks earlier, she pulled from her satchel a large Ziploc. "I went down to see the aunts." Meaning a pair of ancient Haitian crones who live on the South Side and freely dispense both advice and voodoo. Whenever Rosario mentions them, her voice takes on a haunted tone, her r's begin to roll like greased bearings. "They know places"— she pauses for a small wave of the hand to indicate what little trepidation this information gives those who travel with confidence in the shadow world — "where you can buy curses."

Even though Chris considers this mumbo jumbo, she did look at the plastic bag and its colorful contents. (Who could not?) Some streaked stones; some small vials of liquid, one of which looked unsettlingly sanguine; a clump of feathers; what she was pretty sure was a rat's tail — or, as it formed itself in her mind, tail of rat. When she raised a hand against closer inspection, Rosario tucked the bag back into her purse. She accepts that Chris has limits on this stuff, and it doesn't seem to diminish her in Rosario's estimation. She has referred two friends, one of whom then referred another, and now Chris has a small client base of Hispanic straight women, who mostly have a style she thinks of as killer femme — heterosexual panthers with big, dangerous hair, crimson stiletto nails, ankle bracelets — crossing paths in her waiting room with all the lesbians and gay guys. She tries to juggle her schedule to minimize awkward intersections, one contingent freaking out the other.

Chris still isn't entirely sure she is up to counseling these women, who, in spite of their troubles, she mostly envies. She would like to have a piece of their attitude, their plucked eyebrows always ready to arch in contempt, of whatever. She feels neurasthenic next to their breathless anticipation, their fountainlike laughter, their copious, free-flowing tears. Chris can't remember the last time she cried, other than at events outside the periphery of herself: reunions of aged Soviet sisters on *Oprah!*, the crowning of the deaf Miss America.

Sometimes Chris isn't sure that what's happening between her and Rosario is even really therapy. Perhaps she uses Rosario to feel freer, hipper, more colorful by association, while Rosario uses Chris as a totem of status and class. She will come here on Tuesday afternoons to relate her problems in a modern, conventional — if dramatic — way in this atmosphere of fresh, waiting Kleenex and gallery posters and industrial carpet, the late-afternoon sun sifting through the blinds, putting down soft bars of light across the room. Then, when she really needs to resolve a problem, she will go at midnight to a *curandera* who will roll an egg over her naked body, then crack it open into water and read the message it offers.

Chris and Rosario will often arrive at quite disparate solutions to a particular problem. Now, for instance. Chris is thinking that Rosario's next step is simply to get out of harm's way, clear the air of this Tony creep, open some space for an unobstructed look around. But when Rosario locks eyes with Chris, as though the two of them are in perfect accord, what she says is, "You're right, of course. I should have the courage to kill him."

Chris's back twinges with a small spasm.

"Powder, I think." Rosario is rolling now, her voice gone to gravel. "You know. Tap a little into the drink." She sighs richly.

Chris doesn't think she is serious (she has sworn vengeance on others), but their fifty minutes are nearly up, there's no time to let this line spin itself out. "Tell me you're not going to do anything in the next few days. Don't make me an insomniac. We need to talk further about this." She tries to get another eyelock, but Rosario just arches a penciled brow, ducks into the large leather bag that always accompanies her, and brings out a checkbook.

"I owe you for last time and this." She rips out and hands Chris a check printed with tumbling kittens and balls of yarn. "Don't get uptight. I'll think about what you said. About maybe waiting."

After Rosario has gone, Chris can take the ibuprofen and stretch out on the floor while she waits for Jerome Pratt, who initially came to her because of his need to wash his hands quite a bit and check to make sure the burners and water faucets in his apartment were off and the windows were either all open to the same height, or closed. He also needed to check these things a number of times, and certain numbers were not okay. Three, for instance. He would have to check either two or four times. Now he's on medication that subdues these exhausting rounds of activity. Plus he has found a lover, his first in a few years. He is on his way out of Chris's care.

Today he tells her about having sex with the new boyfriend, Keith, in one of the carrels along a forgotten hallway of the library at North-western, where Jerome works. He is quite graphic. There are recipro-cal blow jobs involved and near discovery by a custodian. The story (she can't tell if it really happened or is just a fantasy) and the deadpan way Jerome relates it become arousing. She would like to ask for more details about the blow jobs, instead must stick to busi-ness. She shifts in her chair and clears her throat. "So. Did you experience any urgency to wash your hands afterward?"

She double-checks her schedule: no more appointments. Tuesdays and Wednesdays she doesn't have night clients. She spends an hour or so trying to make a dent in her paperwork — filling in all the blanks as required by the state, the insurance companies, her billing service. Filling legal pads with notes on clients to help her keep track of details and progress, her own hopes for their direction and velocity. Her desk, buried under files and pads and professional journals, correspondence and forms, looks like the workplace of a physicist trying to cull order out of a chaotic universe, and perhaps in this way, the pursuits of physicists and therapists are analogous.

When she's done all she can stand for the day, she checks her voice mail, which is blessedly clear. She is free to go.

Instead, she drops backward onto the sofa, falling into the impres-sion left by Jerome's bony butt. Floating back up to the regular world, she suffers the bends that come with being in this room for too many consecutive hours. She would like someone to come in with a bottle of warmed patchouli massage oil. Someone hot and imperious. Sigourney Weaver in her *Alien* fatigues would be nice. Sigourney Weaver working as a combination masseuse and career counselor. She could oil Chris up while she talked her into some new line of work. Or, she might say, playfully slapping a greased buttock, "Go ahead, keep on doing this, honey, but hey, lighten up about it a little."

But of course this is precisely what Chris can't do. She has entered into all these private compacts, spent so many hours in this confes-sional. She is the repository of her clients' distressing nightmares, witness to their bruises. They bring in all their worst fears for her safekeeping. In return — when she isn't lost in the complex, weary-ing narratives of their lives, or being inadvertently judgmental, or otherwise inadequate to the task — what she offers them is something vaguely, dangerously, in the nature of hope.

The private line lights up. She reaches to answer, sending a jolt of pain through her sacrum.

"Aach!" she says involuntarily into the receiver, then specifically to Taylor, the only other person who has this number, she adds, "Save me."

"Hey. You okay?"

Chris realizes she hasn't answered when Taylor says, "You're just stuck. Come on. I'll take you to dinner."

"It's almost six," Chris says, picking up the Magic 8 Ball from the end table. Silently, she asks it whether Rosario Delacruz is going to do anything homicidal that she needs to worry about and is relieved when MY SOURCES SAY NO floats up to the window. "You probably won't be able to stay awake," she tells Taylor. "I'll have to make all the conversation while you fall face-first into your food." Taylor is just hours back from ten days shooting photos in Morocco, oasis towns in the Sahara, beyond Ouarzazate. Chris asks the 8 Ball if Taylor still really loves her, but gets only REPLY HAZY ASK AGAIN. Sometimes the 8 Ball can be very cagey.

"I took a nap," Taylor says. "Come on. Leave now. Try to beat me over there."

The restaurant is an Italian place they both like, one of a small explosion of new trattorias delivering an atmosphere achieved with what Taylor calls Tuscany Helper, drywall painted to look like the crumbling plaster of a neglected villa. Chris pushes the traffic and has good luck at stoplights and in finding a parking space just around the corner from the restaurant. Still, when she arrives, Taylor is already sitting at a back table, her head tilted against the wall, fingers flat on the table, splayed around the base of a glass of red wine. Her gaze is focused somewhere within, on a vanishing point on some private horizon.

Something cold and liquid and metallic rushes through Chris's intestines, borne partly of not knowing what might be so fascinating, partly of not wanting to know. She watches Taylor turn at the peripheral motion of her arrival, her expression smoothly reshaping itself into something lightly anticipatory and seductive, a rhetoric she uses on nearly everyone. Chris wishes Taylor didn't still need to use this on her, although it was for sure what hooked Chris when they started up.

This was nearly four years earlier.

She had stood in the hallway outside the apartment door, tucking her nose inside the collar of her shirt, to see if she was wearing too much cologne. The invitation was for dinner — she'd assumed her friends Raymond and Jim had asked only her. She was newly single and all her friends were being kind, assuming she was lonely, home in the tub with a bad mystery and a glass of gin, or on the prowl in unsavory places — the sorts of images "single" conjures up among the coupled.

In fact she was exhaling with relief, grateful to the fates for letting her slip out of this last relationship, which had been so embarrassing she couldn't bring herself to refer to it as a relationship. Rather she would say of herself and Lois, "We dated for a while." Or, "I used to see her a bit." When in fact it was nearly a year, much of it spent living together, watching TV, squabbling over nothing, gaining weight together. Chris's friend Daniel still refers to Lois as the Human Pet, a description both terrible and accurate, nearly as humiliating to Chris as it is to Lois.

Coming off this sodden affair, she was leery of starting anything new. She had begun to mistrust her judgment along these lines. She had been looking forward to a semi-serious evening, making small talk about romantic foibles over dinner with two close friends. But there was too much noise on the other side of the door. She was underprepared, emerging into the light carbonation of a couple of dozen people, mostly gay guys, but also a few women, all seemingly paired, holding wineglasses and putting their best selves forward. She immediately felt lacking, in need of some supplemental power source — a battery pack — to participate in this larger evening. To acclimate, she got her own glass of wine and stood near the buffet, watching the other guests harvest a table of small, recherché foods — tiny goat cheese pizzas, tricolored vegetable pâté on rice crackers, brie flecked with mushrooms, salad scattered with flower petals. Then she checked out the crowd, noticed Taylor, leaning against the mantel of the fireplace, brooding, and revised her attitude. Suddenly a party seemed a very good idea.

Of course, anyone would have noticed Taylor. She was out of a full-tilt, no-hitches dream. Mick Jagger mouth. Botticelli hair — dark, long, and tangled up in itself. Pale gray eyes, the eyes of someone slightly haunted, or psychic. In the movie version of this party, the audience would know, as soon as Taylor came into the room, that she was going to turn out to be the main character. The telephone in the foreground that would inevitably ring.

But she was in the close company of her lover, whose radar threw out circles of awareness, blipping up any unidentified craft hovering into their airspace. Raymond eventually introduced the three of them. He worked with the lover, Diane, for Hyatt. Chris wondered if she was a hotel detective; she had the weasely manner, the shifty little gaze. Taylor was a photographer, Chris was told, and she heard a shutter click somewhere inside herself. She began casting about for some way to insult her lightly, having found in her attempts at flirtation that being rude and, if possible, dismissive, was the best approach to great-looking women. Ignoring them completely was the absolute best technique, but this required a situation in which time wasn't an issue. If she were gorgeous herself, Chris might take these women straight on. But she has always been a tall, skinny girl with glasses. She has needed her wits about her.

That night she decided, as an opening strategy, to operate from the deliberately wrongheaded assumption that by "photographer" Taylor meant she operated out of a shop like the dusty ones in Chris's neighborhood, their windows filled with portraits of stunned graduates and brides who looked embalmed, like saints under glass in Spanish churches.

"Do you use a rubber chicken?" she asked Taylor when there was a little space in the conversation.

"Pardon?"

"I was at this wedding once where the photographer used one. He'd hold it up to get everyone hilarious while he snapped the picture. But then I suppose you professionals have all sorts of tricks."

"Not usually anything that clever," Taylor said, and Chris could feel a tug on the line.

Later, when the party got bigger and more oppressive, she went out onto the back porch to try for a little room at the elbows, some unconditioned air. Suddenly Taylor was there next to her. A summer storm was pumping up from over the lake; there were low bursts of popcorn lightning, eerily unaccompanied by thunder. Chris turned her face to feel it.

"My dog does the same thing," Taylor said. "Closes his eyes and puts his face straight into a breeze, for the pure pleasure." Then she brushed a few knuckles across Chris's cheek to illustrate the not-terribly-difficult-to-grasp concept of "breeze."

Chris fought down a nervous impulse to laugh. All through her coming out in boarding school and at college she had longed for precisely this cheesy sort of scenario, the sexually predatory woman, a vamp of an old school with a mastery of situation and technique. Someone who knew all the ropes, who'd brought the ropes along. Now, so many years and so many women down the line, this kind of thing seems purely comic.

Of course, even as she was finding so much to be amused about in this moment, she was also looking over Taylor's shoulder, at the screen door to the kitchen, through which the ever-watchful Diane would surely be emerging any second now. At home that night she took herself to task for flirting with a married woman. She tried to subscribe to a loose system of social ethics: that the world was a less chaotic, more decent place if people got out of one relationship before hopping into the next.

Still, she didn't hang up when Taylor began calling, mostly from pay phones, sometimes from her darkroom or on crackling connections from hotel rooms in the places across oceans where she went to take pictures for *Transit*, "The Journal of Low-Impact Tourism." Or late at night from a phone downstairs from the bedroom where her lover slept.

Nor did she turn down any of Taylor's impromptu invitations — mostly from her car phone — to meet at this coffeehouse on Clark, that wine bar on Ashland. And then Taylor showed up unexpectedly, late one night in Chris's waiting room, sweaty in her running clothes, shorts and T-shirt, just as Chris was seeing her last client out. She led Chris back into the office, tapped the door shut with a Reeboked heel, saying only "shut up" before tackling Chris in a rather dramatic and swashbuckling way onto the sofa. Chris didn't put up any fight at all.

"This is going to be a mess, isn't it?" she asked Taylor some nights later in her kitchen, several cups of strong coffee thudding through her veins. She was angry with herself for buying into the trashy seduction fantasy that was probably all Taylor was offering. Before, Chris had been going along, living a life with at least some reality base, and now she was mired in a B movie, a film noir, where everything happened at night, or on phones with huge heavy black receivers. "I should've done and gotten past this kind of thing in my twenties, right? This is going to just be all sorts of sneaking and subterfuge and in the end your easygoing friend Diane will come by and run her key over the paint on my car. I'll find her sitting in my waiting room with a gun in a paper bag. Or worse, I'll go along with this shabby affair just long enough to become a morally bankrupt, diminished version of myself, and then you'll leave me."

"No. It's just going to be a bit of trouble for a while," Taylor said, pressing Chris against the counter, pulling her head back with fingers laced tightly through her hair. "Mostly on my part. I'll tell her. I'll get out."

This announcement was both thrilling and disconcerting. Even though Chris was by now so vulnerable to Taylor that it sometimes felt as though sharp winds were howling through her chest, she had nonetheless pegged her as a compulsive charmer, all show and no go. The impossibly wonderful words Taylor spent on her were like those colorful but devalued currencies that feature parrots and kings, but buy nothing. She had already resigned herself to some soggy, desultory conclusion with Taylor ducking out, wrapped in a cloak of excuses. She imagined, six months or so from now, running into her and Diane at Whole Foods, around the little bins of expensive mushrooms in the produce department. Everyone would be back in place, only Chris would feel considerably worse than she had before this all started, before she had let it start.

And so she was quite thrown by Taylor's offer to come to her. This wouldn't be simple. Taylor and Diane had tenure, and beyond that property in common — an apartment in Andersonville, and a lot in the woods in Michigan they'd been planning to build on. They weren't just going steady. To come over to Chris, Taylor was going to have to go through a Houdini amount of extrication. First the ropes, then the locks, then the chains around the steamer trunk.

At first, these restrictions were daunting and, in spite of all her big talk, she couldn't get out. After a month or two of being too nervous watching Taylor vacillate, Chris told her to go away until she got things sorted out. She now knew she really wanted her and this wasn't having her.

So she waited, all the time persuading herself that she wasn't really waiting, through what she thought would be weeks, but ultimately stretched into nearly half a year before Taylor actually hired the mover and got into a situation house-sitting for some friends. And then when these events finally dealt themselves out in her favor, Chris surprisingly found herself utterly unprepared. It was like starting out on a great journey at dusk instead of daylight, unpacked and with a map inadequate for negotiating the vague, pastel continent of romance, much less the specific rough terrain of Taylor. That first night when Taylor arrived free and clear, Chris stood inside the threshold as she opened her door and stared and blinked for a few moments, wondering what she was going to do with this prize she had won.

Plus she had a whole other case of nerves that had nothing at all to do with Taylor. Chris had already lived through one uprooting love affair, and its long, terrible collapse, like the demolition of a great palace or temple, had left all her assumptions shaken. She had spent the previous four years dating lightly or not at all, or — for that hazy, now mercifully indeterminate number of months — in the company of the Human Pet. All quite straightforward mechanisms to avoid the possibility of ever experiencing so much pain again. Still, what was there to do after this overture but begin?

Now they sit in this small restaurant and look over their menus. In the four years that have gone by, this alliance has accumulated a small history that, in her more optimistic moments, Chris can construe as a foundation beneath their feet. It's not the same as safety. She can't imagine the decades she would have to have with Taylor before she might actually begin to feel safe. Still, together they are now more than the sum of their individual parts, neither of them quite who she would have been had their meeting not occurred. The fact of their still being together, even in their wobbly, unmitered way, must add up to something.

"What're you going to have?" Chris asks.

"I'm too tired to decide." Taylor looks up, brightly, but not in a particularly good way, like a patient running a slight temperature. "We could order for each other."

"All right," Chris says. "Just don't do anything terrible to me."

"Well, I can't get too treacherous here," says Taylor, going into global mode. "For that I'd have to take you someplace where they serve eyes."

When they are splitting up a *caprese* salad, Chris says, "It was hard this time, I'm not sure why. You'd think I'd be getting used to it by now." Taylor has been to Morocco three times in the past year, not for *Transit*, but to shoot photos for a book, one in a series of travel guides on places difficult for women traveling alone, or with each other, out from under the protective wing of a male companion. If the series is a success, there will be more of this work. Volumes are already being proposed for Egypt, India, Turkey. If she's going to be a supportive partner, Chris can't stand in the way with loneliness and nagging worries about fidelity.

She would like to know if Taylor misses her on these trips. A difficult piece of information to acquire because if she did, Taylor would never be so obvious as to mention it. Chris can imagine that she does miss her, but then can just as easily imagine her relieved to pull back the fresh sheet of a bed that will have no one in it but herself. Or a bed that will have another woman in it with whom she will sleep that night and then never have to see again. Given the options, their equal plausibility and unconfirmability, Chris chooses to imagine Taylor lying alone, tidily taking up only half the hotel bed, propping a picture of Chris against the nightstand lamp before she turns it off and slips into flat, dreamless sleep.

"And I still worry about all the planes," Chris says, hating how she must sound, as though she waits by the window, with a lamp.

But Taylor says, "I do too sometimes. Even after all this time. Sometimes the 'even after all this time' is part of the worry. Like I've used up too much of my allotment of planes that don't crash. Did you read they have a tape from inside the cabin of that plane that went down last month in Pittsburgh? But they won't release it, even to the families, because it contains 'too much human suffering.' What do you think is on that tape? What do you think too much human suffering sounds like?"

This is more talisman than serious talk. If they both touch the cloth of crashing planes, they've appeased the fates. In this way, they carpenter with conversation. A level is placed on things between them, and Chris decides to be content with the moment. Her lover is present and attentive, and the evening rises up gently around them as the butcher paper cover on the table collects bread crumbs and circles of red wine and heavy drops of deep green olive oil.

"This dog is a rasslin' dog," Taylor announces to an invisible crowd in the trailer court accent she uses when she wrestles Bud. She has him flipped on the bed, his paws flailing through the air. While she bats away at them, tapping their leathery pads, she puts her fore-arm between his teeth. "The jaws of death. A bona fide roadside attraction — a dog that bites his own master." Bud slithers out of control, to the edge of the mattress, then onto the floor where he sets himself to rights and shakes out his rumpled fur, gathers up his dignity.

Wrestling is one of the few games they've found that he gets. He gazes bewildered at tossed balls, shies nervously from squeaky rubber lamb chops. They suppose his early years, before Taylor got him from Anti-Cruelty, must have been spent in neglect, tied up in a yard, maybe guarding a store. "I love you, bungalowhead," Taylor says, rolling his soft, furry face between her palms. He is her dog originally. Because she is away so much of the time, though, he wound up being taken care of a lot by Diane, and now by Chris. Even with that, his allegiance is with Taylor — as opposed to his affection, which he divides graciously among all who love him.

When Taylor has returned her phone messages, she tells Chris one of them was from MarySarah, her editor at the magazine, a person Chris finds stupid and pretentious in every way, starting with her stupid and pretentious name. "I need to meet with her tomorrow. She has an assignment for me." She reads from her scribbled notes.

14

"'Taormina, Paradise on the Ionian Sea.' Oh, I can't even think about Sicily, packing up again, getting into nylon underpants."

This isn't like her. She is usually exhilarated by filling her duffel with items either miniaturized or lightened or disposable, dumping a couple of dozen rolls of film into a lead foil bag, cleaning her lenses, calling Flash Cab at the last possible moment. The arrhythmic meter of long-distance travel feeds some need in her for unpredictability. Taylor seems to enjoy being kept a little off-balance, surprised or awaiting surprise.

"You're just exhausted, physically and psychically," Chris says, helpfully explaining Taylor to herself. A terrible habit, she knows. A tiresome by-product of her profession. She looks up into Taylor's weary eyes, and says, "Sorry."

They shower in the dark. With the window open next to them, they can see each other almost perfectly in the infrawhite light of a full moon minus a sliver.

"Christine Snow," Taylor says, as she sometimes does, as though the name holds deeper meanings, has magic to ward off whatever it is that Taylor fears. "Do you want to make love before we go to sleep?" she asks.

Chris nods, shy even after all this time.

This small exchange forms itself into a present between them, waiting to be opened.

The dog clatters slowly into the bedroom.

"Here comes something old," Taylor says.

They listen as he checks on them, then clatters out again, down the hall. He likes to sleep in the guest room, where he has a whole bed to himself.

"Don't be asleep yet," Chris says into the dark a little while later. "You've got a proposition to make good on."

"I'm not sleeping. Not really."

"Are you okay?"

"Sure."

It sounds as though there's a comma after the word, and Chris — adept as she is at interpreting pauses and catches in speech — prepares herself for a confession, but there is only dark air, damp with breath in the narrow space between their faces. Then a leg sliding between her own, hands slipping open the envelope of her T-shirt, a mouth moving over her left breast.

They make love in a rush — because it has been a while, and because they're tacitly racing against Taylor's exhausted collapse with Chris curled around her, bringing her home. Her first night back, she typically gets a few profound hours of sleep before waking into the dawn of whatever desert or glacial plain she has just left behind. She is a traveler even when she is home, in motion even when she is at rest, and Chris feels herself always reaching out, Taylor always slipping through her fingers, like spilled mercury.

CHRIS IS JUST out of an appointment with her chiropractor, Eileen, whose approach is becoming disconcertingly mystical. She has been spending more and more of their sessions with her hands hovering in the air above Chris's back, adjusting energy fields. Today she asked if Chris has been eating a lot of nightshade. Chris would like to keep these ministrations limited to cartilage crunching, which is what Eileen used to do to her. She thinks she might give Taylor's chiropractor a try. This woman is supposedly a hulking gum chewer. Darla. All business. Snap. Crackle. Pop.

Chris shifts around in the driver's seat, her lower back crabbing again, her energy fields, she supposes, slipping once again out of alignment. It is taking her forever to get home today. Traffic up and down Lincoln is glued to itself on account of this first, goofball, way-out-of-sync day of spring, an afternoon that has shot into the seventies. Everyone in the city has come out to contribute to the gridlock. Cars, of course. Rollerbladers and runners. Fat girls in halter tops. Swift bicycle thieves. The homeless, who were already out, but now with élan, and plenty of company. The sidewalk in front of Betty's Resale, a junkyard just south of Addison, is filled with milling customers, as though avocado-colored stoves and dressers covered in contact paper have suddenly soared in value on some secret stock exchange.

Finally, she passes the giant, comic head of Abe fronting the Lincoln Restaurant, and turns onto her street. She pulls up in front of her house and taps the last of a bag of M&Ms into her palm as she listens to Norman Greenbaum pumping out "Spirit in the Sky" on the oldies station. It's an unleavable song and so she sits a moment longer, rocking and rolling a little in her Corolla, contemplating her real estate, this small, shambly frame house with salt-and-pepper asphalt siding and buckling wooden steps.

The neighborhood is changing, upscaling but in an ungainly way. That is, while several houses on their block have been renovated by new owners — Board of Traders, young dentists, and the like — who quickly ensconce themselves behind tasteful, Italianate dark green wrought-iron fences, the tenured residents of the block are people who work in factories and grocery stores and on job sites. So any one of the yuppified houses, for all its landscaping and ADT alarming, might well sit squarely across the street from a two-flat with a rooster in a cage in the front yard.

Chris and Taylor hope to eventually join the ranks of the renovators, but have had the house only a few months and so far have been able to afford only the most meager and necessary improvements. This is the first house either of them has ever owned, and it makes them feel as though they've moved to America. After years of apartments with stairwells full of peculiar cooking odors, ceilings throbbing with other people's stereos, discouraging connections with the flooding bathrooms and stray roaches of strangers, they are now blessed with autonomy and silent nights, and a backyard for grilling and letting the dog out in the morning, for planning a garden. They no longer have to lug everything long blocks from parking spaces in their former, high-density neighborhood.

They have a washer and dryer in the basement, Stone Age machines left behind by the previous owners. The first time Chris ran the dryer it made a huge, chainsaw-massacre noise that rattled the walls and drove the dog up to the attic. She shut off the machine and stood appraising it in ignorance. She tried to guess how old it was. Realistically, thirty years. "Now that I look more closely," she came upstairs and told Taylor, as though she had come to the crux of the matter, "it's not even a Kenmore, it's a *Lady* Kenmore."

"Might be tricky to get that fixed," Taylor said. "I think there's a regulation. I think the repair guy has to bring a female attendant along."

The problem turned out to be nothing. A nail fallen into a baffle. Neither of them knew what a baffle was; they just wrote the check for the service call and went along merrily until the next appliance revealed its failings. First it was the oven, which didn't ignite; then the freezer, which did freeze, but also alternately defrosted at whim.

Chris is aware of the house clearly being, more than walls and ceilings around them, mortar and mortising between them. She and Taylor never speak of these weights and adhesions directly, only natter about the small charms of the place, its value as a sound investment, the dog's kingly happiness here. Sometimes Chris thinks it's kind of sweet how careful they are with each other. Other times she wonders what they are being so careful about.

Having bought the house, they have both become ambivalent about it, although they would never admit their hesitations to each other. Instead, they offset their praise with small complaints about drafts or the cramped clawfoot tub in the upstairs bathroom. In this way, the house has become a rich metaphor for the unspoken, inarticulable nettles they have with each other, about what is happening, or not happening, between them.

Chris is fairly certain that with Taylor's previous lover, it was in some measure the property they held together that freaked Taylor out of the relationship. Taylor once said she felt as though a plastic dry-cleaners bag was being pulled over her head. Chris worries the house is forcing them to replicate that situation.

The concertedly domestic arrangements of most couples of their acquaintance have a sameness, a smugly settled quality that she and Taylor used to make fun of. In the beginning they talked a bit about resisting the subliminal pull toward turning into what Taylor calls the "boring lesbian personality casserole." But in spite of this skittishness, Taylor eventually began lobbying for a house, needing, like most people, to press a thumb down on her particular psychic bruise. In her case, longing to have her affections tucked into the folds of a recognized relationship, even though her heart continues to prowl the night like a werewolf.

And so she scanned ads in six months' worth of Sunday *Tribunes* until she came up with this house and its eager sellers, the Herbsts, who were eager due to Mr. Herbst's imminent transfer to Tulsa, making the house at the price an incredible deal, but one which had to be seized within the next five minutes. This catch left Chris and Taylor no time for long discussions searching the soul of their relationship, plumbing their issues of intimacy and domestic partnership. They only had time to leap, and now, having regained consciousness, they find themselves on the other side, in this place where Chris needs to keep a sharp eye out to try to determine if Taylor is beginning to turn blue inside the bag.

Although she is sympathetic to Taylor's restlessness, Chris quickly winds up feeling worse for herself, having to share a bed with someone who is always tossing and turning, punching at the pillow.

On the surface of things, at the level that would show up on the home videos, Taylor is, aside from her penchant for flirtation, a dream lover — attentive and considerate, surprising. She brings fresh mozzarella home from the Italian grocery, massages Chris's hands with almond oil. Everything truly troublesome about her is buried cable, subterranean trunk line. The closest Chris can get to Taylor's true identity is feeling the vibration of this secret information as it rushes deep beneath the ground the two of them stand on, facing each other with pleasant expressions, good will, and smooth, practiced approximations of intimacy. It's a little like being married to a spy.

She mostly finds this fascinating, and thinks herself quite lucky to have found a partner whose depths are so seemingly bottomless. There are moments, though, when she imagines an alternate life with a person she thinks of as Patti. A homebody who, a little ways into their long, calm, predictable relationship, starts getting her hair cut the way Chris does, then signs them up for ceramics classes together. Someone from whose feet both shoes have already dropped.

Chris pauses a moment on the front porch and tries to call up what they are supposed to be doing tonight. Someone is coming for dinner. Taylor's friend Leigh and her new girlfriend.

She sees that the back door off the kitchen is open and goes out onto the tiny deck that precedes the short flight of steps to ground level. Taylor is out there at the back of the yard, breaking ground for a garden they've planned, prying out one of a pair of generic bushes, legacies from the Herbsts.

Taylor relishes difficult projects. She once hauled a file cabinet up three flights by propping it on the fronts of her thighs. When she cooks, the recipes she takes on are daunting even on the page, projects starting with unhusked coconuts or raw squid, or requiring pastry tubes and springform pans, mortars and pestles, ignition with cognac and match. In the same studied, painstaking way, she is determined to make something pretty out of this rectangle of patchy grass and dusty ruts worn by the Herbsts' anxious German shepherd, Lassie. (All the dogs in this as-yet-untrendy neighborhood are named Lassie or Princess or Rex. Several are offspring of various large females and one busy basset hound. The results are German shepherds and Labradors with six-inch legs.)

On the other side of the fence is the yard of their neighbors Cy and Dolores, whose last name they don't yet know. The yard, in one small plot of ground, manages to contain a pedestaled, sapphire-blue mirror ball, a Virgin in a grotto, a porch rail dripping with wind chimes, and a plastic duck family eternally toddling toward a strip of dirt that Taylor is pretty sure is going to reveal itself as a patch of sunflowers.

"The wind chimes are going to have to go," Taylor told her this morning. "I'm going to have to have a little talk with Cy. Maybe with Dolores."

"I think most people wouldn't find wind chimes a problem," Chris told her. "I myself find them rather charming."

"I myself," Taylor countered, "find they make me want to shoot somebody."

This digging today is a first step in Taylor's opposition to Cy and

Dolores's antic backyard, creating on their side of the privacy fence a traditional English garden. She has already hacked the bush down to a stump, and now, with a pitchfork sunk in at its base, tines tangled in the roots, is prying it up and out. She is wearing long, baggy shorts, her legs dark from having been in the desert, her hair restrained by a bandanna. She is tall, taller even than Chris, with much of her length in her legs. Chris is still a little in love with the way Taylor looks, still grateful for a beautiful lover. It's like having been born in Sorrento, having the rest of life like everyone else, but always also this.

Taylor's struggle with the bush has become fierce. The bush doesn't care that it is offensively Middle-American in the yard of hip urban dykes intent on recasting this landscape with what, in their better moments, they realize are their own pretensions. The bush has tenure here and is not relinquishing its presence easily. Bud sits nearby and watches closely, as though his presence is crucial to the task being accomplished.

"I'll help," Chris shouts, startling Bud, and possibly Taylor, although she would resist showing that. Instead she turns and smiles against the lowering sun. Chris can't see her eyes behind her shades.

"It's okay, I've almost got it," Taylor says. "Besides, you have company."

Only then does she notice that Taylor is not alone in the yard, that Chris's father is sitting at the wobbly redwood table (another legacy from the Herbsts), a glass of iced tea sweating in front of him as he deals hands for a poker game with invisible opponents. His showing up unannounced like this means he needs money.

Chris looks to Taylor for help and in return gets a jaunty little salute. He's not *her* father. Chris goes down the steps.

"Take a seat," he says, gesturing with the hand not holding the deck of cards.

"We're having company for dinner," she tells him. "Girls, but not your kind of girls. I'll have to start cooking soon."

"How about some tea?" Taylor asks Chris, and lopes up the stairs and into the house, calling back down to ask Tom Snow if he wants a refill.

"Mmm," he says, having heard something, but not specifically what anyone has said, then, when Taylor is inside, out of earshot, he prompts Chris. "Pick up your hand. Tell me what you've got."

"Not bad," she says, tapping the side of her nose, pushing her shades up a bit as she studies her cards for a few seconds, then lays down a straight to the jack.

"That's the beauty of this one." He fans a flush on the table to beat her. "You give the other fellow something to bid up, a piece of hope."

"Nice," Chris says with admiration, in spite of herself. "Low-key. Where are you working this?"

"Country club. Golf is great, you know. All those wads of cash folded inside clips, flapping around in all those baggy pants pockets. Money that really, when you think about it, means so very little to them."

She hates when he starts again with cards, leaving behind the small magic shows — for children, for sweet sixteen parties — that make him impatient, there being too little money or risk in honest sleight of hand. Even though he is a first-rate sharp, there's always a good chance he'll get caught out. People — especially men — don't like to think they're bad at cards. They'd rather think they're being cheated. Which puts her father under an unfortunate spotlight because he is indeed usually cheating them. He has been beaten up several times, once gravely, and has been to prison twice, but he is pretty much uncontrite as both stints turned out to be quite lucrative. "The incarcerated," he points out, "are among the few who really have the time and inclination for cards."

Chris takes the deck from him, shuffles, puts it down, and taps it for him to cut. Then she proceeds to deal him a handful of garbage, herself three aces and a pair of kings. When they lay down their hands, fanning out their cards on the splintery wood of the tabletop with soft, feathery clicks and rustles, like sounds from an African dialect, conveying meaning without words, he smiles slowly, swelling up with parental pride.

During Chris's summers and spring breaks and Christmas vacations from boarding school, Tom Snow taught his daughter about cards, and they began working together. Poolside venues. Cruises. He taught Chris everything he knew, and then she shot past him. They didn't know she'd have such a talent for it.

Even if she hadn't been so good, she would have had an advantage simply on account of her age. For their nights out, she dressed like a murderess with a good lawyer, not only in a way that emphasized her youth, but a more innocent girlishness of several decades before her own. Middy blouses, cardigan sweaters with little chain clasps at the neck. The persona they set up for her was slightly petulant, bored on vacation, nagging Daddy to take her horseback riding, sailing, whatever. He would persuade her to stay for just a few hands — why didn't she play? Here he'd even stake her, write out a little crib sheet laying out flushes and straights. And then she'd lose for a little while, befuddled and adorable, then win for just long enough. She would offer to give the money back. "You mean it isn't play money?!" But, of course, no one would ever take her up on the offer. Meanwhile, with Chris serving as a distraction, her father would also be winning in a less conspicuous way, steadily through the night.

The money allowed them, for a while at least, to play at the lifestyle of the men Tom had gone to public school with back in England when he was a scholarship boy. They drove a BMW, shopped at Brooks Brothers and Tiffany, ordered shrimp cocktails and prime rib from leather banquettes and stayed in four-star hotels, able to be their true selves — thieves among thieves — only when they were alone together in the early-morning hours in their paneled cabin or suite, counting up their winnings over large white plates of eggs and bacon, tomatoes and fruit, the food itself arrayed like winnings.

It was her share of their take that got her through school, with a nest egg left over that she never touches, has told no one about. Not her father, who probably assumes it's all been long spent. Not even Taylor knows. Chris has never been able to bring herself to tell her about the money or the sharping, her part in it. It has never felt far enough behind her to work into anecdote. Nor is her reconstructed life of good works and upstanding behavior quite enough of a shield. There is still hardly a day when it doesn't cross her mind that she could get on a plane to Vegas, check into a small suite at the Four Queens, go downstairs to the poker tables, and, in a couple of hours, before she attracted too much attention, leave with more money than she makes in a year of private practice. It is an extremely peculiar power to hold, unused.

Today her father has come to ask for start-up cash, membership dues for the club. When he sees the reluctance in her expression, he says, "Tell yourself I'm taking up golf. It'll be good for my health." He has been idly shuffling the deck and begins turning over jacks and queens in alternation.

"Show-off," Chris says. Then, "How much?"

"Eleven hundred?" It is always an odd amount, to imply the seriousness, the direct applicability of the money requested. She looks at her father from a greater distance than she actually sits from him. Bud's chin is on his thigh. The dog selects his own friends from among their visitors. In mulling over her father's request, Chris silently runs through a series of calculations, not all of which have to do with money.

"We're a little house-poor at the moment," Taylor jumps in, back with glasses and a pitcher of iced tea, which she sets on the table. Tom tamps, and then pockets, his deck of cards.

"Ah, a bit pinched, eh?" he says. He's English by birth and milks this. In his line of work a dash of class helps. Chris's mother met him on a cruise ship. She was traveling with her parents, was young and deeply naive. Their affair was as silly and inconsequential as an Astaire-Rogers movie; it should have had lyrics rather than dialogue. But pregnancies come out of far less, and there they were, under-acquainted, ill-suited, and about to be parents. Which is how, nearly forty years later, Chris comes to sit across from this childish man, bound up with him in ways that make her feel, irrationally she knows, that Taylor is at the moment interfering, rather than only trying to help.

She notices that his hair — reddish with faded dye — has thinned out a bit since she last saw him; his scalp looks pink and exposed between the comb marks raked along the sides. His throat has caved in so deeply that an egg could fit inside the hollow. The buttoned collar of his sport shirt loosely circles his ropy neck. Because he has always been overly fastidious, she takes this lack of fit as a sign of decline. One of her most indelible memories of the time she spent with him, when they worked as a team, is the waiting for him to be ready. Hours at a stretch on the sofa with teen magazines, itchy on the crushed velvet upholstery of the sofa in this hotel room, that stateroom, waiting as the ritual moved toward its eventual completion — waiting for the shower steam to evaporate and the minted scents of shave cream and toothpaste to recede as the air from the bathroom began to deliver the bracing cologne that signaled he was done. It was like being the child of a great diva preparing to walk out onto a stage filled with elephants and extras, to sing *Aïda*. When in fact all her father was primping for was another evening of cards.

Now his glory days are quite a ways behind him, and he seems so terribly diminished to Chris, reduced to waiting for her to decide if she's going to give him a bit of money. She's not interested in holding this cheap power, and so she goes inside for her checkbook.

Chris stands back, Bud's tail swishing against her leg, as she watches Taylor under the tree overhanging their parkway, the sunlight thin and watery on her as she shuts the door of Tom's car (a fairly new Bonneville won in a long night in Miami Beach) and leans through the open window to graze his cheek with her lips. She is courtly with him, as though he is their most valued visitor. As they watch him drive off at about fifteen miles per hour, though, she says, "We could have used that eleven hundred. To replace the worst of the rotting windows, for one thing."

"I know," Chris says, and prepares herself for the hard words they're going to have about her misplaced generosity. Which will doubtless lead into a lecture on how much more Chris could contribute, not to mention how much better off she'd be financially, if she weren't such a soft touch for the deadbeats among her clients.

But the lecture doesn't come. Instead, Taylor runs a hand through Chris's hair and smiles, which is worse somehow. Usually money is a great opportunity for an argument between them — their lack of it at any given moment, the different uses to which they each think it should be put. Chris's spendthrift bent in opposition to Taylor's skinflintiness. It's dispiriting, Taylor taking a pass on a fight when she has Chris dead to rights.

Chris tries another test of Taylor's mood. She watches as Taylor pulls a bunch of carrots out of the vegetable bin in the refrigerator and takes them over to the sink, starts running water, finds the peeler in the drawer. Then Chris comes up behind her, reaches inside her shirt, traces fingers around her waist, then up to her nipples.

She feels Taylor tense beneath her touch. This is much worse than a worded rejection, worse still for not being the first time. Through most of their relationship, they've accommodated each other's impulses, moods, open to stopping on a dime in the middle of a day or a project and finding their way to the bed or sofa, or just down onto the floor they're standing on, which is what Chris is negotiating at the moment.

It is just lately that she has been apprehensive about making passes, fearful they will, as in this moment, get snagged on Taylor's unspoken reluctance. There's been more of this since she got back from Morocco, and Chris is too afraid to ask about the connection. It would be pointless anyway. Taylor would just lie, Chris knows it. Of all the feelings Taylor can engender in Chris, the one she hates the most is feeling a door being ever so gently and kindly, but firmly, shut in her face.

After so many thousands of hours spent listening to the misery of clients at the hands of troublemakers, Chris knows certain warning signals. Unfortunately, her own lover came with a full complement. From the first, red flags fluttered through the air around Taylor. If one of Chris's clients had fallen in love with this woman and brought in a detailed description, she knows she would have put up a licked finger to discern the sharp, tricky winds ahead.

Leigh and her new girlfriend (the women who are not dating material for Chris's father) are due to arrive soon. All of Leigh's girlfriends are short-term. She attracts them easily by her charms, and by her mild celebrity status as a reporter for the Channel 5 news. She likes to bring them by for Chris and Taylor's approval, an exercise that seems particularly pointless to Chris, in that by the next time they have dinner with Leigh she will be with a new date.

"Tish?" Chris says, mincing an onion, trying to remember the name of this latest one.

"Tiff."

"What can that be about?"

"Short for Tiffany, I think."

"Tiffany's the name of Myra's bird. A cockatiel."

"Well, it's also the name of this girl we're going to be very nice to tonight." This is another sign. There is too often lately a color to Taylor's tone, some verdigris of irritation or weariness, covered quickly, softened and brightened with the next sentence, but still.

"She's going to be terrible," Chris says.

"Maybe she'll be okay" is all Taylor says, purely out of devotion to Leigh. They were involved with each other for a short time a million years ago. Lesbians, even in a place as large as Chicago, draw their friends and lovers from the same pool, which often leads to some confusion at the start of things and some awkwardness in the aftermath, but also to friendships like Leigh and Taylor's — fine, sturdy houses built on some nearly forgotten rubble of romance.

Tiff stands in the middle of the living room, her hands flattened against an imaginary pane of glass between herself and her audience, which is composed of Chris and Taylor and a rapt Leigh. Tiff's face is a child's twist of consternation. The only sound in the room is the sticky creaking of her leather jeans.

"She's trying to break through the fourth wall," Leigh finally explains, as though to a meeting of the Dunderhead Society. "Her pieces are self-conscious; they're about the failure of performance to obtain meaning." This line sounds suspiciously to Chris like a sentence cribbed from an art magazine Leigh picked off a coffee table. A lot of Leigh's conversation has this air, as though she has been, five minutes earlier, briefed on the subject by a researcher, given a digest report while she's jogging.

Tiff falls onto the sofa, dramatically exhausted, and nuzzles her girlfriend.

"Hasn't mime kind of fallen into eclipse?" Chris asks, unable at the moment to address Tiff's performance directly.

"Everybody just thinks that," Tiff says.

"Tiff's work is different," Leigh says. "She's interested in stretching the boundaries of the form." She locks eyes with Tiff as she pleads her case to the cultural philistines.

In the kitchen, Chris and Taylor rev up the cappuccino maker.

"What can the attraction be?" Chris says as Taylor opens with a stagy flourish an imaginary bag of coffee beans and measures them into the grinder with an imaginary scoop.

"Come on, she's hot, don't you think?" Taylor gets the real coffee out of the freezer. "Skinny blond girls in black leather, come on."

"But you'd have to talk with her afterward."

"From what Leigh says, afterward doesn't come for a long time, or very often. And she brings along a product, some unguent or poultice or something that takes away the marks from the thumb cuffs."

"What are thumb cuffs?"

"Think you could shout that a little louder? There might be a small chance they didn't hear you."

Chris grabs Taylor's arm, presses her mouth against a shoulder to blot her laughter. "Tell me. I need details. Diagrams. Greasy Polaroids."

"I'm not telling you anything. Especially not about the prison scenes. You're indiscreet. You're very unreliable."

"Please."

"No way," Taylor teases. "Besides, cappuccino's ready. We don't have time for idle gossip."

When they are done in the kitchen, she tightropes down the hall with grave concentration, carefully balancing two cups, which nonetheless slosh milky foam onto their saucers.

And so Chris thinks things are back to being easy between them, that Tiff is a joke she and Taylor share, until late into the evening when she has come downstairs from the bathroom and passes Leigh, who is at the wall phone in the kitchen, having been beeped by the station.

"Train wreck in Indiana," she says to Chris, who nods soberly at this distant tragedy. Then, in search of a mislaid corkscrew, Chris comes upon a smaller, domestic, misadventure: Taylor in the living room, by the bookshelves, pushing aside with her hand the great wave of pale blond hair that falls over Tiff's left eye. For her part in this vignette, Tiff is playfully biting the base of Taylor's thumb.

"Please," Taylor says later, when they are alone, gathering up glasses and dessert plates. "Let's not get into some big scene about something that was nothing." The standard response Taylor gives whenever she is found out. Like the night Chris belatedly decided to go with her to walk Bud and caught up at the 7-Eleven, where she was hunched over the mouthpiece of an outdoor pay phone. Or the time she found a small, folded piece of heavy gray notepaper in the back pocket of a pair of Taylor's jeans, which she was throwing in the wash, and written inside (in a studied, squared-off script Chris didn't recognize) was "Madly."

"I'm assuming it was nothing," Chris says. "I'm not accusing you of getting matching tattoos and asking her to have your children. I just want you to see that you've made me feel extremely lousy in this particular moment. Which is not nothing."

Chris is furious at having her nose rubbed in all of Taylor's pathetic subterfuges and diversions, the very sort of insignificant liaisons she thought they had both given up. She herself has not so much as made a flirtatious remark to anyone else in these nearly four years. To be honest, she hasn't had the impulse. So the discrepancy doesn't seem unfair, only sad. They're both white mice in this test cage of commitment. Chris sits content, though, while Taylor still hunches over the bar, pressing. She still needs girl pellets.

"You knew this part of me from the start," Taylor says in weak defense. "If I hadn't flirted with you at that party, we wouldn't be here tonight."

"Yes, but I wasn't looking to be the next person who'd lose you."

"I didn't really love Diane. You know that. You knew it that night. And you know I do love you."

"That's not quite what I'm looking for at the moment. I'm hoping for something more along the lines of an apology, some promise of reform, even if it's a lie. Giving me nothing backs me against the wall, do you see that?"

Taylor shakes her head. "You think you love me, but you don't even know me. You don't have a fucking clue."

They lie together but apart, facing the outer edges of the bed. Chris evens out her breathing so Taylor will think she's asleep, although she worries Taylor's own even breathing probably means she simply *is* asleep.

After a rubbery length of time during which Chris shuttles between sleep and a kind of racy mulling, Taylor slides out of bed.

"I'm just restless," she says, clearly lying, when Chris turns over and lifts herself a little off the bed inquisitively. "I'm afraid of keeping you up."

"It's okay."

"No." She's taking the extra quilt off the armchair in the corner. "I'll just go downstairs for a while. Read a little, maybe."

"Hey," Chris says, not sure what she's going to follow with. But Taylor is already on the stairs, Bud's toenails clattering after her down the wooden steps.

Near dawn, Chris finally falls into a profound, dreamless sleep after a couple of hours tuned in to the sounds of Taylor's limbs pulling the quilt on and kicking it off, the creaking in the springs of the sofa. The faint signs that she is there, even if "there" is becoming an increasingly tricky place to define.

IN THE MORNING, Chris feels as though she has barely slept at all, although the evidence around her contradicts this. When she comes downstairs, the kitchen air is still ticklish with turmeric and cardamom from the curry they fixed for Leigh and the mime. Taylor is already up and has been gone — by all signs, for a while. The dog is lying half-asleep in a wedge of light on the floor of the living room, so he has been fed and walked. Otherwise he would have been nosing around Chris's side of the bed, lobbying for her to open a can of food.

The coffeemaker is on with the glass carafe still half full, a bag of Starbucks and a carton of milk on the counter next to it. Chris pours herself a mug and goes wandering through the house. Taylor's camera bag is not by the front door where she usually leaves it, nor upstairs by her side of the bed. Her Cherokee isn't out front, nor in the garage when Chris goes to check.

Wherever she is, it's just as well she's not here. Chris would like the opportunity to tear into her a little, especially now that her arguments have had a few hours to simmer in the dark. She is fed up with Taylor maneuvering off the defensive with a quick skip onto the offensive. The problem is that — enough of the time to make it worth her while — this cheap trick works. Chris finds anger hard to sustain; its fibers break down in the solution of time and enforced silence. Too soon, usually in the middle of the night, she gets to where she just needs the fight finished, Taylor okay again. To obtain this equilibrium, she'll give over quite a bit of ground.

This time, though, the morning light falls hard and bright on the extreme reason of her position. This time she can withstand the freeze-out; she is up to it with so much right on her side, a quiver full of right. Taylor (Chris sums up for an invisible jury) simply has to maintain more fidelity than a cat, has to go beyond searching out sunny sills and hands ready to scratch. All of us — especially those of us who have had a few glasses of pinot grigio — would like to run an idle hand through the hair of this or that dinner guest. But we don't; we behave ourselves.

Behaving is something Taylor finds tiresome.

Tough.

She thumps the brake hard. Fascinated by her compelling and continuing inner diatribe, Chris hasn't seen that traffic has ground to a halt. There's a sickening second or two when it's not clear if she's going to stop short of, or slam into the rear end of, the convertible ahead of her. She misses by an inch or two; if cars could breathe, the convertible's bumper would be fogged.

Her heart is still racing as she pulls into the lot next to her office. She presses her forehead to the top of the steering wheel, an emotional tourniquet. She needs to come down off her personal life. She checks her watch. In thirteen minutes, she is going to have to be listening with full attention to Nida Louis, her first Thursday appointment.

Daniel is already in his office when she comes in; she can hear him grunting from the waiting room. She pokes her head in. "Can you do a quick consultation with me on Rosario Delacruz?"

He looks up from the floor, where, toes hooked under the couch, he is doing sit-ups. "Sure. No problem."

Chris drops her stuff on the sofa and perches on its broad arm. "Well, I guess I'm worried I like her too much."

Daniel lifts an eyebrow slightly as he raises his shoulders off the floor, hands pressed behind his head.

"Not like that," she says. "Give me a break. She has a furry mustache and nails so long she could sell them in China or somewhere. Not to mention that she's straight, with a vengeance. Not to mention that she's a client. No, I just mean I plain like her. She's very charming in her goofy way, and I worry it's making me go too easy on her. She's been coming in for over a year and she's just stuck — one abusive relationship after another — and I can't seem to get her to budge. I'm just sitting there letting myself be charmed and empathizing like crazy, but where's it getting her? Like, I think she may be close to breaking off with this latest creep, but she'll probably just take up with another in his wake. She seems to have an endless supply. She must have a dating service for big-fisted bruisers."

"She's got a background of abuse, I remember?" he says, the words spaced out by the sit-ups. His back is even worse than hers.

"Mmm-hmm," she says. "Her father was the Tequila Monster. Got drunk at the corner tap, came home and beat everybody. Her brother's worse, but her and her sister, too, for good measure. But that's old territory. We've been over it, she and I."

"So what do you think this is about then — self-esteem issues?"

"Are you doing these" — she taps his chest with an extended foot — "for your back, or are you buffing up?"

"If you must know, I'm trying to shape myself into a babe magnet. I bought one of those machines where I'm cross-country skiing except I'm really in my living room. I feel like a complete fool on it, but I do forty-five minutes a day. Then a hundred of these. I'm expecting dramatic results soon. Why don't you try to get her to focus on the self-esteem issues, direct things away from the sexual arena; that's probably not the source at any rate. You said she was financially successful. It may make her feel unfeminine, unworthy of male attention. But you probably need to get to there from someplace easier to talk about. If you get the feeling she's trying to charm you, that in itself is probably a tip-off to self-esteem issues."

She nods. "I don't know which are harder, the clients I like, or the ones I don't." She picks up the thick paperback spread open on the back of the couch. Proust. She puts this together with the sit-ups.

"You've put in another ad," she guesses.

He looks gloomy. "I signed up for this service. It's supposed to be low-pressure. It's called Lunchables. You just meet the person for lunch. At a restaurant. They set it all up."

"When's your lunch?"

"Today. At one. At the Swedish Kitchen."

"I hope the Swedish Kitchen wasn't her pick for the restaurant. I don't think that would be a really good sign."

"I like Swedish Kitchen," Daniel says, and Chris sees it was his choice.

"Well, of course, it's a fine place. But you have to concede it kind of has an ethos that's built around creamed meatballs and lingonberries. It's not really a place where a spark would be likely to burst into flame."

He nods, contemplative and downtrodden, dark stubble already peppering the pale skin of his cheeks. "I thought it would be cheery."

"Well, and I'm sure it will be." Chris tries to sound encouraging and sincere, a difficult combination to summon up around Daniel's dating, which is a conveyor belt of sad misunderstandings and crossed purposes. "What's her name?

"Ariadne," he says, already defeated. Daniel longs to marry, or rather remarry, in spite of a turgid first marriage to his Finnish massage therapist, and a three-month acidic second one to a psychiatric nurse. Both women tired of him before he got around to tiring of them, and the rejection has left his confidence undermined. It was the turgid first marriage that yielded up his daughter, Camille, who is now fifteen and lives with Daniel part of the time.

Although he has been talking to Chris for a few minutes, he only now, as he rolls over, really looks at her.

"Hey. What's up?"

"What do you mean?"

"Well, for one thing, you look like you slept the night in a boxcar full of hoboes. You're wearing different socks."

She sees this is true, although it's not so bad really. One blue and one bluey purple.

"Taylor's back from Morocco, feeling frisky. She was cruising last night. Unfortunately, this was in our living room."

"Oh, Christine."

"And so she's taken off in a huff. Nothing serious, I don't think. A small huff." She has learned to minimize her domestic dramas.

The door from the hallway opens behind her and they cock their heads to the noise, an arriving client, then drop their conversation.

"So I'll get back to you on that matter."

She nods. She's actually relieved that they've been interrupted. She doesn't really want to continue this conversation. He has never thought much of Taylor. He thinks she leads Chris on too much of a merry chase, keeps her off-balance just for the sport of it, because she can. Chris thinks this analysis is reductive and tries to point out how much more subtle and layered the relationship actually is. When she is put out with Taylor, though, she uses him as sympathetic audience. Too sympathetic, really. It's too easy getting him worked up on her behalf.

She has trouble holding her focus during Nida Louis's hour. Part of this distraction is attributable to Taylor, but in truth every session with Nida is tough going. Her problems are dull and, while not insoluble, the solutions Nida comes up with don't seem likely to take her in any good direction.

"He came home early Tuesday," she says, referring to her husband. She has an angry cold sore at the corner of her mouth, as she often does, adding to her general aura of beleagueredness. "Caught me totally by surprise."

"And . . . ?" Chris prompts. Sometimes Nida ends her lines of thought in the middle. "You and Pam were up to some mischief?"

"Oh no. I was alone." Another hallmark of Nida's life is the non-occurrence. "But she *could* have been there. I hate to think what would've happened."

Pam is Nida's lover, sort of. They've only gone so far as heavy petting, Chris gathers, rubbing around on each other, that kind of thing. No further on account of Nida's Catholicism, which proscribes both extramarital affairs and homosexuality. The marriage has been long and dreary, the husband a drill sergeant with her and the kids, inspecting their dusting and bed-making, dominating the airwaves of their house with an audiophile stereo system on which he plays big band music. He enforces a strict laundry routine — socks one week, underwear the next — which he helps with, but still. He's pretty much the standard five-hundred-pound gorilla.

What Nida longs to do, but can't just yet, is pack up the kids (there are two) and bring them along with her when she moves in with Pam. She tells herself she is in transition between two lifestyles. Chris, for her part, sees Nida crawling out of one airless bunker, down into another. That is, when Nida visits Pam's apartment, she is not allowed to wear cologne; Pam is allergic. When Nida gets up from the sofa, Pam pats the indentation out of the upholstery. The books on Pam's shelves are arranged alphabetically by author.

Nida sees her dilemma in terms of coming-out issues, agonizing over whether she is really a lesbian, while Chris thinks what she needs to do is become the type of person — gay or straight — who doesn't need to be in the keep of an Enforcer. Helping her see this will be the barge-towing, the hod-carrying part of this therapy.

When dealing with clients whose issues involve coming out, Chris tries to quell her impatience by dragging herself back into the muddle of her own sexual defining, reimmersing herself in that protracted period of false starts and bad choices made out of desire too long suppressed. She tries to recapture those initial impulses, which she can still remember, like blades glinting through her — as though she were a circus performer, assistant to an apprentice knife-thrower, quivering and wounded in her fringed dress, bleeding against a colorful backboard, surrounded by untouched balloons. Secreting these painful pleasures, thrilled by them while at the same time not being able to see how they would possibly fit into any larger context, specifically a world that structured itself around attractions between male and female.

This exhilaration and confusion began late into her time at boarding school, first with crushes on a spate of older girls, then with one girl in particular, Alison Beale, the focal point of a brooding obsession Chris chested like a dicey hand at a tough poker table. Queerness wasn't an acceptable avenue back then, back there. Mostly it wasn't mentioned, and when it was, only as the vague butt of tacit, indirect, universally accepted jokes. Don't wear green on Thursday, that means you're queer. Don't look at other girls in the shower, what are you, queer or what? The subject was never opened for head-on discussion the way other topics were — such as was there life after death or did boys really wake up every morning with erections.

Now she looks back and wonders if anyone was fooling around with anyone else in those dorm rooms, those showers, but she can't pull up so much as a possible pair of suspects, so absorbed was everyone in the miracle of boys, the mystery of maleness. Which even caught her up for a while. She can remember getting agitated before mixers with nearby boys schools, going into the city to pick up guys they had met at rock concerts. The mixer boys had shorter hair and wore aftershave, the ones at the concerts were slightly grungier, less about them was comprehensible, but what any of them wanted on couches at parties and in cars and against support beams under the El was pretty much the same. And while it was stirring in the moment, in the between times Chris's imagination always alighted on one or another of the haughtier senior girls, and then on Alison, who returned the interest in a hot and cold way or, more accurately, warm and cold — looks that could be interpreted to have deeper levels of meaning, but might also be only vaporous or ephemeral. Occasionally, though, there would be the remark that seemed unmistakable in its meaning.

One time, for instance, Chris gave Alison a present, for her birthday, an enameled pin in the shape of a cat. "I remembered purple is your favorite color," Chris said, going for extra points. They were by the lake, on the rocks. Alison's birthday was in April and the weather was not quite nice enough for those in a normal frame of mind, just nice enough if you were in love, and Chris took it as a good sign that Alison seemed content to be there with her, pulling her jacket more closely around her rather than suggesting they go back to campus.

"But it's not really purple," Alison said, "not quite. More lavender or lilac, or, I don't know. Sometimes it's a little hard to think."

"Why?"

"Oh," Alison said, smiling, looking at the rock she was sitting on as a way of not meeting Chris's eye. "Come on."

Another time. A night Alison had gone off with Curt, a guy from Lake Bluff who would wait late at night for her in the lot behind the dorm in his Corvette, its massive engine idling in a deep, auguring way. Usually she wouldn't return until nearly dawn, with Chris listening for her, and then for her allusions to Curt in the days that would follow, always veiled and cryptic and maddening. This night, though, she came back via Chris's room, not bothering to knock at the door, first kite-high, then collapsing onto the floor next to Chris's narrow, shiplike bunk. She was filled with bottled whiskey sours and some nonlinear chat that was about absolutely nothing on the surface, everything underneath. Then she went down the hall to the john and, when she returned, slipped in beside Chris. They slept fitfully, tangled up in each other, but not doing anything identifiably sexual, only turning to press mouths against each other's hair, backs against breasts, fingertips grazing each other's shoulders and legs — anything that could be excused by the limited confines of the single bed. Alison's predawn departure signaled the end of this one-time event. It was never repeated, and never commented upon by either of them.

Chris would replay these and the rest of her small collection of Alison tapes until they wore thin, trying to extrapolate from them a further reach of whatever was happening, but lacking the imagination to get there. She had only the blurriest vision of where they might be headed, and no idea at all how to maneuver. And so things never progressed much beyond these freighted moments, which were separated by long stretches of Alison being wrapped up in her world history paper on Otto von Bismarck, or in work on the Spring Fling decoration committee, or in Curt.

In the alumnae bulletin, which Chris's mother still passes on, Alison was once mentioned, living in Marin County, outside San Francisco, working for a software company. No husband or married name or mention of children, and Chris wondered if Alison eventually found her way to the same place she herself did, if what the two of them had been doing with each other was reconnaissance.

Chris tries to put what Nida Louis is going through into a similar cha-cha pattern — one step forward, two back — and is vaguely hopeful about her eventual arrival at a better place, but is also resigned to a long meanwhile of listening to soggy installments about Pam and about Barry, the husband. (An enormous amount of what she listens to is the same story, which the client presents as a hundred amazingly different stories.) Today's is about how Barry makes them change rooms at hotels on their vacations.

"Either the bed is too soft, or the carpet doesn't look really clean to him," she says, pressing the wadded corner of a Kleenex against the fever blister, which gently weeps.

"Does it look clean to *you?*"

"Well, I guess my expectations for motel carpeting aren't that high. You know. So many toes passing through. But just because *my* standards are low —"

"Why put it that way? Maybe it's just one of a million tiny points where you view the world differently from him. Maybe it just means you're a person who doesn't sweat the small stuff where carpets are concerned."

"Hunh?" Nida says, and Chris watches her point drift off toward the ceiling, as Nida dabs at her lip with ChapStick.

Nida suffers from many small maladies. She had pinkeye last summer and then something troublesome in the bunion family had to be removed from her foot and she hobbled into several sessions wearing a podiatric shoe. Chris has to work hard to keep from thinking less of Nida for these small, unglamorous ailments. Her crummy inclination is to admire the healthy, to ascribe virtue to the athletic and good-looking. She hates herself for this weak-mindedness, which runs absolutely counter to the set of personal ethics she likes to think she holds solidly. It's as though there is a boring evil twin inside her — not someone wicked on any interesting scale, only a puerile, callow jerk hanging around making the most superficial judgments. Sometimes the jerk surfaces, unstoppable. A couple of years back a hugely fat friend from college visited and wanted Chris to take her to the women's bars. Chris faked stomach flu rather than risk being spotted by someone who might assume they were an item. Chris fears there will be a cosmic payback for these lapses in character, that she will come back in the next life as plankton.

After Nida, Chris sees one of her few straight couples — the Sidelmans, both of them painters, she quite well known — given to dramatic gesture. Most recently, she dumped a bowl of cereal (with milk and bananas) into his leather portfolio. He retaliated by going through her dresser drawers and cutting the sleeves off her sweaters.

Couples therapy is both tricky and exhausting — like being stuck in bad traffic. Often what's put on the table in sessions isn't enough to work with effectively. One partner is already out of the relationship, or having a clandestine affair (although Chris can usually spot the signs). Another may be too frightened of fallout from the sessions to be forthcoming. There is frequently a hidden agenda — one partner feigning interest in working things out while actually trying to build a case against the other. Negotiating all these variables, managing the text without seeing all the subtext, often leaves Chris exhausted, as if she has worked a shift on a construction site. Today, after three couples sessions, at eleven, noon, and one, she is completely drained by the time she finally gets a break and checks her messages. The one she wants isn't there and so she relents and calls first home, then the *Transit* darkroom. No answer at either place.

"Fuck her," she tells the empty room.

She tries calling again when she's back from getting her hair cut (badly; there's a tufty aspect to the right side), then quits trying. She will see Taylor when she gets home tonight. No matter what, Taylor always takes care of Bud. The dog walker comes in the early afternoon and Taylor is usually home by seven so Bud doesn't have too many hours to wait to be let out, to get his dinner. He's an old dog and they try to cater to him.

But even though it's eight by the time Chris gets back, Taylor isn't there, and the dog is agitated and jumps on Chris when she comes through the front door. She senses her mood shift, out of anger, but then it is unable to find another gear. It occurs to her that something is more wrong than she has been thinking, but wrong *how* she can't tell.

Perhaps if she acts as though things are normal and regular, the gods of normal and regular will rise off their celestial sofas and move into action. In this spirit, she feeds Bud, changes into sweats and a Walkman, takes the dog and Don Henley, who's singing "The Heart of the Matter," and heads up through her neighborhood park, over to the river. By the time she gets back, Taylor will be there, or at least the red light on the phone machine will be blinking.

It doesn't work. The gods are still asleep. The house is empty, the phone tape blank.

She calls Leigh.

"Hey. Have you seen my girlfriend? We had a fight." She doesn't mention its subject. Why make Leigh feel lousy about *her* girlfriend, too? "Anyway, she's off somewhere, toughing me out."

"Not over here," Leigh says. "You know she's always weird and antsy when she gets back to town."

"Especially from Morocco, don't you think?" Chris fishes.

Leigh says, "I wouldn't know about that," an expression that, in Chris's experience, is a lie about ninety-nine percent of the time it's uttered. "Call me later if she still hasn't turned up. We'll go sniff out her trail."

Chris looks at the phone for a moment and thinks about calling Audrey, then decides this will be a low-yield enterprise. Then calls anyway. Audrey is her oldest and least likely friend. These facts are doubtless related. That is, much of what brought them together initially, so long ago in college, has dissipated with the tangents they've taken since then, so that what they have accumulated is mostly history and a large accommodation of their differences.

These past few years have really been the second installment of the friendship. There was a long breach when Chris couldn't accept Audrey's ruthless retreat from the margins, from being involved with women and reasonably out about it, into the safety and perks of heterosexual marriage.

Now Chris has come to accept that while Audrey may prefer women in her bed, she does not want to dangle off any societal cliffs. These days Audrey lives far back from the edge, blocked in by a nice-guy husband and a preoccupying baby. Chris can accommodate this choice, or forsake the friendship, and she has chosen the former.

"Is this a good time to call?" Chris asks when she gets her on the other end of the line.

"As good as it gets these days. I put Horace down and he's quiet now, but that could change at any moment. What's up?"

Chris tells her about the fight with Taylor, about Taylor going off in a huff, even as she can gather from the silence on the other end that she's not going to get much sympathy.

"Oh, Taylor. So theatrical. Don't you ever get tired of it? Of always being on tenterhooks?" This isn't what Chris wants to hear. "How long has it been, a couple of years?"

"Nearly four," Chris says, reluctant to give up this piece of information.

"Really? That long? Well, that makes my point even stronger. Don't you think that by four years in, you ought to get to relax a little? Put on your slippers, your old flannel robe. Oh, I wish you and Renny had worked out. I know she was terrible in her own way, but —"

"Don't say her name. Please. It just jangles me. And of course I could say the same back at you. Why don't *you* go back with Helen from the bookstore?"

"Well, maybe because I'm otherwise occupado along those lines."

At first, Chris thinks Audrey is referring to her husband, Tom, and the baby, but then she deciphers the meaning of "along those lines."

"Along those lines *what*? I'd think you were too busy and too heterosexual these days for anything 'along those lines.' Shouldn't you be overwhelmed with motherhood? Stitches and weepy breasts and postpartum depression? I mean, haven't your social opportunities been a little limited lately?"

"This is a woman from my Lamaze class. She was her girlfriend's birthing partner, but then they broke up and — "

"Ah," Chris says, "life in the suburbs."

"Don't be sarcastic. I'll quit telling you anything." Audrey is the only person Chris knows who would still use the word "sarcastic." Recently, she referred to someone as "conceited." It's as though she was socially arrested in junior high. Now she says, in a much bigger voice, "Hi, honey." Meaning her husband has entered eavesdropping range.

"Call me when he's not around," Chris says. "I'm not sure why, but I want details on this."

Chris showers, finds some jeans and a sweater, a pair of socks; it's suddenly cool and damp in the house. She kicks up the thermostat. Bud paces. She rummages through the kitchen cupboards and finds him a rawhide strip. Usually this is good for half an hour's distraction. Now, though, he only drops it on his corner of the rug in the living room and sits guard over it.

She calls Daniel at home. She won't get sympathy from him

either, but at least she might get supper and a bit of company. For shrinks and Spaniards, ten is a reasonable dinner hour.

"How did the lunch go?" she asks, putting off telling him about Taylor.

"A dead end, I'm afraid."

She waits for more.

"She doesn't have a stove," he says finally.

"How much could that matter? How did it even come up?"

"I told her I loved to eat in restaurants and she said she wasn't interested in eating, period. Or cooking for that matter."

"Was she thin?"

"Actually she was quite a large woman. I think she might be a salty-snack-foods sort of person. Or a one-food sort of person. You know. English muffins. Potato salad. She was bleak more than anything else. Bleak and doughy would be my capsule description."

"You wonder why they matched you up with her."

"I always assume clerical error in these situations. Any other answer is too depressing."

"Hey," she says, "remember how you wanted to be nice to me this morning? Well, now I'd like to take you up on it. Can you have dinner with me? Taylor is still gone and I'd like to be casually out when she decides to slide back into the house." Chris has in mind that they'll go out and grab something at a restaurant, but he persuades her to come over to his place.

"I have a stove. More crucially, I have a microwave. Plus I have Camille with me tonight. I was going to fix dinner for us anyway. Something low-fat. I've put myself on a strict diet."

Chris thinks Daniel is a fairly good looking guy, in a recessive way. Still, he is undeniably short, and she knows this is a problem for men. He is also slightly overweight with, unfortunately, a large proportion of the extra baggage in a wide, matronly butt. He also has an excess of hair. Not just head and chest hair, but on his neck and inside his ears, dark tufts on his shoulders. He is convinced that these two aspects of his appearance are serious liabilities.

Chris has told him she doesn't think women care about the hair thing. "I mean it's not as though you have a tail."

He responded by arching an eyebrow of mystery.

He can be self-mocking, but he is also quite determined to revise himself along more conventionally attractive lines. He is, for instance, undergoing electrolysis in the back of a beauty parlor in the far, deeply Polish reaches of Milwaukee Avenue. And he has signed up to take a biking-and-hiking trek through Utah in the fall. From the brochure, there don't appear to be any horizontal stretches along their route, only varying degrees of vertical.

"Where's Camille?" she says as he leads her back into an empty kitchen. It turns out the late supper he was going to fix them all is Lean Cuisines and Diet Cokes.

"In her room doing homework. They give a lot at her school. Too much maybe. She always seems burdened. I keep thinking this should be the time in her life when she's just having fun, not being so purposeful. There's something . . . I don't know . . . joyless about her lately."

Camille, whom Chris has known since she was born, has always been a slightly magical girl, fey and fun, a storyteller, producer of elaborate puppet shows, editor of tiny newspapers. She has always made childhood seem a more wonderful place than Chris remembers it. For the past couple of years, though, she has been steering a hard course through her adolescence. The particular difficulties are hard for Daniel to determine because they mostly manifest themselves in broody silences, but from little things Camille has let slip, he suspects she is terribly alienated from the person she is becoming. She can already see that the venues of adulthood are not going to allow her to be the self she is best at. She is tobogganing full-tilt into a place where life is conducted on flat, dry ground. A place where there are few stuffed animal tea parties or cardboard castles, and no imaginary friends.

Daniel goes to shout down the hallway, calling her down for dinner. When he's back, he says to Chris, "She keeps you too much off-balance." He means Taylor.

"You only hear my side of things."

"Why are you defending her?" He opens the freezer door, fanning away clouds of frosty steam, more like special effects at a bad rock concert than the workings of a normal freezer. He points to a stack of white boxes with orange lettering. "Go ahead. Take your pick."

"I don't care. Any of them."

He pulls out roast turkey and stuffing.

"Not turkey," she says.

"How about Mexican?"

"Can I use your phone for a second?"

"Not to call home, no, I don't think so," he says, reaching over, taking the receiver out of her hand, placing it back in its cradle. "I think the better thing would be to have dinner with us, and then go home. That way, you look like you're over here really having dinner. If you call, it'll be obvious you're just trying to *look* as though you're over here having dinner."

Camille comes into the kitchen looking sleepy. One side of her face is imprinted with the crosshatch texture of her bedspread.

"I guess I crashed." She smiles lopsidedly and kisses Chris on the ear, missing the cheek she was aiming for. The older Camille gets, the more she looks like her father, which is probably not the best news for her. Her mother, Bibi, looks like Joni Mitchell, ethereal and intellectual. Camille seems to be getting her height; she is already as tall as Daniel, and will almost surely pass him by. But, like him, she is dark-haired, with broody, hooded eyes.

"What's for dinner?" she asks.

"I thought we could just have something of the frozen persuasion."

"We can't eat that stuff all the time, you know. They had a nutritionist come to our life skills class. You can eat boxes some of the time, but you have to have real food, too."

"You didn't tell them we microwave all the time, did you? I don't want a visit from some social worker, some home visit where she shows us a laminated pie chart of the food groups. Tomorrow we can make a stir-fry. You can help me. We'll make it with tofu. I don't want you to have to be ashamed in life skills."

"Oh, I'm not nearly the worst. Janine Handelman told the class she has a 7-Up and a Slim Jim for breakfast every morning. And Eric said sometimes his whole family has Pop-Tarts for dinner. We're only about in the middle." She is poking around in the refrigerator, on her knees, which are exposed through raggedy slashes in her jeans.

Daniel mans the microwave while she concocts an idiosyncratic salad of lettuce and olives and cashews.

She is writing a script, Daniel tells Chris when they are all settled on high stools at the kitchen counter. "For her video class," he says.

"It's called 'Something's Alive under the Stairs,'" Camille says.

"A romance," Chris guesses.

Through the short meal, Camille is animated and talkative enough, happy to see Chris, as usual. They have been friends since the beginning, Camille's beginning.

As soon as she is done eating, though, Camille excuses herself and disappears. About a minute later, Chris notices the red light go on on the wall phone next to her head. The private line is in use.

"Who does she call?" Chris asks.

"Some fellow named Doc. He goes to Columbia, downtown. Which as you might note is a college. Which means he has to be at least eighteen. Eighteen is too grown-up for her."

"Have you met him?"

He shakes his head. "Bibi has. He has one of those little goatees. A neohipster is what I'm picturing."

"You know, she's always been such a great person," Chris says. "First a great little person and on from there. I don't have any major worries about her. I don't think you should either."

He nods, as though he wants to believe. "I just have to bear the anxiety and keep an eye on her and hope she comes through to some other side."

"I'm trying to picture what this other side would be. Group dates with wholesome teens who climb mountains and sing? The Von Trapps?"

They sit in silence for a little while, riding their separate trains of thought.

"How about some cognac?" Daniel says.

"No thanks," she says quickly.

"Not the stuff you said you wanted to borrow to strip furniture. This is a really good bottle, a farewell gift from a graduating client, actually."

"Oh, well then. Sure."

They go into the living room, which holds a stereo and a sofa and matching recliner in purple velvet that Daniel bought without checking with anyone. This was on his way out of his second marriage.

He puts on a CD of Parisian cabaret music from the thirties and forties he knows Chris likes.

"You think I can do better," she says. "Than Taylor."

"A little better, yes. There are, as they say, other fish in the sea."

"People say that, but then they never have any other fish to offer."

"Maybe I do."

"Not that I'm looking."

He doesn't say anything.

"Who?" she says, finally.

"Well, I met this Natalie Weyman. I know she's gay. I've been on a committee with her for the crisis hotline. She's — " He catches a glint in Chris's eye.

"Too late," she says.

"Christine. Are there any women in Chicago you haven't been involved with?"

"Don't act as though I'm running through the alley with my dress over my head. I really don't have such a shocking résumé."

She's blowing smoke. He has hit upon a truth. The few times she has filled out sexual surveys, she has been surprised to find herself in the next-to-top category with regard to number of partners. This isn't too comforting, considering that the top category, she knows from designing these sorts of questionnaires herself, is invariably reserved for the people you see at the Y cozying up to the whirlpool jets.

She has all sorts of excuses for her high numbers. Some of them are even good excuses. Most of this surplus of liaisons occurred in her twenties. A lot of these connections were one-night stands attributable to the seventies and women's music festivals and coming out relatively early in her life as opposed to other dyke scenarios, such as languishing for a decade or two in a dead marriage, or frittering around for years in a closety way with ambiguous friendships.

Seducing women, letting herself be seduced by them, taking things, with a little eye contact and a few well-chosen words, off the plane of not happening, onto the plane of about to happen, then tilting the plane, this variety of fooling around became addictive in her late youth, a prolonged celebration of having come out — of her indecision, the closet, her strained one-year marriage, which she

48

realized was a mistake during the wedding reception. Finally free of all these self-imposed restraints, she spent her freedom aggressively. For quite a long while, she had no interest in monogamy or commitment. As soon as she made a passing attempt — because it was expected by somebody, or everybody — circumstances inevitably and quickly intervened. The wild party. The soul-searching talk on the late-night beach walk at the personality disorders conference. The tryst at the health club. And once, an amazing, after-hours event in a dentist's office involving an agile hygienist and a lot of nitrous oxide.

Early on in her own therapy, with Myra, this aspect of her character was the most difficult for her to crack open. At first she tried approaching it anecdotally, passing it off as a kind of jolly eccentricity.

"Making love with women," she tried to say, "is the easiest thing for me to do with them. Everything else leaps so quickly into difficult and complicated."

Myra, with the sum of her years in the listener's chair, didn't subscribe much to the notion of jolly eccentricities. "Of course," she said, "covering a lot of territory means you're never wholly vulnerable in any one place."

"Do you ever think," Chris asked, having already spent her own share of time in the listener's chair, "that making oneself vulnerable is something of an overrated enterprise?"

Of course, this was a question posed by an earlier version of herself, when she was still sailing along on the surface of her life, unknowingly on the brink of experiencing the transforming power of love, a baptism of fire, the terrible, improvident, ill-considered — unconsidered, really — opening of herself to the Person She Still Can't Talk About.

If she had been shrewder or more self-investigative, she might have seen this cataclysm coming. If she had sat in a chair opposite herself in her own office, she would doubtless have seen herself as one or another textbook case, isolated throughout her childhood, left — after all those years spent as her mother's burden, her father's accomplice — too unembraced, unflourishing, spongy with longing for merger. She could have seen that any client with such a thwarted emotional start in life was doomed to take a tumble into one or another pair of outstretched arms. But she didn't see, and her unpreparedness was part of the cataclysm, allowing as it did for the pure thrill of being ambushed.

The relationship with the Person She Still Can't Talk About — Renny — was a disaster, but one that had, as disasters do, exhilarating highlights. Like a flood leaving her sitting atop her own house, floating on roiled waters along with everything else around her that she had previously considered stationary. Or like an earthquake that had sent her floor shuddering.

And, also in the spirit of disaster, the affair left her irrevocably changed. In its aftermath, she couldn't go back to being an agnostic about love; she became an atheist, fearful of her own belief. She couldn't erase the information she now possessed. She might be ashen and wary, but she had also come to know the amount of pure feeling available in connection. Most of the time following Renny she spent cautiously alone with her understanding that what she had experienced was a new truth, and was her future — a future she wasn't nearly ready for. And so, when she did venture out, it was only into the most tepid liaisons, such as the one with Lois, the Human Pet.

But then Taylor came along and rode in over her fences, a prophet in black jeans, bearing precisely the message Chris longed to hear. Everything about her said she was someone with whom Chris could validate her vulnerability, make something important out of it, something beyond merely another experiment in terror. Finally it seemed Chris had stumbled upon another person who longed for this kind of fierce connection as much as she did.

. . .

In bed together, one of the first times, in the huge, ridiculous king-size four-poster belonging to the friends for whom Taylor is house-sitting. They've been making love for hours, through an afternoon, into the evening. Time in this room has become a rubber band.

They are both exhausted and galvanized. Taylor is dead on top of her, sweaty, smelling as much like Chris as like herself. Her mouth is pressed against Chris's ear.

"Whenever you get scared about us," she says, "think of this. You and me with no space between."

In the face of everything Chris knows to be true about the

fundamental isolation of humans, their imperviousness to real connection, or the failure of connection to alleviate the isolation, Chris wants this image to be true. With Taylor, she longs to reinvent her virginity, slip back to the place before unbelieving.

· · ·

When Chris is leaving, Daniel says, "The thing is, it's not really important that I appreciate your girlfriend. It's only important that she's coming up with enough of whatever it is that's essential to you."

"What are you talking about?" Chris says, leaping up from the defense table in an imaginary courtroom. "She listens to my troubles, takes care of me when I get a cold. She'll usually make love to me even when I'm too lazy or tired to make love back to her. She opens stuck jar tops."

"Oh. Well then," Daniel says, knowing enough to fold. "I didn't know about the jar tops."

When she pulls up in front of her house, the same configuration of lights are on as when she left. Bud comes wobbling sleepily down from upstairs; she rumples him a little, then phones the darkroom again. No answer. Then she tries her voice mail at work. It's clear; no clients, no Taylor. Then, reluctantly, she dials MarySarah's office, in case Taylor is there, working late into the night, as they sometimes do when they start to get crushed by layout deadlines.

"Mary" — about the only fun in talking to MarySarah is pretending not to get the compressed hipness of her name — "it's Christine Snow. I'm trying to get hold of Taylor and I thought maybe she'd forgotten to tell me she'd be working with you."

"Christine?" MarySarah says, as though laboring through a vast Rolodex of acquaintanceship, fingers rifling through the C's, the S's. "Oh, of course. No, hon. Haven't seen our girl all day. Just chill, though. I'm sure she'll be home soon." There was a distinct spin on the way she said "home," shaping it into a kitchen bathed in the glow from a hearth fire. A plate of warm brownies sitting on the table next to Chris, who waits while Taylor is out living a real life. Five seconds of conversation with MarySarah — any conversation, they are all as bad as this one — and Chris begins to feel a touch homicidal. She doesn't bother saying goodbye before hanging up.

She doesn't know what to do next. She doesn't want to be here alone, doesn't know where else to go. Somewhere, though. Pulling on her beat-up bomber jacket, she runs a hand through her hair, which reminds her about the new, bad cut. She goes into the bathroom and runs a wet brush through the tufty part, which seems only to reactivate it, like those compressed sponges. Recently, she has begun to notice enough gray stealing away the original pale brown that she supposes it's time to consider coloring. Maybe a chanteuse red.

She takes Bud along with her for the ride. He sits in the passenger seat, staring straight ahead, as though performing some crucial function, a mode of his Taylor refers to as the Pseudonavigator.

She pulls over into the 7-Eleven lot and buys some Marlboros. She quit smoking some years ago, but emotional extremes can still drive her to the red-and-white box. She sits with the window open, absorbed by inhaling, then rolling the smoke out into the night fog. What she thinks is, *I would never do this to her.*

She drives past Leigh's, past their friends Jane and Tina's house, looking for Taylor's Cherokee, but no luck. She tries the apartment building of a woman Taylor had a brief fling with a couple of years back. She even knows which windows to check out from having done a little light stalking while Taylor was having the affair. She can't find the Cherokee, but the woman's lights are on. Meaning nothing. She's having trouble finding meaning anywhere in this expedition.

Driving fast down emptied streets, she experiences — between the fear and growing craziness — moments of pure exhilaration, as though she and Taylor are playing some cosmic variant of hide-and-seek. And then, just as suddenly, she loses any sense at all of Taylor out here, of any presence tugging on the other end of the rope, and she is stunningly, utterly alone.

By now, it's almost one in the morning. She scans the parking lot at Paris Dance. She doesn't know what she's doing. They almost never go to bars. Taylor hardly drinks, hates smokiness. Chris is not going to find her inside sucking on a vodka tonic, tapping her toe to "I Will Survive." She knows this, but doing something, anything at all, is suddenly crucial.

And so she drives down to Belmont, parks in a tow zone outside Berlin. Inside, Chicago in the nineties is Germany in the thirties. Everything is very Weimar Republic, the girls updates of Sally Bowles with stylized, as opposed to styled, hair. White-blond crewcuts and black clothing dominate the room. Lovely fresh-cut tattoos.

The lesbian strippers are extremely audience-interactive tonight. Chris orders a glass of red wine while standing next to one who is topless and stretched out on the bar, face-down, humping the surface. Another has come down from the tiny stage, into the milling crowd, where a chunky butch is kneeling to slide a five-dollar bill from between her teeth into the top of the stripper's G-string.

This place is the domain of girls not yet, or not ever going to be, on any particular track. Women with nothing so pressing awaiting them on Friday morning that they can't give over a Thursday night to whatever might happen here. There's a broody flirting going on among them, and an arousing sour ripeness to the air, the whispered promise of sex.

Chris edges onto a stool and pulls out her cigarettes, lighting her way back a decade. Before the match is out, there are two hands clamped on her shoulders. She turns around. "Teresa."

Teresa is a looming figure with a buzz cut and massive arms and thighs barely restrained by tight jeans. She's hulky in a purple satin baseball jacket. She looks like a bouncer, although by day, in a shirtwaist dress, she teaches Shakespeare at a community college in the western suburbs. More to the point, she is old friends with the Person Chris Still Can't Talk About, although now it looks as though she will probably have to.

"How's it goin'?" Teresa shouts into the air next to Chris.

Chris nods by way of reply. The music is an engine in overdrive. Conversation has to be abridged, rechanneled into whatever gets minimal meaning across.

Teresa nods back and looks off at the dance floor. Chris hopes she'll move on, but she just keeps standing there, head bopping a little to the beat, sipping her drink. Finally, she leans in, and says, "You still with the photographer?"

"Yes," Chris tries to sound emphatic, although as she speaks, she realizes that her answer, at the moment, is only provisionally true.

She waits while Teresa processes the information, then leans in again. "She'd like to see you," she says, then adds, unnecessarily, "Renny."

Chris feels herself flinch a little, beneath the breastbone, some tiny piece of snapping cartilage. She never uses her name, has a hard time hearing it, and is really not prepared for this piece of information. By the time she works up a response, she knows she has taken way too long, shown Teresa that the message holds weight. Information that will, she knows, get relayed.

"I don't think that'd be such a good idea" is what she finally says.

Teresa nods like the Godfather, full of burdensome knowledge. She shrugs, and then is gone.

Chris is left rattled. She wonders, frightened, is there already an empty space next to her where Taylor should be, one that Teresa was able to pick up on? Her whole past and present full of women comes tumbling down on her like soft, heavy coats worked loose from an overhead train rack, an avalanche of women — none of them here at the moment, though, in this place full of women.

She has three glasses of wine in rapid succession, more than she has drunk in a night in a long time. The wine is accompanied by more Marlboros as the next stool becomes transiently occupied by a sweating stripper, then more permanently by a woman older than Chris only by a few years, but years that look to have been longer and harder ones than Chris's. Her hair is muddy blond with a dull finish of missed retrieval, a failed reappropriation of however it looked when she was young. In most other ways, though, she appears not to be trying at all, which has its appeal. Her face looks prewashed for softness. She's easy to talk to in a bar-ry way. She doesn't take Taylor's disappearance seriously.

"Some girlfriends don't like to come home nights. Not every night anyway."

While she understands that this woman might well come out of a part of the culture which is less invested in permanence, Chris nonetheless takes consolation in the notion of a whole body of lovers, a pack of wild, roving women who don't like to come home at night. She sees them skinny in zippered black leather jackets, haunting all-night diners, talking low across the cramped, smoky interiors of parked cars, heaters running on high, exhaust fanning out lazily from the tailpipes. Or kick-starting their Harleys in alleys, following each other out of town. She imagines Taylor as part of this clan.

When Chris slides off her stool and signals the bartender to settle her tab, the woman pulls out a pen and offers her phone number inside a match pack.

"In case some night you get tired of waiting for her."

The dog has been sound asleep while she was inside the bar. He stirs himself, his fur rumpled, his eyes bleary, and stands and turns around a few times on the seat, then slumps back down and shuts his eyes and begins his deep, rattly breathing as she drives through the dead end of this night.

She called home at three from the pay phone in the club, again at three-thirty, and so at least there's no shock in walking in to find the house still empty. She crashes on the sofa and sleeps for a couple of hours, but terribly, as though she's being driven around at high speeds by a blind man. As soon as she has closed her eyes and begun to doze, she wakens sharply, feeling as though the car is hurtling toward a wall.

SHE'S UP FOR GOOD the next morning — Friday — at seven, dragging herself off the sofa to let Bud out. Walking into the kitchen, she notices the soles of her feet hurt, her lower back aches. A shift in a mine would have been as restorative. A shower helps some in cutting through the gray feeling. Coffee dispels the lint in her brain. This is better, she thinks, then almost immediately has to sit down on a chair in the dining room in total defeat.

She has seven clients scheduled for today and tonight — at nine, ten, eleven, two, three, six, and eight. She simply has to go in. She starts by finding some socks, putting them on, one foot at a time.

"Hey," Daniel says when she comes in. He is doing his billing. She started farming hers out last year after she'd fallen months behind. "Everything work out last night?"

"Oh," she says, understanding after a beat or two that he assumes Taylor came home. Her first impulse is to tell him the truth, but she squashes that. "It was a nowhere fight, like I told you. We're fine." She can't remember ever having lied to him before; she's not sure why she is doing it now.

"Do you have a minute?" he asks. It's just another workday for him.

"Barely," she says. It's the truth.

"It's about James Altgeld." This client has been troubling him for some time. He is in his early forties, with a history of compulsively romancing lonely women, who he meets mostly through literature classes at the Newberry Library. He lays siege to them for a few months. There is usually money involved, debts of his paid off. Or large gifts received — significant vacations, once a boat. Then after the engagement has been announced, sometimes a little earlier, maybe right after the trip home to meet her family, he breaks off in a ruthless way, usually with a note. His reasons, as he voices them to Daniel, are always in the nature of the discovery of some fatal flaw in the beloved. Once he admitted to Daniel that he writes the notes on his computer and uses the previous note as a "template."

"I'm beginning to feel like I'm Charles Manson's therapist. Or Mengele's. You know. Like I'm sitting there fatuously asking, 'Oh, well then, how do you see your work for the Nazis fitting in with your medical career goals?' I mean, these poor women. I envision them dropping their wedding dresses off at the consignment shop, steaming the stamps off the invitations."

"Do you think he's a con man? My father had a friend who used to fleece manicurists. Apparently they're real nest-eggers. Loaded, though you wouldn't think it." She is trying to be of help even though she can barely focus this morning; she's racing through her memory, trying to call up what Daniel has already told her about James Altgeld.

"No, I don't think the money, the gifts, are the real issue, just corroboration of his prowess. I think it's more a straightforward power trip. And of course, he's misogynistic as hell. He lived with his mother until she died a couple of years ago. He claims to have worshipped her, but I'm beginning to wonder if he wasn't slipping strychnine into her cocoa."

"He doesn't see there's a pattern to any of this? A problem?" She knows she is offering only the most banal analysis.

"Just the stuff at work, like I've told you. He's misunderstood there.

Passed over for promotions. Lackluster evaluations. He's in a rage about this stuff most of the time."

"Do you think maybe you need to get him talking about the women?"

"Oh, he's only too happy to oblige on that. All their faults and flaws. The hopelessness of a man today trying to find a woman of real character. He doesn't have sex with any of them, you know."

"You never told me this part," Chris says. "How could you have left that out?" For a moment, he has her full attention.

"I'm sure I told you."

"What does he do?"

"They neck, as he puts it. He's Catholic. He doesn't even jack off. I asked."

"Doesn't that do some bad thing to a guy's dick?"

"Christine. It's like I'm talking to another sophomore by the lockers in high school."

"Well, that's about where I left off with dicks. I was just asking."

Daniel sits down on his sofa, looks like he's puzzling out the problem.

"Maybe as a way in, you could get him to talk about his start with girls, work forward from there. To how he feels after he kisses them off. See if you can get him talking about the high he gets from dumping them. Force him up against it. You've got to crack the wall somehow or this stalemate could go on forever."

He nods. She can tell he's feeling defeated, but this is all the advice she can come up with. Plus there's no more time. She heard her nine o'clock come in several minutes ago.

"Let's talk later. Call me at home if we don't get to touch base before we get out of here."

He nods again, but it's not a persuasive nod. She worries that she's failing him, which she hates. Worse this time than usual because she is also lying to him. She's protecting someone, but who — Taylor or herself, or some presentation of them as a happy couple?

It is impossible to hold on to her own troubles through a day spent listening to those of seven clients, one of them new. This is Clarissa Sims, who Chris expected, from her name, to show up fresh from the Greyhound station off a bus from downstate, carrying a cardboard suitcase, wearing a calico dress with a flower in her hat. Instead she is a wiry stone butch in her twenties with razor marks on the insides of her arms, on which she doesn't choose to remark. Chris doesn't like to rush people. She has spent enough time at poker tables, is adept at waiting for others to show their hands. Which are not always composed of the cards she expects.

When Clarissa leaves, Chris asks the 8 Ball if Taylor is coming back today, and gets VERY DOUBTFUL.

During a break in the middle of the day, Chris's mother calls. For once, her presence on the other end of the line is a relief. Her mother never mentions Taylor, so no lies or evasions will be necessary.

She wants to schedule dinner and a play with Chris. What she specifically has in mind is *Tommy: The Rock Opera*. (This is how she identifies it.) Chris stops for a moment in the conversation, trying to imagine the evening. It turns out her mother has already seen the show once. "Maury and I caught the road company at the Parker Playhouse." This theater is near their winter place in Florida. "Fabulous. We were wrong about rock and roll if it's all like Tommy."

See me, feel me, touch me, hear me, Chris thinks. "Sounds like fun," she says.

Listening, politely, to her mother, she realizes she is precisely at the intersection of the tragic and the ludicrous. Here she sits with a problem so daunting it seems that by rights it ought to stop everything in its tracks, but in fact it doesn't even slow things down. She is still going to have to make plans for *Tommy*, pay attention through the rest of the day's appointments. Feed the dog. Buy groceries and drop off her dry cleaning. Taylor's leaving is not going to let her off any hooks.

By the time she gets home, exhaustion has taken the edge off her fear and depression. She feeds and walks Bud, checks to make sure she has a clean outfit to wear tomorrow, then eats dinner — crumpled foil surprises — while standing in front of the open refrigerator. She plays back the phone tape. There are three messages, all for Taylor. 1. MarySarah wondering why Taylor missed their appointment. She refers to it as a "rendezvous." 2. Diane saying Bud is due for a rabies booster. Her voice is clipped, all business, which Chris knows is a cover for the fact that she'd take Taylor back in a minute. 3. A vapid-sounding girl from someplace called Peepers with the news that Taylor's glasses are ready. As the tape rewinds, it occurs to Chris she didn't know that Taylor needed glasses.

She goes to sleep easily and has a wonderful dream filled with color. A party on a terrace in Italy, overlooking the sea. Waking up, though, drops her about forty feet. She knows in the first minute that she won't be able to make it through another ordinary day, a day she will have to pretend is ordinary. It's Saturday. She has only two morning appointments and calls to cancel them, pleading a toothache. She stays in bed except to pee or tend to Bud, and the day passes, as if lifted outside of real time.

She spends the first part of it in a deep humiliation — like a mud bath, heavy and oozing around every part of her. Taylor has left her. How will she manage? How will she tell their friends? What posture will she be able to find that will allow her to walk into a party and appear not to notice the whispers? At what point will she no longer be waiting for Taylor to return?

But there is an essential falseness to this stance and by the afternoon, she has run out to the end of self-indulgent fantasies of rejection and unrequited love. In their absence she is left with something harder, colder; the truth is, she can't see much about herself in the equation of Taylor's departure. She's still not sure what Taylor's absence is about, but it is beginning to seem that it is probably not her. Yesterday, Taylor was first not yet home, then late, then not back. Today, some much further line has been crossed. Walking out onto the front porch into the dusk, Chris understands that Taylor is gone. In this way, one door closes, allowing another to open and let in the first cool, damp breezes of terror.

Chris goes looking through the house. Maybe she has missed some crucial piece of information, a note perhaps. But there is nothing. Everything is ordinary and usual. Taylor's dirty clothes heaped on the floor of her closet, a tube of sunblock poking out the opening of her toiletry kit perched on the toilet tank. A copy of *The Waves*, open, its binding sprung, on the floor next to her side of the bed. Aside from Taylor's car and her camera bag, all Chris can be sure is gone is her resale shop gabardine jacket. Her keys. Chris can visualize outlines of these things — dotted lines around shaped pieces of air. After a moment or two, she realizes what she's doing — creating a picture of Taylor as she was when she left. Working up a description.

She calls 911. They tell her to hang up and wait, they'll have someone from Missing Persons call her back. This happens within minutes. The woman on the other end has a form in front of her. Chris can feel it sitting there between them, a comfort, implying as it does that what is happening to her, to Taylor, is so common that there's a standard form to accommodate it. They'll need a description, a name.

She hesitates a moment, trying to hold things for just a fraction of time, back where they were, in the clouded realm of before. Then she crosses the threshold. "Taylor Heyes," she says, trying to think where to begin, to come up with a first point in a galaxy of points. Any one of them will be inadequate, so she picks one at random. "She's tall."

CHRIS THROWS UP — the pizza Leigh ordered for them earlier in the evening, and what looks to be most of the coffee she's had through the day. She can't remember having thrown up since childhood; it brings with it a flash memory of the flu, her mother's hand on her shoulder, then lifting the damp, matted curls off the back of Chris's neck. The bathroom with yellow tiles, the mint green ceramic fish, three gold ceramic bubbles eternally suspended above its placid fish face. She has so few memories of being mothered that this recollection runs a thin vein of happiness through her misery. Then her stomach wrenches and heaves again.

She presses her cheek against the cool porcelain of the toilet bowl. After a while, she gets up slowly, testing for steadiness, then flushes. For a brief moment, balancing like a ballerina at the towel bar, she feels dramatically better, cleared out. Then the headache begins to rise again, an internal tide. If she tilts her head, it washes through that side of her brain; she needs to hold very still. Very.

There's a great knocking on the other side of the bathroom door, imperious and commanding, a visitor out in the storm at the door of the old mansion. She tries to sort out what proportion of this loudness is her own internal amplification and concludes that the knock was probably just a regular knock, maybe even a polite one, light knuckles on thin, old wood.

"Everything all right in there?" Leigh employs a brisk voice, the saleslady outside the fitting room in budget sportswear. She is here, mercifully, without Tiffany, who has a performance tonight.

Chris opens the door. "No."

"Mmm. Smells good. And you *look* good, too."

"I had a terrible headache like this a couple of times before. I think it's stress-related. That, or caffeine overload."

"It's a migraine," Leigh says matter-of-factly. "What you have is a classic migraine. I have a little potion that'll take care of it." Leigh has something for whatever is ailing anyone. She is friendly with a pharmacist of casual ethics, also with an international flight attendant who picks up tough-to-come-by drugs that are, however, over-the-counter in other parts of the world. Knowing Leigh is like having an amazingly sympathetic doctor who knows just what you need and also happens to have it with her somewhere in the deep reaches of her bag.

Chris expects the potion to be a pill and pulls back a little at the appearance of what looks like a marker pen. Leigh has a foot up on the edge of the tub and is loading the device with a tiny syringe.

"What's that?"

"Shut up," she says as she presses the nose of the marker hard to Chris's upper arm and fires.

Leigh has a slightly dated, hard-boiled quality that makes her seem, not older, but from an older-fashioned time. She reminds Chris of Eve Arden. Now she puts the lid down on the toilet. "Just sit here for a minute. I'll tell Mr. Tough Guy you'll be right along." She's referring to the cop waiting in the living room.

Chris does as she's told, waits leaning against the wall with a weird buzzing in her jaw, but the headache does begin to recede.

A sequence of calls earlier in the evening has filled her house, yielded up Leigh, then Daniel. Calling him was nearly as hard as calling the police. The two of them tell each other everything (a fact that bugged the hell out of Taylor; once, in bed, in the middle of trying an adventuresome bit of technique on Chris, she stopped and said, "I wonder how you'll describe this to Daniel"). They have been closest friends since graduate school. They set up in practice together straight off, consult on each other's cases, also on the cases that they themselves are. Their intimacy is based on telling each other the worst, showing each other their most vulnerable undersides. When Daniel threw out his back, Chris sat with him, came by for four days, emptied the mayonnaise jar he peed in before he was able to walk the distance between bed and bathroom. He sat up with her the night after her iffy mammogram, before the doctor went in with a needle and found the lump to be fluid and innocuous.

They have seen each other through broken hearts. He is the only person she could ever have confided in the time she stupidly brought someone home from a bar one night and left her sleeping the next morning when she had to run off to make an eight o'clock appointment, then came home to discover, over the next couple of days, that she was missing some jewelry and a leather jacket.

And so her hiding Taylor's disappearance is a sad marker. He came over as soon as she called, and will, she knows, put his hurt aside and do whatever friendship requires from here on, but there is a tear now in the smooth fabric of their relationship.

While she was in the bathroom, Daniel sat in the living room with the cop who has come by to begin the investigation. This cop is a guy in a suit and a fifties crew cut that doesn't appear to be a hip, retro version, but rather the real thing. He taps tiny breath mints into his mouth from a small container. There is dandruff on the shoulders of his jacket. He is Detective Sikora. Ted.

First he fished for simple information, a bland cataloguing of Taylor. Age and weight and occupation, names of her immediate family members, and do they know what she was wearing when she left the house? A little while in, though, he seemed to be shifting onto some offensive. Any problems at work? Had she seemed depressed lately? This was where Chris needed to leave and throw up, although the connection between the cop and the nausea was not exactly clear to her. Now, although her esophagus is raw, her face is scrubbed and she is fresher, readier to field his questions.

"Your friend. She got a boyfriend or somebody like that?" he asks.

"I guess I'd be the somebody like that," she says, throwing him for only half a beat.

"You two have any kind of domestic dispute?"

"Nothing big enough to cause this," Chris says.

"What about drugs, any problems there? Bad debts? Enemies?" He's looking at her as he talks, but his hands have put down notepad and pen and are softly wrapped around Bud's head, thumbs rubbing behind the dog's ears. She's a fool for anyone who appreciates the dog. Of course, she realizes the dog rubbing could just be part of some tricky, good-cop thing.

She doesn't want to talk about Taylor to someone who doesn't know her. It makes Taylor seem scarily out of the loop. Why can't Leigh handle this part? She's used to dealing with cops, mostly at crime scenes where she arrives breathless, her sound and camera crew in tow. She and Sikora even know each other in passing. This familiarity, though, is not turning out to be much help tonight. Leigh makes him nervous because she's a high-profile media somebody watching him doing his job up close. In turn, he makes her nervous because he's sniffing around a powder keg with a lighter in his hand. Leigh is deeply closeted. She even has a cover, a fiancé, a banker named Frank Weiss. They've been "engaged" for years.

Neither she nor Leigh nor Daniel is his or her best self tonight. It's as though each of them is a student actor looking for a way to play an unfamiliar role. The manner Daniel has assumed has been pragmatic, calm, implicitly upbeat — the way he would be with a distressed client. Together — the three of them and the police — they're ready to take on the situation and dispatch it. As though Taylor's disappearance is a small matter of misscheduling, an overdraft at the bank, resolvable with a few phone calls, the right attitude.

Earlier, before Sikora arrived, Daniel clasped his hands like a camp counselor working up a volleyball game, and said, "What we need is lists." As though assembling stacks of friends, or books Taylor has read, patterns of movement from her old Filofaxes, is going to produce a hologram, 3-D and virtually realistic, which will then metamorphose into Taylor herself. This brisk, businesslike approach has done nothing to lift Chris's spirits, only backed her into a small, nihilistic corner.

Leigh is a different kind of useless. She has taken an indignant high road, her manner edgy, caffeinated. As though being pissed at Taylor and her missingness will whip everything back into shape, as if the circumstances are merely tricky and inconvenient. Chris hoped Leigh would be a steadying force; her stock in trade is, after all, tragedy, but of course these are the tragedies of others. ("Here in Aurora tonight, residents are stunned at what has happened in their once sleepy, peaceful town.") Here in this small living room, Leigh has lost her voice, her command of catastrophe. All she has been able to do is punt with a jazzy irritation.

"Why do I feel nothing's being *done?*" she says to Chris but really to Sikora, who is sitting across from them. "Why do I feel this little chat isn't the sort of priority treatment you'd see if it was a person with a slightly higher profile who disappeared — Sharon Stone or Oprah or the Pope? The Pope having a Grand Slam breakfast at Denny's and *pffft!*"

Actually, Chris thinks the police have responded pretty fast and heads-up. She doesn't want to get them pissed off right away. She begins to see what Leigh is up to, though — using irritation as a way of holding open the door through which Taylor will be able to walk with some nearly reasonable explanation. *You won't believe what happened,* Taylor will still be able to say as Leigh and Chris and Daniel roll their eyes at each other and issue stage sighs and laugh with release and embarrassment that they reacted so precipitously, bringing in the police. Leigh's tactics are a way to fend off fear, a way of not allowing it a jinxy seat in the room. She is trying, even in this late moment, not to let down the conceit that what they are waiting out is just a fluke, which will smoothly reshape itself into anecdote as soon as it's resolved, which will be any moment now.

What Chris would like is a break. She would like Daniel to settle down, Leigh and the cop to stop sparring, the cop to stop asking all these wrongheaded questions.

"Taylor's not a weirdo." She tries to simplify for him. "She's not a peculiar person with dark secrets. You're on the wrong track. You're on the 'Unsolved Mysteries' track."

He nods, clicks his pen point in and out. "A person who has disappeared has been taken out of what appears to be ordinary life. Which means, either something peculiar has happened to them, or their life wasn't really so ordinary. It helps us if we know which type of situation we're looking at."

"You mean whether Taylor was kidnapped from choir practice," Leigh asks, still jacking up the conversation, "or whether it will turn out that the sweet little Hallmark shop she ran out at the mall had a satanic ritual rec room in the basement?"

"Something like that. Did she, do you know, have an address book? One of those little date keepers maybe? Anything along those lines would be a big help."

"She does," Chris says, "but she keeps it in her bag and that seems to be gone with her. I know her family. I'll call them."

"Even an old one might help." He's stuck on the address book. "Maybe it's lying around and you've forgotten about it."

"I can give you numbers of everyone she knows."

"Maybe," he says in a way Chris doesn't like. "And while you're looking around, you can help us out by calling anybody you can think of."

She has become possessed by certain images. She regrets all the docudrama TV she has seen, all the ponytailed maniacs driving aimlessly across Arkansan landscapes, their trunks stuffed with trussed women nabbed from mall parking lots, women with rags crammed down their throats, their mouths sealed with duct tape. If Taylor is gone and not calling, perhaps she is someplace she can't call from. This is both the likeliest excuse for Taylor's absence and the one Chris least wants to consider. Still, the pictures force themselves on her. Her inner eye has no lid to shut them out.

She tries to imagine being inside a trunk. Sealed off in a basement. She holds still and can hear a rutted dirt road thumping beneath the tires of the car. Or, alternately, a dripping in the corner of a remote, rural cellar, behind a water heater that goes on periodically with a small, explosive sigh. Dry leaves scud past the boarded-up casement window. The rest is dead air waiting to be split by the sudden sound of a footfall on the stair.

Sikora leans forward and the holster under his suit jacket creaks. He's a lean, rangy guy, probably a basketball player in high school. Now, though, in his early fifties, he has sloped shoulders, a small, hard-looking gut nudging against the beltless waistband of his synthetic trousers.

"I want to be helpful," Chris says. "That is, I want you to find her, of course. It's hard, though, all this picking around at who she is."

"I'll just need a photo for now," he says, "and then I'll be out of here."

Chris turns and pulls one off the door of the refrigerator. A magnet shaped like a piece of shrimp sushi clatters to the floor. She hands over the picture.

This is one Chris took. In it Taylor is sitting in an Adirondack chair, although the setting is nowhere near the Adirondacks, but rather up in Door County, where they rented a cabin for a week of last summer at the Three Sisters resort, the only place they could find that would take Bud, too.

• • •

They're up at the lake, the one with the cabin and the Adirondack chairs. It's an August night, warmer than would seem possible for someplace this far north, this deep into a country of pine forests and deep water.

They go into town for a fish fry supper, then afterward walk along the main street, looking into the windows of shops that sell printed T-shirts, taffy, painted weathervanes. Then beyond, past the small city hall. There's an old school, a looming sort from the 1920s with dark brick and small windows, designed, it would seem, to frighten small children.

There's a playground around back, a scattering of weather-beaten teeter-totters, a set of rusted parallel bars, a slide worn shiny by a million thrilled descents.

The two of them settle into side-by-side seats on the splintery boards of the swing set. At first they're idling, talking in a small way, but then they fall into silent swinging, sinking back into their separate girlhoods. Pushing off the cracked ruts of dirt

68

beneath them, then, airborne, pumping backward, stretching forward, hands gripping the sweaty metal chains.

Chris looks over and sees Taylor's feet, big and kidlike in her Teva sandals, their soles pressing against the night sky. And then she is dragging these soles along the ground, lightly with each return, until she has slowed herself enough to leap onto the grass beyond them. She almost falls, rights herself, turns — a winner in some private game — and grins at Chris with her whole being.

In this instant, Chris realizes she has never seen Taylor this happy, this kind of happy. It implies someplace within where a wholly gleeful Taylor resides, someone whose acquaintance Chris has yet to make.

■ ■ ■

Now, Chris notices that in the photo Taylor is holding a copy of *The Bell Jar,* and she thinks, who over the age of nineteen would be reading Sylvia Plath? Everywhere now she is looking for some dark cast to Taylor's soul which she might have missed, or not wanted to see.

Sikora stares down at the photo, too, as though he's going to be quizzed on it in detective school. Chris looks at it again, through his eyes, and can already see Taylor's wide smile, the teeth too white against her underexposed face on a mail flyer or a toll booth.

"She could just be starting fresh somewhere," he says. "Sometimes that happens." All his words are measured, marked.

Chris tries to imagine this possibility — Taylor in a motel, going through job ads, having breakfast on the road, kidding with the waitress in the diner, inhaling the sizzling bacon scent of her new life, having left everything old behind — but she can't. Taylor doesn't have to start anew; she fine-tunes herself every day. She doesn't need to secret herself in the folds of some hotel; she travels constantly. How could there be any unfulfilled need to vanish in someone who is always disappearing anyway?

And if it was simply that she was tired of Chris, she had only to announce her departure before making it, as she has in the past with other women. Why would she need to leave Chris in a worse way?

"Maybe we'll get some answers for you right away, but sometimes these things take a little time," Sikora says at the door. Chris has no idea what he really thinks, although surely he thinks something. She has already imagined him into a guy who has seen too much in his years on the job and has come down to operating mostly on flinty, sharp-edged hunches. She wants to ask if it seems to him that Taylor is some particularly bad variant of gone, but because there's only one answer she could bear, she can't take the chance.

"He's okay, really," Leigh says, nodding toward him as he gets into his unmarked car, a boxy brown Chevy.

"Nobody's okay," Chris says, shutting off the porch light as he pulls away.

Daniel goes upstairs to sleep in the guest bedroom. "I thought I'd stay over. Just to be around. In case." Chris can tell from the exchange of looks passing to the side of her that he and Leigh have had a discussion out of her presence. She gives him a hug to show she's glad for his kindness, his presence, although she's not sure she wouldn't rather they both left her alone. She's growing weary with being buoyed by all this bonhomie.

To appear polite and seem appreciative, Chris stays down in the kitchen, sits at the table and watches as Leigh cleans up, tossing everything into the trash with insouciance; recycling has not really crossed over into her consciousness yet. She litters on highways, too — whole sacks full of burger wrappers and congealing fries go sailing out her open window, the sort of full-throttle landscape pollution no one does anymore. Chris worries about adding anything larger than a nail clipping to the global slag heap.

While Leigh washes their few dishes, Chris tells her about the car trunk she sees Taylor folded into. "Sometimes it's a basement. I can see it so clearly. Perfectly."

"Yes, and that's why you're not a professional clairvoyant, why you don't have your own 900 number, because you're not really seeing anything. You're only cooking up your version of the worst."

Chris wipes her eyes and face with a paper towel and slides her glasses back on. "What would be the *best?*" she says.

Leigh stands thinking a long moment, yellow rubber gloves dripping onto the wood floor. Chris only now notices that Leigh's nose is raw beneath the nostrils, and under her eyes are shiny maroon hollows. She hadn't considered that Leigh might, off on her own, loosen her tough upper lip to weep for Taylor.

In the ordinary run of life, Leigh is not really Chris's kind of person. A little too abrasive, her judgments a little too packaged. If it weren't for Taylor, they probably wouldn't be friends. Still, even though she is at the moment quite tired of Leigh, Chris is nonetheless deeply grateful for her presence here tonight. If nothing else, she and Daniel add physical weight to this situation, which more and more seems in danger of coming completely untethered.

"You two had a fight," Leigh constructs her best-case scenario. "You say it wasn't bad, but maybe it was from her end. Bad enough."

"Bad enough for this?"

"Honey, she's always packed anyway. She's used to leaving. And coming back. Which she will. She even left me once." It's clear Leigh thinks she is coming up with an extraordinary scenario.

Chris brightens with the news of a precedent. "For how long?"

"Oh, a few days, as I recall."

Chris is nodding with relief when Leigh adds, "She called that time, though. She was staying at my sister's, which really galled me."

"It wasn't at all the same thing, then," Chris says. "This thing, what's happening now, isn't the same as anything before it."

"Maybe not," Leigh admits. Her beeper goes off. They both look up at the old Blatz bar clock on the wall. It's after midnight. She picks up the receiver on the wall phone and calls the station to find there's been a major murder. A teenage brother and sister in Kenilworth have blown away their parents and grandmother with a nine-millimeter semiautomatic they bought from a friend at school.

"I hope the parents don't turn out to be shrinks," Chris says. "I hate when that happens."

Leigh shakes her head. "He's an ad exec. Super-rich. Anyway, I've got to get up there pronto. Before they bring out the bodies. That's the crucial shot — the bag on the stretcher. Will you be able to get some sleep?"

"The thing about sleep is that it becomes less and less interesting," Chris says. "You know?"

Early the next morning, she is still sitting in the living room, on the chair by the window, immobilized. Bud climbs up into her lap, even though there really isn't enough room for both of them.

"You're a big baby, you know. For such an old dog."

A car pulls up out front. For a few seconds she's sure it's Taylor's Cherokee and suddenly everything she has constructed — all the scaffolding around her fear — collapses, is unnecessary.

And then she sees it isn't Taylor's Cherokee, isn't a Cherokee at all, just a small van. She recognizes the guy who gets out of it as one of their neighbors from across the street. He's compact, muscle-bound, wearing a Grateful Dead T-shirt, now unloading flats of impatiens to fill in his garden. She hates him for his easy possession of a perfectly ordinary Sunday.

When Daniel finally wakes up, he needs to hurry to make it to church. He is recently Unitarian, joined up with a progressive congregation in Evanston, she suspects, as another way of meeting likely women. At any rate, they made him an usher and so he has to show up for the service.

He offers to come back later; he has some idea of going through Taylor's clothes and books and papers, trying to see if they could fill in the blanks, figure out what she had taken and, by implication, what kind of journey she planned. This seems like an extremely low-yield enterprise to Chris. What's in it for her? If Taylor has taken nothing, she's in the psychopath's trunk. If she has packed her car to the gills, she has left Chris in a horrible, bloodletting way from which there will never be any getting back together.

"Oh. You're not really up to this, are you?" he says in a talking-to-your-aged-aunt sort of voice. They have both developed, over time, professionally sincere tones, which she knows are manifestations of real sincerity. Nonetheless, she has begun to hate hearing them, particularly when they are directed at her.

"Actually, I'm busy," she says in an attempt to adjust the conversational level down a notch or two. "I have a date with someone new tonight."

She has given Leigh all the phone numbers she can think of. The only people she has to contact herself are the ones she least wants to, Taylor's family — her mother and her sister, Desta. These reduce to one when Desta says she will call Ardith, her mother. It will be better this way, she assures Chris.

"Do we know what's going on here?" Desta is a pediatric dentist. She uses the dental "we" a lot, as in "We're going to look *way* back in here." The suspicion behind the question, if Chris has gauged accurately, is not that Desta thinks she has Taylor chained to a pipe in the gardening shed, but that she has done something shabby or hard that would drive anyone as decent as Taylor away.

"I think she's been a little down lately," Chris says. She can hear her voice breaking and hates that she can't control it. She pauses and tries to phrase things in the flattest possible terms. "She's been traveling even more than usual, on account of the Morocco book. It wears her down. The time zones. It even throws her periods off. Warps her moods. They've done studies on this sort of thing with flight attendants — "

"And I'm sure they're fascinating. Have you contacted anyone?"

"Pardon?"

"A detective agency?"

"Oh, the police are handling things."

"I can't imagine they're doing anything but going through the motions. I'll talk with Ardith."

The Heyeses feature themselves artistic and progressive. Ardith was a painter in her day. She did portraits of the moderately famous. A series of governors. A few socialites. Two of Taylor's brothers are writers, a poet and a playwright. But as far as Chris can see, they are really quite a conventional lot. The money for the artistic endeavors came from machinery — a line of machines Taylor's father manufactured to repair other machines. Taylor once tried to explain it to Chris. The father made the money and was generous with it and patted the precocious heads of his wife and children. But all of them knew enough to keep things within bounds. No nude performance pieces. No sacrilegious sculptures. The poet brother has published two small books of inspirational verse, rhymes to help the troubled get through this or that bad day. The playwright specializes in historical pieces on whaling. Chris hasn't seen any of these. She has dismissed the whole family enterprise as middlebrow, and only sometimes feels snobbish for holding the sentiment. (And of course because she loves her, Chris chooses to think of Taylor as the family's exception, the one true artist to come out of all this posturing.)

She tries to listen patiently whenever Taylor reminisces about her whimsical childhood. How she and her siblings all went to ungraded free schools, were allowed to sing at the table and fingerpaint on the walls and first-name their parents. Desta is, in a way, the least pretentious of the lot. She gave up on her budding noncareer at the pianoforte and lurched straight into dentistry.

"We'll get back to you," she tells Chris. "I'll probably have to come out there." She sighs to indicate all the small patients whose appointments will have to be rescheduled, all the time stolen from her life with her family. But, nonetheless, it must be done. An adult presence must be brought to bear on the situation.

"I think we're doing all right out here as it is," Chris says, summoning up a "we" of her own.

"Christine. We're her family. These are *family* decisions."

Chris hangs up on Desta, which doesn't seem nearly enough. She longs for a phone feature to help her: call-exploding.

She sees herself moving into a crucial cycle of darkness and light. The heat-seeking part of the rotation draws her into the presence of others. The great thing about humans, she thinks, is how they talk and move about, shut the windows when it grows cool, turn on the lamps against the spreading gray of dusk, put on a CD to ward off silence. All of which is comforting, for a while. And then exasperating when she suddenly, desperately needs to curl in on herself, to be amorphous, aquatic, eddying on a sea bottom. It is only in this place that she can still have Taylor with her.

Taylor's darkroom is in the same old warehouse building as the magazine, but with a separate entrance in the back, what was once the loading dock. Chris has a key because Taylor loses hers regularly, along with wallets and sunglasses and notebooks. Gloves in theaters.

• • •

"Nearly everything I've ever owned is gone, disappeared into some sucking black hole," Taylor tells Chris, having looked unsuccessfully through two trunks and a footlocker for her high school yearbook. "Where are all my great old albums? I don't even know. My Mamas and Papas and Jefferson Airplane — pre-Starship. And my Peggy Lipton record, from 'The Mod Squad,' a gem. It's my irresponsibility of course, but also all the moving I've done, boxes stored in friends' garages, but now I've forgotten the friends. Those spacey Jesus People movers leaving things in closets. That bad breakup with Janine, where I couldn't get my stuff out."

"There's an old piece of conventional wisdom about all that, you know, about losing stuff behind you as you go through life," Chris tells her. "Ben Franklin or somebody like that said that three moves are as bad as one fire."

"I feel like I've had seven moves," Taylor says, then reconsiders. "No. Make that seven fires."

• • •

Chris fiddles with the key in the stubborn lock tumblers and, once inside, has trouble finding the light switch. She tries to think if she has ever been in here without Taylor.

The place is a genial mess. There are two rooms — the darkroom at the back, and in front an office–waiting room, although there are really no customers to do any waiting. Still, there is a sofa (which has always bothered Chris in its lack of a strictly business *raison d'être*, idle cushions being the devil's decorating) and a low table covered with dead cans of pop, grease-blotted pizza cartons, opened mail. Stacked everywhere are shallow yellow boxes of prints, numbered and titled in heavy marker scrawl. There is a neatness beneath the surface disorder, the cataloguing essential to photographers, providing access to the thousands of tiny squares of light and dark, the contact sheets and negatives, the rights and permissions material, the urgently needed one thing in the midst of everything. Taylor says taking the pictures is the easy part.

Chris sinks into the squooshy sofa and is taken by surprise when it releases a light gust of Taylor's smell, incredibly faint really, but it is enough to send her off the rails. Tears begin sliding down her face. This is the first time she has pulled the focus off Taylor and onto herself, seen herself as a suffering figure, left so terribly alone, a hitchhiker on some untraveled highway, without any idea if she will ever see headlights.

Ever. Never. The vocabulary of her thoughts has come to rest on absolutes.

She goes into the darkroom. Evidence is everywhere of the developing and printing of film Taylor shot this last time in Morocco. Negatives hang from clips over the bath. Pushpins hold contact sheets on the corkboard wall. Shots meant to induce tourism: open trucks piled high with oily olives; medina stalls barely big enough to contain their owners and wares — jars of colored buttons, mounded conical towers of spices. She flips through the contact sheets, finding nothing that offers a clue. She has turned to leave before it strikes her. She goes back to the last contact sheet on the right. There are only four strips of negatives printed on it. Each of the other sheets has six strips. There'd be no reason to leave off any negatives unless they were so badly ruined — over- or underexposed — that there was no point to printing them. That, or else they were shots not of colorful Morocco, but of something Taylor didn't want hanging from a clip, even in this private place of work.

Chris begins going through the files of negatives.

It doesn't take too long; what she is looking for is in the envelope, marked "Merzouga," with the rest of the roll. They are thirteen shots in rapid sequence, one not terribly different from that before it, an automatic-drive riff.

The subject is a woman. Chris sets to work. She pulls developer and fix and stop-bath bottles from underneath the counter and pours them into trays, turns on the enlarger. She learned the basics from Taylor. In the beginning it was part of the heat. They would take pictures of themselves together — in bed of course, but otherwise too, and develop and print them. Another way of being together in the dark.

Two hours later she stands bathed in red light. In front of her, clipped up to dry, are thirteen damp, slightly curling prints she can go crazy with.

The woman is older than Taylor, or at least has a face that has accrued a few more lines. She is interesting-looking in a way that's from someplace else. There is an intensity of expression American women don't typically rise to. Her features are carved from broad planes. Her eyes are so dark that, in the photo at least, it is impossible to distinguish pupil from iris. Her mouth slouches, like Julie Christie's, Jeanne Moreau's. And that is, in fact, her essence. She looks like a real-life version of a sixties film vamp. Like someone with a big past and a face she has earned. She is startled, looking over her shoulder with an expression of surprise and vulnerability that makes it clear she is in love with the photographer.

What was an indecipherable jumble on the negatives has blown up and reversed itself into a clear background — an azure wall, worn away in patches, exposing a crumbly terra-cotta. A sign hangs above the woman, off to the right, the Coca-Cola logo in Arabic script.

Who she is in these photos, more than anything else, is who Chris isn't. Which feeds Chris's private nightmare of losing not because of anything she does, but simply because of who she can't be. Now here is the nightmare incarnate, this non-Moroccan, non-American woman nonetheless in Morocco. The problem Taylor left behind, what has been holding her gaze on some inner middle distance.

The basement and car trunk vanish, along with the image of Taylor hiking the Himalayas in a white robe, on a spiritual quest, as Chris's fears begin to reshape themselves along more familiar lines.

"I DIDN'T KNOW where else to come." Chris is worried that she might be making a mistake, opening up what was carefully, professionally finished and closed.

"No need for apologies," Myra says, waving them away. "No excuses called for. The conventions, they're for the ordinary course of affairs. Now you have — you have these unfortunate circumstances." She pulls a stack of bloated appointment books, their corners curled, out of the bottom desk drawer and begins rifling through them. "How long has it been? Since we last met?" Chris notices the stains on the pages, crusty patches of this or that solitary working lunch between sessions. Soup from a widemouthed thermos.

A little over five years. She tries to accommodate how old Myra has grown in this short time. How much older. She was already old when Chris started seeing her and that must be eight or nine years back. Now she seems ancient. Her face has fallen in around her mouth in great, sucking creases. Watery brown spots float on the backs of her hands. Her movements are more deliberate, visible mechanisms of fulcrum and lever and pulley.

She has made them tea, two cups with a single bag. The cups are old and cracked and not as clean as they might be. Myra sets them down, one on the low table next to her chair, the other on the wide, threadbare arm of the chair in which Chris is sitting, the fabric stained with the concentric circles of a hundred transient cups before this one, some of them surely tattoos of cups sipped during her own past hours in this room.

A sharp ruffle and flutter, and the air turns metallic with tiny screeches, followed by more subdued chatter from Myra's cockatiel (the other Tiffany) as she totters along the edge of a bookshelf over Myra's shoulder.

"She's drunk," Myra says, reaching out toward the bird with a beckoning finger, which Tiffany rejects coyly with back-and-forth bobs of her tiny head. "She licks the Windex off the lamps after the cleaning lady has come. It gets her loaded."

Tiffany alights on the toe of Chris's running shoe and begins picking at the laces. She tries to imagine the cleaning lady armed with a mere bottle of Windex in the face of the stupendous clutter of this office, its Tiffany droppings and seed hulls, its way too many chairs, crammed and sagging bookcases, carpeting layered over with Navajo rugs. Now the room is further crowded with the two of them. Even the air is overoccupied, dense with smoke that is as much an element as the furniture, Myra sitting like Jabba the Hutt, enveloped in her own exhalations. She has already lit a Pall Mall to get things going, dropping the match into a standing brass ashtray that looks to have wandered in from the lobby of a cheap hotel.

"So," she says. "Tell me what it was like with her before she went away. Sometimes if you look at the first act of the play, you can see an outline of the second." Myra's association with Chris predates Taylor and so she doesn't know her. But her question is too large, and Chris can't immediately see a way to begin breaking it down.

"Well, of course, it's been complicated," she starts, "like trying to hold on to smoke." She opens and shuts a hand in midair. "Or grabbing at something aquatic. All that's available, really, with some-one like her, is hoping the waters will suit her enough to stay. Well, that and always being a little nervous."

Myra considers for a moment. "I can't believe you didn't find this tiresome."

"Actually, it's the opposite. All along I've been off-balance, of course, but I'm also fascinated by the power she holds over me. She is only my second venture into giving over. There was . . . well, you know . . . the Person I Still Can't Talk About — "

"Renny." Myra has little patience for the worship of love objects.

"Yes. And now Taylor." She cocks an ear. "Do you hear a sound, a little ping-ping-ping?"

"Mmmm. Hearing aid," Myra says, lifting a piece of lead-colored hair (where does she even find anyone to dye it this awful, prison-matron shade?) to reveal the piece of tan plastic nestled within the recess of her left ear. She catches Chris's smile. "I know. It's like a joke. The blind surgeon, the deaf confessor. But really, it works wonderfully. Improves things, actually." She taps it happily, as if in a commercial. "I'm hoping it will extend my years of practice indefinitely." She pauses a moment, shutting her eyes, then says, "I'm wondering how this slipperiness of hers went for you, really. This elusive lover. Weren't there, I'm guessing, moments when you wished she would disappear just to put an end to your waiting for her to do it?"

"Well, of course, a hundred thoughts haunt me now. Everything was so complicated. But now nothing is. Complicated sits way back there across this wide divide. Now the sum of her is that she's gone. The sum of me is that I'm waiting. I wait. And miss her. It's an extremely reductive situation."

She mentions the photos of the woman in Morocco. She means for this revelation to be a bombshell, but Myra only shrugs.

"Perhaps significant, perhaps nothing. She could have been a minor distraction." Chris hasn't been allowing for this possibility — that there could be this other person at the edge of the frame *and* that her existence would not be the crucial piece of information. She doesn't particularly like this theory, but she knows Myra might be right. Even on her own she has come to see that Taylor's casual faithlessness might be insignificant, only a way of bleeding off restlessness while still being in the relationship, or at any rate always returning to it. Still, she was almost hoping this woman, this time, signified somehow. It was calming to have a focus for her anxiety, a villain.

Myra tugs a shred of tobacco off her tongue, pulls her thin, brightly colored shawl around her shoulders. The day outside is blustery; in here it is alternately dank, then broily when the space heater kicks in. "I'm thinking aloud now, and my question is for you as a colleague as much as for you as my client. We try to manage loss and staunch grief — such a large piece of the work we do. But perhaps these are emotions based on perilously false assumptions. You know, that the other will be there indefinitely, that this is the normal state of things, what happiness should be predicated on. When in fact, eventually everyone leaves, most sooner rather than later."

"But then what would be an appropriate hope?"

"Well, there you have it. A good question. And I'm not sure what the answer is. Perhaps living in a series of authentic moments?"

Chris finds herself suddenly impatient. "Oh, Myra. Emotions don't have any interest in lining up for authentic moments, or for being cautious. Everyone wants love, important love, stretching to their horizon. What does it matter that this expectation is loony, that we're all walking along I beams or passing under falling safes, headed for trouble? When you love someone you want them to stay, against everything you know is cosmically positioning itself against that."

"Yes, of course," Myra says. "I'm just trying to get you to think a little about accepting a certain measure of powerlessness. It's hard at your age, I understand. When you get a little older, you start surrendering to the idea a little more. Now that I've lost two husbands and one of my children, I'm becoming close to philosophical. But you aren't there yet. You can't expect to be. You want her to come back, and we have to hope that happens. And also . . . also prepare as much as we can for the possibility that she might not."

"I don't sleep much these days," Chris says. "I've got plenty of small hours to think my way through, and read. I've been raiding Daniel's shelves. He has a ton of material on loss and grief. But all the information I can get only seems like so many blotters dropped into this huge waterfall, my Niagara of fear and misery." She stops, feels herself balking the way her own clients do when they hit one wall or another. "All of a sudden I feel ridiculous sitting here. As though we're having some fatuous little salon. You're holding out a tray full of small, stupid canapés while I'm starving and what I really need is bread and meat. A sandwich."

Myra nods and leans across the space between them and takes Chris's hands. "Darling, this is what the books can't say. There are some terrible times when knowledge isn't power, when being sane won't save you. You are standing in the middle of the night in an arctic sea on a flaming ship that's exploded. Maybe I can help. I'm going to try. But perhaps all I can do in this moment is make you slightly less alone on deck."

Chris calls from a pay phone in the lobby of Myra's building — first to the most stable, least needy of her clients, to cancel their appointments for this week. She is torn between not wanting to abandon any of them, and fearing that if she tries to manage everything whirling around her at the moment as well as her full client load, she will crack, do something unseemly, break down in a session, let the mess of her own life bleed into the controlled white therapeutic space. This is something she has avoided in all her years of practice.

She tries Rosario's number.

"Look," Chris says as soon as Rosario answers. "I have to cancel for next time. Something has come up."

"What is it?"

"I can't really go into that," Chris says.

"Boundaries," Rosario says witheringly. She thinks Chris is overly concerned with professionalism. Last year, she couldn't understand why she wouldn't come on a cruise with her, a trip Rosario had won through a radio station.

"Rosario?"

"Yeah?"

"I'm going to get cut off here in a second," Chris lies, "and I don't have any more change."

"You should go cellular. Get a little flip phone like I have. You don't have to push your mouth against public germs."

"Right. Listen, I'll see you next week, the usual time. Okay? And if anything comes up, be sure to call me." She belatedly thinks to ask, "How are things going?"

"Okay. My sister's at the hospital having her baby. There are two fathers, did I tell you? They're both at the hospital, so things are very tense."

"How can there be two fathers? I know I paid close attention during sex education class in high school."

Rosario giggles childishly, a different laugh from her usual self-conscious, throaty sex-bomb laugh.

"Well, both guys think they're the father. You think they'd run away like crazy, but both of them want to stake a claim. In case it's a boy, yes? Hey, this problem of yours, it's serious, then?"

Chris realizes Rosario is clinging to their connection. She is frightened to let Chris evaporate with the dead metallic click of hanging up. Chris knows she should be generous in this moment. The client-therapist relationship is so peculiar and fragile, an unhatched egg. Clients need to be prepared for absences, even small, finite ones. Chris needs to push against the door of her self, and come out for just a minute to take care of Rosario.

"I'll tell you about it as soon as I can," she tries. "But don't worry about me. I'm okay. You take care of yourself and know I'm thinking about you." And the amazing thing is that she will be, even as she negotiates her own, at the moment, terrible circumstances.

She calls Sikora, to find out if he has run the check on Taylor's passport, to see if she has used it in these days — a little more than a week now — she has been gone. Gone. Chris doesn't like to say "missing," even to herself.

But the check has turned up nothing.

"We've also run through hospital admissions, including DOAs, and we've got queries in on all her credit cards," he says. "People have a hard time going on their merry way these days without credit. So hang in. We're zeroing in on the car. That Cherokee is our best shot now."

"What do you mean *now*?" Everything he says sounds loaded to her in some way she can't quite get.

"At this stage of the investigation," he says, disappearing into bureaucratic vagaries.

"How many stages are there?"

"That depends how many we need."

She tries to shape her silence into something rigorous, something he won't toy with. Talking to him makes her jumpy. She's the monkey in the old psychology experiment, the one strapped down, getting ulcers, while the happy monkey next to her is free to press the button that stops the zapping.

"Hey," he says. "Hang tough. We'll find her. We find ninety-eight percent of them. Missing is a hard place to stay. Eventually people use a credit card, or get a new job and have to put down a Social Security number. They get a parking ticket. It's hard to live a life now, even on the lam, without generating a paper trail."

"You're assuming she's alive, then?"

"We don't assume anything. We're hoping, like you are. But even if she's not, we'll probably find her. Even the dead have a tough time disappearing."

"I can't think about that yet," Chris says.

"I appreciate that," Sikora says. "But I'll tell you something I know from years of being in this business. The place you're in right now is the hardest. Knowing even the worst is easier."

"You think something terrible has happened to her." Chris feels irresistibly drawn to the scab, to picking at it.

"I don't think anything. I don't have enough information to think anything yet. You don't either. And there are things you can find out easier than we can. Did you call her family yet? Her friends?"

"Leigh's calling everybody. I talked with Taylor's sister. She's talking with the brothers and their mother today. The mother had a stroke last year and no one wants to freak her out. Then she'll check with the brothers. There are three. I don't know them as well, but Taylor's in touch with all of them. The whole family is close, in a sick way."

"Sick how?"

"Nothing juicy enough for you. No drama, just the standard dysfunctions."

"Hey," he says before hanging up. "Try to keep remembering I'm on your side."

Chris picks up her home messages by remote; the tape is full of friends. Audrey, who says she wants to stop by with a casserole. She is from a small town originally, and every now and then this legacy will turn up in odd ways — dropping by without calling if she's in the neighborhood, frequenting rummage sales and church pancake breakfasts, using expressions like "Don't be a stranger, hear?" Sometimes this all seems a little too much like *Our Town*, but today, Chris is charmed by the offer of the casserole, and by her tact in not being inquisitive.

The others — the friends Leigh has contacted — are fiercely inquisitive. Now, already, they need to know, whatever. "Do the police have any leads?" they say, having watched an aggregate million detective shows. So they know leads are what's being looked for. And beyond that, suspects. A composite portrait drawn from eyewitness descriptions. A .45 semiautomatic. An abandoned car pulled from a swamp. The key to a locker at the train station. Secret connections to drug lords, slave traders. Stains, lipstick and blood.

Chris presses the code for rewind, letting the tape eat up all this curiosity. If she calls these questioners back, she can only pose as a victim, along with Taylor, of so far unseen outside forces. When in fact, she may simply be someone who has been left behind in a manner slightly more dramatic than usual. Or maybe all these friends already know about the woman in Morocco. If they do, any conversation with them would hold this information in its creases, which would make her even more queasy.

She fishes through her jacket pockets for more change and calls Leigh. Who answers in a husky voice, as though she is barely able to crawl out of a sexual haze.

"I need to talk with you," Chris says.

"I got your messages. I was about to call." Chris can tell Leigh is lying, that she is in the middle of something. Something being done to her, silently, by a mime. How can she? How can she be having sex? How can she have gone back to regular life already?

"Are you there?" Leigh interrupts Chris's inner tirade. "Have you talked with the cop?"

"Nothing. They know nothing. What I need to talk with you about is something I found out on my own. I don't want to do this on the phone. I need to see your eyes when you try to lie for her."

"Sure, honey," Leigh says in the voice she would use on someone with half a dozen sticks of dynamite strapped to her chest. "I'm on my way in to work soon, though. Come by tonight. I'll be home by seven. We'll fix you dinner."

"I'm not eating."

"Well, of course you're not. But you should be. Tiff will fix up something organic. That twig and thistle casserole she does. Ouch!"

"I'll probably be late," Chris says. "I've got clients until eight." She is looking down at her Filofax. She actually has only one appointment, at seven. She needs the intervening hours to be alone. The image that comes up is one of folding herself into a drawer, pushing the drawer shut, closing out everything in the world that is too uncomprehending.

Bud is waiting when she gets to her car, parked in the exorbitantly priced garage next to Myra's office building. He's sitting in the driver's seat, facing seriously out the side window, watching for her. His expression doesn't change when he sees her, but his ears stand straight up.

"Dogs in the back," she says as she slides into the warmed seat. The whole inside of the car smells wolfy.

She takes the Drive up from the Loop. The lake is a gunmetal gray, churning its way through spring. She has been in this city nearly her whole life, has seen this stretch of water a hundred different colors. It has become for her not a stationary sight or landmark, but rather an emotional entity.

She takes the little exit between Belmont and Irving Park, the one that shoots straight into the park. The day is wet; there's a mist enlivening the air. The parking spaces by the tennis courts at Waveland are empty except for a couple of guys in a couple of cars, cruising or waiting for a dealer or customer, ancillary enterprises of the park.

The courts are too wet to play on, although the nets are up already, one of the defining signs of spring. Small leaves the color of lemons are plastered across the surface of the courts. Chris pulls open the heavy, rusted, chain-link gate and, while Bud noses around the court, she sits in a corner a little away from the flotsam that has collected — more leaves and sodden tennis balls and pull tabs from their vacuum containers. She closes her eyes and hears the hiss.

• • •

Chris is standing at the baseline, putting a sports strap on her sunglasses. The sun lies like a heavy, transparent drape across the late morning. Taylor slides her racquet from its sleeve and pats Chris on the backside with it.

"This butt," she says. "I'm going to wipe it all over this court."

"Right," Chris says, watching the workings of the tiny muscles above and behind the knees of her lover as she walks to the other side of the net, picturing for just a moment a tongue tracing them. She sees small teeth marks. When she hunkers down into position to receive Taylor's serve, she realizes she is slightly wet between her legs, the endpoint of this particular imaginative highway. Her concentration is blown, and she hears the terrible woosh of her racquet entirely missing the easy shot that has obligingly come her way. She hears Taylor's magnificent laugh riding on the air, and thinks, She only knows half the joke.

■ ■ ■

Chris and Bud ride home together. At lights, people in cars pull up beside them, look over and — ignorant of their shared sorrow — smile.

SHE UNWINDS from a fetal position to drive down to the office for her seven o'clock, Laura Wheeler, who is in her late twenties and going through a rough patch, a nasty breakup in the fall. Her girlfriend left her for somebody else. Until then, Laura thought things were fine between them, the relationship on sure footing. And from everything Chris has been able to elicit, it does sound as though the relationship was good and sustaining, at least on Laura's end. The girlfriend simply fell headlong in love; Laura simply got dealt a bad hand. Sometimes there aren't any childhood traumas or chemical imbalances or bad patterns of interaction. Sometimes it's a bad hand, no face cards, no aces, you're just holding junk.

An additional factor is that Laura hasn't had all the opportunity she might to repair herself because she and the ex, Marcie, are nurses in the same ICU. Five nights a week they work elbow to elbow, helping doctors jolt the failing hearts of old men, pluck bullets from the stomachs of gang-bangers. And then at seven A.M., Marcie walks out the door, to the far edge of the parking lot, where her new lover, who is in real estate — slightly older, much richer, business-oriented, an unfathomable choice to Laura — waits with take-out coffee in an idling Saab.

Chris thinks Laura is basically okay, solid beneath her shakiness. She will come through to the other side. Time is really her greatest ally. Chris's function is mostly to be there, ready with Kleenex and sympathy, accessible by phone for wig-out moments.

Today, though, she knows that underneath, just barely below the surface of the empathic gaze with which she is trying to meet Laura, she is envious of the small, contained quality of her client's dilemma: a girlfriend who has exited visibly, demonstrably, in an upscale Swedish automobile.

The session is desultory. Chris tries to persuade Laura that switching to another shift at the hospital, getting away from the daily friction of rubbing up against Marcie, might be helpful. In response, all she gets from Laura are complicated reasons why a different schedule wouldn't work. It would upset her already fragile sleep rhythms. She likes her other coworkers on the night shift. The P.M. supervisor is a harridan. The excuses mount, block by block, into an unassailable fortress of logic. Chris sees between these bricks to the probability that Laura wants to maintain the proximity, that she feels continued contact is her best shot at getting her lover back.

What's happening in this session, though, is more difficult for Chris to pin down. Laura seems oddly shy of Chris, or worse. Distant, a little edgy.

It's only afterward, in the bathroom, that Chris catches herself in the mirror and sees what the problem might have been. She hasn't changed clothes or showered or touched her hair in the past couple of days. She's wearing the same sweater and old jeans — by now heavily creased at the backs of the knees, bagged out at the fronts — and a T-shirt imprinted with her smell and stretched to the shape of her shoulders, the same one she was wearing when she called the police. The only changing she has done since then has been stripping to the T-shirt and underpants to sleep. And now she will show up at Leigh's this way. There's no time to go home and regroup. But then, why bother? Dressing up, showering, brushing her hair, would only misconstrue this dinner as a social occasion rather than an information-gathering mission.

And, even in normal times, there would be no point trying to impress Leigh, who is way out of her fashion league. Chris's style — basically taking advantage of having good hair and being thin — comes down to lots of black, and tight jeans, a leather jacket, a few resale-shop forties shirts. She doesn't want to look as though she's trying too hard. Leigh and Taylor, on the other hand, read *Vogue*; they know the names of several supermodels. They have certain kinds of outfits they wear to gallery openings, arrays of sunglasses from various times (the forties and fifties) and places (Germany and LA). They have a profound comprehension of accessories, which Chris finds as complex and impenetrable as a branch of science. Luckily, she's not expected to join in. They've told her not to bother, that her lack of concern for all this makes her a different kind of interesting.

These days not even interesting is expected of her, which is just as well because she couldn't come up with it. Even the minimal preparations necessary to getting out of the house are nearly beyond her. Everything seems staggeringly difficult now, the way her depressed patients describe the mechanics of getting through a day, an hour. Seeing clients, for sure, but even smaller stuff stymies her. Finding her keys, which are now lost nearly every time she needs them, sets her off on a fatiguing scavenger hunt. Feeding Bud and walking him around the block seems like an expedition to the South Pole, a north-face climb.

On her way out the door of her office, she notices (as Laura Wheeler probably did) a crusty stain on the knee of her jeans. It almost seems like a badge, as though she is Jackie Kennedy going through that whole long day starting in Dallas in the same blood-stained pink suit. She has to censor these sorts of melodramatic thoughts more and more often, has to remind herself that this tragedy is not hers nearly as much as it is Taylor's.

"She understands that we need to talk," Leigh tells her in the cavernous foyer of her vast apartment, nodding back toward the open kitchen where R.E.M. and Tiff are singing "What's the Frequency,

Kenneth?" Guitars shudder behind them. She is cooking while she karaokes with the radio. "But she wanted to fix you dinner. She wants to make a comforting gesture and isn't sure what the right thing would be."

Chris nods and feels lousy and tries to banish the attitude she came in with, attitude that had a lip curled and was saying that with everything she is going through right now, doesn't she deserve a temporary dispensation from social interaction with Tiffany?

As they come back into the kitchen, Tiffany says hi but barely looks up. She's not being rude; it's simply that the chopping of carrots has absorbed every molecule of her attention. She is like a stoned person, like the girl at the Seven Grains Shop who used to take five minutes to wrap the slice of whole-wheat pizza that Chris would pick up for supper. Next to her tidy pile of carrot bits, acorn squash halves sit on the counter, scooped out, waiting to be filled with some complex, recombinant mixture of the carrot bits and nuts and spinach. Chris sees corn kernels in a dish, a mound of shredded orange cheese. She has noticed that she sees differently lately, with more intensity. Sometimes scenes freeze into still lifes; certain pieces pop into relief.

She sees, for instance, that there are dust motes drifting through the air of the kitchen under the bright track lighting. Tiffany is wearing black tights and a fatigue green tank top. An overshirt, faded yellow cotton, has been abandoned and is now hanging on the back of one of the chairs around the dining table. It's hot around the stove, and there's a film of sweat across Tiffany's back, setting off the tattoo on her right shoulder, a design done in black and a pale fern green, obscurely Asian. Yin and yang are both in there. Tons of Deeper Meaning beyond that probably, although Chris will never know; she's reluctant to enter a conversation with Tiffany which would involve asking what her tattoo means. Then it occurs to her that this is precisely the conversation Taylor would have with Tiff if the two of them were alone in this room together, Taylor tracing the tattoo's outline with a pressureless fingertip.

Leigh's part in this dinner is to kneel in front of the wine rack, hunkered down in serious selection. When Chris first knew Leigh, she thought of her as one particular version of embarrassing dyke, someone you wouldn't really want to serve up to straight people as a representative lesbian if they could know only one or two. Not as hair-raisingly mortifying as the woman from one of the bar teams in Taylor's softball league who showed up at a game last summer with her girlfriend on a leash. Leigh seemed embarrassing in a more conventional way — a guy in sheep's clothing, an imitation of one of the crummier clichés of the straight world. She usually picks younger women, middlingly naive girls, puts in a couple of labor-intensive weeks seducing them, then another persuading them to move in. The jobs these girls hold are never of much consequence, the money never anywhere near what Leigh makes on television. And so quite soon they've given up the part in the play, or are now just working on a consultant basis in whatever, spending the bulk of their time shopping for birthday gifts for Leigh's mother, cooking dinners for company, collecting rents from tenants in the six-flat Leigh owns over on Belle Plaine, by the cemetery. For her part, Leigh shoulders the burdens of being a midlevel local celebrity and assumes a husbandly position around the house, selecting the wines, driving the Legend, lingering on the phone with her broker.

But what Chris didn't see until she'd been around long enough to watch the pattern repeat itself a few times is that Leigh really falls in love with these women, is enthralled by their newness on the road of life, their lack of past or bitterness or bad experience. Most often, this rather straightforward affection is not entirely reciprocated. The beloved turns out to have been attracted to Leigh's money or her mild fame. When things don't work out, Leigh tumbles into a terrible grief over the loss of this love, which was going to have been perfect. Chris has come to see that Leigh is really the unlikely naif in these pairings, her belief in their possibilities ever-renewable, even as the lovers move off briskly, acquiring edges and calluses.

This dinner, which Chris has been dreading, turns out, surprisingly, to be the most successful collection of moments she has had since everything started, since the bottom fell out. For stretches of two or three minutes at a time during the long meal, she is able not to think about Taylor.

The stuffed squashes are merely a side dish. The centerpiece of Tiffany's menu is a fish fondue, which goes so astray that it's comic even to the chef. Despite the earnest application of canned heat, the oil never gets really hot and so the three of them sit with long forks holding flaccid strips of snapper and sole which never pass from warm and greasy to cooked. Tiffany is so ingenuous, leaning against Chris at the counter, putting her head on Chris's shoulder in embarrassment over the fish, that hating her stops being a possibility. Perhaps what Chris saw between her and Taylor that night, Taylor's fingers tangled up in all that hair, Tiffany's teeth pressing gently into the skin of Taylor's thumb, was only a normal set of reflexes between two people with an easy physicality, unguarded reactions. She can be generous now, when so much that seemed to matter no longer does.

Through the whole dinner both Leigh and Tiffany treat Chris with great kindness, as though she is a stray in need of a bath and a blanket, warm milk, a hot water bottle to hug through these nights spent in terrible solitude. When Chris picks up on their charitable tone, she begins crying silently onto her pile of limp fish strips. Leigh and Tiff wait quietly until she finishes.

"I'm sorry about the other night," Tiffany says when Leigh is in the bathroom and she and Chris have the table temporarily to themselves. She draws tears down her cheeks with her index fingers, mime shorthand. Because she is saying what Chris wants to hear, though, Chris does not leap across the table and throttle her. "It was stupid," she goes on. "It wasn't about anything. It was stupid fooling around. For days now I'm, like, Tiffany, what were you *do*-ing?!"

Chris relieves her of any responsibility, explaining, she hopes tactfully, that Taylor's leaving wouldn't be about anything so inconsequential.

After dinner, Tiffany stays behind in the kitchen while Leigh and Chris repair, like gents, off to cigars and cognac in the living room, with its two stories of windows overlooking a stretch of Clybourn that has not yet been strip-malled, that is still factories and warehouses. From Leigh's boneless filet of sofa, at the right hour, the rust-belt sunsets framed by these vast windows are thrilling. The first time Chris witnessed one, it felt like a show just for her.

• • •

Sipping a better chardonnay than she could afford for herself. Arrayed before her, an artful arrangement of things to eat with drinks — mustard pretzels, fried Chinese peas, tekkamaki. The immediate setting causes her to consider money and wine and views, to think about the power in being able to purchase this dramatic palette of ocher and sienna and umber made metallic by the dying sun. As opposed to the small, underlandscaped courtyard that her own living room looks onto, or the view from her kitchen, which is that of another kitchen in an apartment in the building next-door — extra interest value provided by the elderly, overweight woman who lives there and often cooks in just her bra and an amazing, old-fashioned girdle.

This slow train of thought is stopped by a body tumbling over the back of the sofa next to her. Taylor. They've been together — or rather together without the specter of Diane on their horizon — for only a week or two. Chris has been brought to Leigh's, she knows, so Leigh can see how wonderful she is. A standard rite of relationship, lover offered up to best friend for inspection. But since they've been here, Leigh has been on the phone with Jessica Ann, the woman she's seeing, who is in telemarketing, as Leigh puts it. Which is to say, she sells magazine subscriptions by phone. According to Taylor, she is about to be fired for spending so much of her time at work pretending to sell these subscriptions to Leigh. There are supervisors who monitor the calls and are adept at cracking the flimsy codes of lovers.

Taylor comes back from trying unsuccessfully to wrestle Leigh from this particular conversation with Jessica Ann, and falls onto Chris's lap, then pulls Chris on top of her as they stretch out along the length of the sofa, keeping an ear out for Leigh's distant voice on the phone. "Boy, before you I didn't even really have an idea, you know?" she says, then presses her teeth tight against Chris's nipple, leaving a wet mark on the front of her silk shirt. "I wasn't even close. This is so much more than I had in mind."

"What was it then, what was it you had in mind?"

"Oh, I guess something I could see the borders on, where I'd know what was in the picture and where it left off and the frame began. This, with you, just slides over all the edges."

"Does that make it a better thing?"

Taylor doesn't respond immediately; they lie silently together listening to Leigh's low laughter floating in from her kitchen phone call. Finally, Taylor says, "When I'm with you I think it's better. When I'm alone, sometimes the bigness gets scary."

"Then just be with me," Chris says, muzzy with new love, her hearing slightly impaired in the high registers of warning signals.

. . .

Tonight it is Leigh who pulls Chris down next to her on the sofa, and much more decorously. Today's sunset is long past, the lights of the city have already come on, brilliant against a navy sky.

"When is Desta coming? She's such a wonderful person. I'm sure she'll be a big help to you in your hour of need." They both loathe Taylor's family.

"Tomorrow," Chris says. "Do you think I have time to move to Tibet before she gets here?"

"What does she think she's going to be able to do that we're not already doing?"

"Oh, I suppose she wants to throw those big hips around a little. The Heyes clan always likes to put its own mojo on things. She and Ardith have decided the police aren't colorful enough in their pursuit of resolution. No high-speed car chases. They haven't taken DNA samples from the house. It would work for them pretty well — in terms of their belief system — if it turned out I'd bludgeoned Taylor with a waffle iron, then stuffed her in my crawl space. And if I'm not suspect, I'm at least incompetent. So they need to hire somebody to poke around, you see. They're always more comfortable when they can pay for whatever. Then they know it has value. I hate the idea of them getting into the search, not to mention some bozo detective. Everything is already so invasive, and now to have them pushing their way inside, when Taylor has always worked so hard to keep them out."

"Can you manage?" Leigh asks. "I mean by yourself?"

Chris laughs. "I don't know. I couldn't deal with Taylor's family in regular life. Now they just seem like one more terrible thing, and who's counting anymore?"

Leigh rubs the back of Chris's head, as though Chris is a puppy. Leigh is extremely physical in these offhand ways. "So. You've tripped onto a secret and we need to talk about it," she says. Chris can't find a trace of surprise in her voice. Which makes her think there are whole constellations of secrets orbiting around Taylor, that she has tripped onto only one of them.

"Wait," Chris says, and goes to fetch the pictures. When she returns, she fans them out across the burled wood of the coffee table. The woman standing before the desert wall looks at them over her shoulder, then straight on, across half the earth's circumference, a suddenly significant stranger in their midst. Chris expects Leigh to blow smoke around this, but all she does is nod and look at them a long time, as though they are merely fascinating, not horrifying.

A thousand years pass in the silence. Chris feels significantly older by the time Leigh finally nods, and says, "Well, her name's Stéphane Michaud."

"Yes?"

"Well." Leigh turns her hands palms up, smiles out of nervousness.

"Please. Tell me she's the nice lady at Travelers Aid in Marrakesh. The flight attendant who helped Taylor when the air-conditioning unit started leaking over her seat. Tell me," she says, reversing the position she took with Myra, "tell me she's just another one of Taylor's tiresome flirtations."

Leigh marks her words before speaking, but Chris can hear her anyway, even before she says, "I think Stéphane was a little more than that. But she's married. Two teenage kids, one possessive husband."

"Meaning?"

"Meaning it wasn't going anywhere."

"Well, that's a real comfort." Chris races through a few scenarios, but anything she can think of comes up as fairly improbable. Finally, she's relegated to asking flat out. "How did she even meet somebody French and sexy? I mean aren't all the girls over there in chador, or one of somebody's four wives?"

"I gather there's a significant French community, vestigial colonizers. Stéphane and her husband own some little hotel on the edge of the desert. She's an old friend of Jacques's, apparently." Jacques Aumont is Taylor's buddy over there, a gay guy who works in the lab at one of the film studios in Ouarzazate. He lets her use darkroom facilities when she's shooting down that way. Chris has never met him, knows him only by Taylor's description, which is rhapsodic. She sees him as a kindred spirit, living in an iconoclastic, mostly isolated way. He has a small house with a Moroccan toilet and a gas burner, a tiny yard where he cultivates flora that will tolerate severe aridity. Few possessions and few friends. An ascetic. Although Taylor reveres him (maybe because she does), Chris has always thought she'd find him insufferable. Now she augments her opinion with the new information that he also procures exotic girlfriends for Taylor.

"It's not an important thing is what I'm trying to tell you," Leigh is saying. "At the moment Taylor thinks it is, but it isn't. Not really."

Chris is having trouble getting enough oxygen out of the available air in this suddenly too small room. "Boy, I should be feeling great by now with all this reassuring news. Taylor's gone and there's this vampy item in Morocco, who someone might think is a problem unless they talked to you and were made to understand that she's not a problem at all because her husband is going to get in the way and, anyhow, you've got the tea leaves and can see Taylor's future and know for sure this Stephanie — "

"Stéphane."

"Right. Isn't in it."

"Stop." Leigh puts a hand on Chris's arm. "I could have lied, you know."

"A lie might at least be colorful. What you're telling me is so gray, so pathetic. Taylor infatuated with a straight woman. I mean, isn't it a little late in the day for that sort of thing?"

Leigh's mouth gets small with seriousness. Smaller. It's already small, like the rest of her features. (She says this is very helpful for TV, which essentially puts your head in a box.)

"Is that where Taylor's gone to?" Chris finally thinks to ask. "To be with her?"

Leigh shakes her head. "I called." She knocks her forehead with her knuckles. "Dumb. I only wound up unsettling someone else."

"Oh, I feel so bad about disrupting her well-being," Chris says. "Now that she's upset too, though, maybe we could all form a support group."

Leigh folds Chris up in her arms.

"Is this what the Morocco book is really about — an excuse to go over there every few months for something femme and fatale? Why do I know she has a husky voice? From all those Gauloises." Chris feels the ashy colored hairs at the nape of Leigh's neck stir against her lips as she speaks.

"I think it's the other way around," Leigh says, pulling back. "She fell in love with the place, and this woman is a part of it and so she fell in love with her, too."

"I thought she was supposed to love me."

"That's beside the point." Leigh looks past Chris for a moment, clearly preparing her response. "Taylor does things to make herself feel better. I think you don't understand because you already feel better."

"Do you know where she is? You don't have to tell me where, only *if* you know."

Leigh shakes her head. "I wouldn't do that to you."

"But you know more than I do, don't you?"

"I think I know more than you do, maybe — where Taylor is inside her head. I just don't know where she is in this world."

A few days later, at the mall that also contains her health club, Chris runs into Alan Browning, her ex-husband, although so much time and sociability have passed in the years since their blip of a marriage, a grad school linking of mistaken identity (Chris's mistake, this being in the period after she had begun sleeping with women but before she began thinking of herself as a lesbian), that she hardly ever thinks of him in these terms, more now as an old acquaintance. Which puts him in the small legion of people she, at the moment, finds it imperative to duck.

"Hey," he says, coming out of a store called Bad Boys, looking much the same as the last time she ran into him, which, she realizes, must now be a couple of years back. He teaches philosophy at Circle, is a Buddhist, a vegetarian, at peace with himself, and all this mellowness keeps him from aging or even looking at all weathered or burnished by life. "How's it going?"

There is no spin on the question. They bear each other no ill will. They actually bear each other nothing. And so she tells him everything's going great.

"Still getting people's minds right?" he asks, and she tells him she's busier than ever. She finds out he is remarried, again. He was redivorced the last time she ran into him. This time it's a woman who lives in his ashram and so he is more confident of it working out. She didn't know he lived in an ashram, pauses to think about this for a moment, grown people sharing a belief system and a toaster. It has its appeal.

"Are you . . . I don't know . . . seeing anyone?" he says. "Weren't you with somebody when we last talked? A photographer?"

She has begun to see that one of the worst aspects of her life now is that it has turned into a sequence of events that's happening to her rather than anything she is effecting. The situation with Taylor has robbed her of her status as an active agent, left her a person to whom something bad has happened. She is someone to be pitied by casual acquaintances, and this is unbearable. And so she tries not to miss a beat before telling him, in lieu of telling him everything else, "No. No one special."

The other members of Chris's health club are twenty years younger than she is. The place is mostly neon and mirrored and carpeted in pink or purple, a disco of health.

She is always uplifted in this artificial ozone, breathing its atmosphere of jaunty narcissism. She enjoys watching the gay guys hang around one another in sweaty, ironic-manly ways that, she guesses, eventually wind them up in bed together. She also likes eavesdropping on the conversations held on the two phones in the women's locker room, mostly calls to agents about modeling or acting jobs. She has come to understand that everything about their lives is important, crucial even, to actresses and models. Actresses and models and women who sell real estate.

She hasn't been here in the days since Taylor left and is hoping a workout will seal her away from her pain for an hour. She changes into a pair of black stretch shorts and the crumpled T-shirt in her gym bag. She puts her Walkman on and Taylor's tape comes up inside her ears, a gift from a past phase of their relationship, a mix of old favorites. Dolly Parton is singing "Single Bars and Single Women." The song yawns around her head and swallows her whole.

. . .

They're in the park, sitting on a bench with their bikes propped against their knees.

"Do you have a fantasy person?" Taylor says, idly, early on, when Chris would tell her anything she asked.

"How do you mean?"

"I don't know, like a movie star?"

"This is really embarrassing."

"Come on."

"Dolly Parton."

Taylor lowers her sunglasses, peers over the top of the frame.

"There's just something about her. She's like a secret agent butch. It's something around the eyes."

"But what would you do with her hair? I mean, it seems like there's Dolly, and then there's her hair. Don't they seem like separate issues?"

"It's wet in the fantasy. She's just out of the shower so her makeup's all washed off, too. She's au naturel and sexy in that pert way she has."

"You'd have sex, then she'd want to talk about the week's grosses at Dollywood."

"She's very smart," Chris says. "I can tell."

Taylor pushes her shades back in place, finds half of an old candy bar in her backpack, and untwists the wrapper. "People have no sense of humor about their own pornography."

• • •

Chris methodically works through the circuit of machines. Not varying means not having to think while she's in here, only do. She works out here at the club, runs in good weather, plays a little tennis, but is mediocre at all of these pursuits. For one thing, she doesn't care about winning, about stacking herself up against anyone else. She is content to keep in shape and nurse along a few Walter Mitty fantasies. She would, for instance, like to possess great arms. Something along the lines of Sigourney Weaver's arms when she's driving the giant earth mover in one of her *Alien* movies, ramming the gearshift into forward, reverse. Arms so great that Chris could walk into the most low-life bar, in the middle of summer, in a muscle T, and stop conversation. Serious arms that in reality, she knows, are a little out of range for someone who is overscheduled and in the practice of therapy, a profession that instead lends itself to serious butts.

All the while she is sweating, bench-pressing, and doing military pull-ups on the Gravitron, she is inside Taylor's tape. Dolly Parton bleeds into Shawn Colvin into Michael Stipe, and hard reality begins to recede into the background. After going through these motions so attached to regular life, cutting experience into reps and sets, muscle memory kicks in and overrides pain and uncertainty in this contained piece of time.

And so, when she walks into the women's locker room and sees Taylor's marvelous back disappearing into the showers, her long, narrow hips wrapped in a heavy dark green towel, Chris doesn't hesitate or call out. She follows the sure, steady pounding of her heart with her footsteps and, when she gets to the stall, throws back the curtain with the momentum of reunion, the sureness of everything about to be set to rights.

The woman in the shower is at first confused through the shampoo in her eyes, then freaks out. "Hey!" she shouts, like the graduate of one of those self-defense courses.

"Oh," Chris says. "I'm sorry. I'm just so sorry."

She doesn't change, just stuffs her street clothes into her duffel even though it's too cold and rainy to be outside in stretch shorts and a T-shirt. She supposes she's beginning to slip over the line of the acceptable and socialized. She will now become peculiar in her grief, use it to allow herself bad behavior, or worse, not even see that she is behaving badly. She has become an exception to the rules of regular people, who still travel with the assumption that their tomorrows will look pretty much like today. There is, just past the place where she's appalled at herself, a small element of exhilaration in this unfettered sadness, a release accompanying this propulsion into vacuum and void.

SHE HAS BEEN assiduously trying to get back on track, keeping up with her schedule of clients (although not taking on any new ones to replace those who, like Laura Wheeler, after the lackluster session, have dropped away). She has tried to keep the house straightened, Bud fed and walked on time. She talks to him in the jolliest voice she can summon. She's doing all right, she tells herself, until the next time she falls into the covered pit of a lion trap.

She never knows where one will turn up. All of the self-help books on loss and grieving she borrowed from Daniel tell her there are key moments when you miss the departed. Anniversaries, holidays, Sundays. Nights when you go to bed alone. As it turns out, she is too consciously prepared for these easy pitfalls for them to be the worst. She's a tougher nut to crack. She can bear solitude through all but the stormiest nights. The phone can go unringing through an entire Sunday afternoon and evening and she's glad nothing has interrupted her paper reading, household puttering.

For her, the worst moments of missing Taylor turn out to be much smaller, and almost never predictable. The latest beat in a running joke, for instance. They used to cook up a tour of oddities they'd find on their routes around town. The Sanitary Fish Market. Germ-Proof Cleaners. The Très Ambiance Beauty Parlor. A collection of stores Taylor grouped together as "Huh?" — their dusty display windows crammed with andirons and Avon products, old shoe boxes, sleeping cats. What did they sell? What was their corporate marketing strategy? This week Chris was driving along Belmont and spotted a new addition to the tour — three adjoining storefronts, windows crammed with the jetsam of basements and attics — Itchy's Stop-n-Scratch Flea Market.

Her heart soared, and then in the follow-up instant she broke down so completely, suddenly sobbing so violently, it was like trying to drive through hard rain. She had to pull into a parking space and wait for the ions of normalcy to regroup around her.

Taylor may have been withdrawn at times, ultimately closed in on herself, and certainly not a committed partner in any conventional sense, but she and Chris did move through the world together in a way that Chris is only now realizing was crucial to her experience of life. With Taylor no longer present to get the cosmic joke, Chris fears she will lose her sense that there is one.

At the moment, she desperately wishes Taylor were here to meet Jon Folan, the detective who is going to try to find her. Together they would find him hilarious. On her own, Chris can only work herself up to being contemptuous and dismissive. She has written him off entirely, although she has been in his office only twenty minutes. She can't imagine that anything significant is going to come through him, and she is already sick of sitting opposite him, sick of smelling his cologne. She has run out to the end of her initial fascination with his hair, which is frozen in a daytime-drama actor style, an aspic of hair. She is already up to feeling sorry for the pie-faced wife and children in the oak frames on his file cabinet, the small cluster of people who have Jon Folan in every one of their days.

More to the point, even though he's billing Desta four hundred dollars a day plus expenses and wearing a thousand-dollar suit, Chris doesn't think he's going to turn up anything that the cops, in their cheap sportscoats and Supercuts, won't find for free. And so she has convicted Folan of superfluousness, strapped him into an electric chair of her imagining, allowing him a moment to squirm before she throws, with a flourish, the switch. This fantasy has kept her just shy of paying enough attention to follow what he has been saying. Which is working out all right, however, because he's directing most of his conversation toward Desta, keeper of the checkbook and legitimate next of kin. Because Chris isn't even in the kin line, her function in this room seems to have settled into that of interpreter.

"Your sister — does she have any places she retreats to?" Folan says. "You know. When she wants to get away from everything and everybody?" When Desta passes his question along to her with a shrug, Chris turns back to Folan and says they don't know.

Although Chris realizes the country of Morocco might well qualify as a retreat, and though she is holding the name of someone there who might have a key piece of information, she is not impelled to mention the country, or the north of Africa in general or the town of Merzouga in particular in this office, leaving Jon Folan to trail off with a little speech on hideaways, telling them, "You might not believe it, but we've had our share of 'missing' persons (when he sets off something he's saying in quotation marks, which he does quite often, he traces tiny, two-fingered hooks in the air) who merely turn out to have gone fishin', as it were."

"Taylor didn't fish," Chris says, concocting a look she hopes is earnest and full of helpfulness.

Desta appears to have developed an opposite response to Folan. As he explains the essentials of missing-persons work, and fills in their answers on an elaborate, often inscrutable, questionnaire (Is Taylor right- or left-handed? What sorts of music does she listen to?), she watches him with unblinking eyes. She is frightened, Chris can tell, every bit at sea as Chris herself. But Desta would never be so weak as to let this show. Instead, she has transformed her panic into a white-knuckle grip on her belief that the problem will be resolved by bringing it to another professional.

"Fascinating how you detectives can assemble the puzzle pieces of someone," she says, with a secular reverence. But Chris knows Desta well enough to understand that her fundamental interest is not in anyone else's power, but in her own. She is looking to Folan to give her leverage in taking charge of this situation. Together, the two of them are softly seizing control; Chris can see it being transported across the room, away from her.

Leigh has cautioned her to watch out for signs that she is being pushed out of the picture by the family, that this is what often happens to lovers when gay people fall sick, and could as easily happen in this situation. The truth, though, is that she doesn't care much about being included in the family grouping. Although she understands that Taylor is also missing to her relatives, their loss seems pale and formulaic beside her own profound emptiness.

Desta is a bit younger than Taylor, somewhere in her mid-thirties, already with a full shelf of life trophies. Her lucrative dental practice. A first husband (an investment analyst) who hasn't worked out and is being replaced by an older but richer one. Three children either doing well in private schools, or excelling in sports that originated on the other side of the Atlantic. She is big in Junior League in Burlington, heads up the annual Thanksgiving Food Drive, and at Christmas organizes Make-A-Wish for terminally ill kids — good works that don't require actual physical contact with anyone poor or sick.

She has narrow-set eyes that cling vaguely to a point in the middle distance, lips that part slightly when she's at rest. Chris sees her as a dopey woman at the height of her dopey powers. (It was thinking about the insouciant ignorance of Taylor's family that first got Chris to admit that Taylor herself, although Einsteinian in this bunch, nonetheless probably falls shy of brilliant.) The Heyes arrogance comes out of their money, but also goes beyond it. Taylor wears it with style and charm. On Desta it looks bulkier, less graceful, more bullying.

Chris excuses herself and goes into the ladies room. The key the receptionist hands her is attached to a small spyglass.

She has tried to keep better track of her clothes, that is, has tried to remember to put on fresh ones every day, but she sees she has fallen down in other areas of maintenance. Her hair, she notices in the mirror, despite the flattering, peachy lighting, is quite greasy, its curls separated from one another, like doll's hair. The lenses of her glasses are dusty and filmed with fingerprints. She holds them under the tap, rubs at the glass with a paper towel, which only adds a breading of lint to the sticky surface. She thinks of giving her hair a quick wash with the liquid soap from the wall dispenser, but catches herself (in plenty of time, she thinks), seeing that this is the sort of inappropriately major toilette you'd find in the ladies room of a Greyhound depot.

When she returns, she tries to cut through the thick camaraderie Desta and Jon Folan have forged. The questionnaire is finished, and they're now basking in a kind of afterglow, going over Folan's plan for what he refers to as the "independent investigation." Chris cuts in, saying she thinks the police are on the case in an active way and she doesn't especially want to step on their toes.

"The Chicago cops couldn't *find* their toes," Folan says. "With both hands." He shoots a wrist out of the sleeve of his suit jacket. Both the pale creamy cotton of his cuff and the band of his watch are so flat they barely stand out in relief from his skin. Chris settles back into her chair and imagines Jon Folan burdened with a sad, expensive fetish, a standing Thursday afternoon assignation with a bored hooker who pees on him in the bathtub of one of those sex motels north on Lincoln with light-blocking drapes eternally closed across their sixties-style, big glass windows.

"We'll talk again in a couple of days," he says, standing to indicate that the meeting is over, bending to brush down the knees of his trousers, so the material falls back in place around the crease. "Unless something breaks before then, of course. Which could happen. Could very well happen. There are several aspects of this case that I must say look very promising."

Chris fights down the impulse to ask him just what those aspects might be.

"We were wondering," he turns to her, "do you have access to Ms. Heyes's darkroom?" He catches Chris a little off guard. She realizes she must be responding with a question-mark look when Desta helpfully prompts, "He means do you have a key?"

"Oh," Chris says. "No, actually. I don't." In her absence, Taylor seems vulnerable, in need of protection. Chris is not about to hand her over to anyone on a platter. Especially not to fools.

Just when she thinks she is getting some footing back, getting a toehold in the middle of the avalanche, everything is suddenly, stunningly worse, and all of it inside her. She spins down into free fall. At home, she becomes wedded to her sofa. She tries to remember to feed Bud and take him out, to turn on the lights when it gets dark outside. She looks at these tasks as accomplishments. She tries to keep things very small, narrowed down. When she looks any further, all she can see is nothing. Although she knows this is rationally absurd, the future doesn't seem to exist without Taylor in it. All their plans are canceled, the little soft snags on time — movies they were going to see, the cheap vacation to Nassau they were planning, the Asian cooking class they'd signed up for — have been snipped away, leaving only a vast barren plain ahead with no markers, no resting places. And she will have to take on this interminable distance alone.

Sometimes when Chris wakes up — usually around four — she gets a brief reprieve, a few minutes of light haze in which she is deluded, thinking things are still all right, still the way they were before. She will roll onto her side, moving to hook a leg over Taylor's, then realize with a forty-foot drop that she is alone in the bed, that nothing is any longer all right. The drop is into the driver's seat of a bumper car careening through a vacuum. Huge waves of anxiety surge through her, electric nausea, detached from any specific thought or worry, their lack of focus making them only more harrowing. By seven she has managed to peel herself off the bed, shower, and get to the office, where she works very hard at doing an impersonation of someone sane.

She sits and tries to focus on what her clients are saying. While she waits for the next one to arrive, she paces the room, often finds herself crying with no advance warning. The need to get away somewhere is suddenly imperative, but the somewhere is away from herself, the one place she can't get out of.

After a few days lost and alone on this forced march, Daniel surprises her by stopping by the house late one night.

He sits in a lotus position atop one of the counter stools in Chris's kitchen, his legs wound around each other like sausage links. For a chubby fellow he is amazingly flexible, the result of years of yoga. She doesn't know why he hasn't met someone there. Any yoga class she has ever been to has been filled with single straight women. Single straight women with bad backs, but still.

She sets a mug of tea in front of him. Making it was, at her current ebb, a culinary victory. She had to boil a kettle of water and rummage around in the cabinets to find some tea, chamomile, that was herbal as opposed to real. And then, because the tea was loose, she had to scrounge up a little bamboo strainer from under everything else in the kitchen implement bin. Now that all this effort has assembled into a cup of warm and pale liquid, she feels as though she has performed a colossal feat of entertaining — Martha Stewart topping a cake with a detailed marzipan replica of the celebrant's life milestones.

As she brings the cup down in front of him in triumph, they lock eyes across the counter. She can't tell what he's thinking. Something, though. She knows he has been keeping an eye on her around the office lately. They are both fiercely independent and their friendship has been fostered by knowing how much space to give each other. He knows that, even in a crisis, overattentiveness would be oppressive. That he has come by tonight indicates to her that she must seem in bad shape indeed. She senses that he's about to spring a surprise on her, but is nonetheless startled when he hops off the stool, and says, "Come with me for a minute," and leads her upstairs. When they're in the bathroom, he pulls a bottle of shampoo out of the shower caddy, and says, "I'd like to wash your hair."

"It sounds like that dating service isn't meeting all your needs."

"Don't take this the wrong way . . ." He sits on the edge of the tub.

"Oh shit. I hate sentences that begin like that."

". . . but you need a little fluffing up. What I'd really like to do is give you a bath, but that doesn't seem like us somehow."

"No. That seems much more like those old Westerns where the ranch wife gets sprayed by a skunk and the cowboy has to drag the tin tub out into the yard in front of the ranch and suds her up." Tears begin pushing up through her ductwork, and she tells him, "Leave me alone."

"No. You're going to take a bath and I'm going to wash your hair. My treat. Please. Let me do this for you. Can I use this hose?" He is on his knees rummaging around under the sink and has come up with a sprayer. "I mean, is this what you use to wash your hair?"

"No. We're not English working girls after the war. We use the shower. That's what we use to give Bud a bath." She stands there knowing she looks foolish, that they both look foolish, then relents. "Okay. I'll get in the shower, but I don't think we need to do the hair.

I don't think it's that bad yet." She is obligated, for pride's sake, to put up at least a small defense.

In response, he stares her down, and wins.

"I met someone," he confesses as he sits on the closed toilet while she showers and washes her hair.

"Met?" she shouts, holding this information off for a beat. "Where? The lunch thing?"

"No. This one came out of the bluest blue." He has to shout back over the noise of rushing water. "Her mother is in the same nursing home as mine. I see her there sometimes when I visit, and I always thought she was attractive, but she wears a ring and . . . well, it turns out it's her grandmother's wedding ring, some family heirloom. She's single. Divorced." He's suddenly quiet, then explodes with a small, detonated laugh.

Chris pulls back the shower curtain and looks to see what has stopped him. "What?" She turns off the water and takes the towel he is holding for her. "What's so funny?"

"Well, I'm startled, I guess. Finding a great person in such an unlikely spot. I mean Raleigh Manor is the last place I would have expected anything romantic to, you know, happen."

She starts to smile along with him, but it turns almost immediately into crying.

"What?" Daniel says. "What is it?"

"How can you go on like this?" she says. "How can everybody? I know I'm being unreasonable, but it seems crucial for you all to stop until Taylor gets back. So she won't have fallen too terribly behind."

When she is clean and dry and swaddled in her old chenille robe and the two of them are burrowed in next to each other on the sofa, Chris puts on the tape of the Flowbee infomercial. Taylor made this off cable a while back to cheer Chris up. Lately she enjoys replaying it. It's a way of still being able to share a joke.

"*I used to throw my money away on expensive salon haircuts. Now I can cut my whole family's hair at home with our Flowbee,*" says an insanely cheerful woman in mid flow, grinning like a jackal, her long hair being sucked on one side into the clear plastic jet chamber of the handheld Flowbee, where the ends are being snipped off.

"We could trim you up real nice with the Flowbee," Chris tells Bud. She runs her hands through his fur. "Do a poodle shag."

"It's good seeing you relaxed," Daniel says. "Not all buzzed. I think you're doing a good job of processing your emotions." This line of talk, she can tell, is out of some book or seminar. He doesn't use this peculiar, lilting tone when he's being his normal, hesitantly earnest self. He has seen her through other breakups and bad stretches and never used this tone, which makes her suspect that this time he finds her not merely troubled, but crazy, in need of some professional ministering.

Her hackles are up. What she wants from him now is plain friend-ship, not counseling. She wants him to shut up and be there for her and not say anything about her current state of affairs which might hold implicit in its folds an I Told You So. She can't brook any criticism of Taylor now that her own anger has so dissipated. How can she rail against someone who has been forced by such profound sorrow — what else could account for it — to leave her entire life and sail off with a camera bag and a Cherokee, into the mist?

And too, how can she work up any decent sentiments about herself when she must surely have been part of a totally unworkable equa-tion for her lover? She must have (worse, for being unaware of it) failed so utterly at offering the kind of prop or guyline partners are supposed to provide each other. She not only couldn't hold Taylor upright, she didn't even see that she was toppling. And while she tells clients they are not ultimately responsible for the happiness of those around them, she can't cut herself this same slack. There is blame someplace in this situation and part of it comes down on her and under it she sinks to the floor. Past the floor. She can't any longer feel where the floor would be.

"I mean I understand of course you must be agitated underneath," Daniel prods.

"No," Chris lies. "Really. I've calmed down quite a bit. I mean, there's only a concrete wall for me to bang my head against at the moment. Hurts less if I don't bang."

Daniel nods understandingly. He can't help it, she knows. It comes from years in the therapist's seat; after a while you can't help nodding sincerely at anything anyone says. The nerve pathways get stripped; someone starts talking and you start nodding. "You don't know how relieved I am to hear you like this. I was a little worried you'd do something crazy."

"Like what?"

"I don't know. But when I talk with you on the phone lately, you have this about-to-jump-off-the-line nervousness in your voice. Like you're on some starting block, ready to spring into action. Take matters into your hands. I don't know what I imagined. Anyway, it's irrelevant now because I can see you've reached some further stage."

To stop him from laying out whatever preformatted phase he feels she has reached, she says, "You know, I think I really have," then yawns and stretches her arms inside the oversize robe in an attempt to look as much as possible like the bear on the Sleepytime tea box.

"I could stay here until you drop off," he says.

"That's okay. I'm going to stay up a little while, I think. Read some uplifting inspirational verse before I go to sleep." He flips her the finger, but she can tell he's pleased that he's done such a good job, left her in such a better place.

While he's backing his tanklike Volvo out the driveway, a heavy spring rain slashing in front of his headlights, she stands in the window, waving. She looks at her schedule for the rest of the week. To get away through the weekend, she will have to cancel fourteen appointments, five with clients she already canceled in the first days after Taylor disappeared. Still, she knows she will do it.

She closes her appointment book, gets her billfold out of her briefcase, slides out her highest-limit Visa, and thumbs through the phone book for the reservations number of Royal Air Maroc. It's both frightening and thrilling when a voice comes on the line, even at this late hour, and can put her on connecting flights late the next afternoon, first to New York, then to Casablanca, then a short jump down to Ouarzazate, at the edge of the Sahara.

SHE IS NOT a returning native, and is too underprepared to be a tourist. Although she has been cramming on the plane with a couple of Taylor's old guidebooks, cross-referencing with a map so worn it is shredded at the creases, she is nonetheless an anomaly among the passengers on this flight — neither going back to a place firm in her memory, nor forward to one fashioned from longings or imagination. She has been locked in transit, first by her obsession with finding Taylor, or rather finding out who she was — heading toward a person, not a place; then further sealed away in the non-stick channels of airports, the air-freshened, gray-carpeted interiors of O'Hare, replicated by those of Kennedy, yet again by those of Casablanca.

And so it isn't until she looks down and out from her window seat on the jump flight southward over the High Atlas mountains, as the plane descends into Ouarzazate — a garrison grid of squat mud- and putty-colored buildings huddled on a plateau of scrub and stone, in the shadow of a brooding wall of mountain — that it strikes her directly: she is about to emerge into the alien and unknown.

Aeroport Taorirt is hyperactive, but in an inaccessible way. More seems to be going on here than in an analogous American setting. Women, foreheads tattooed above half veils, men in robes, rush along the corridors, or huddle in conversations punctuated with much gesture. A fluid stream of congress and transit, with currents and countercurrents.

Also, she immediately sees she is not up to speed, any speed. She caught a couple hours of head-lolling sleep on the plane over and felt almost refreshed by the prearrival orange juice and coffee, the bracing peppery airline aftershave she splashed on in the lavatory. But now that she is grounded and ambulatory, she feels fogbound, gray (and smelling, she notices, like the guys she dated in high school), entirely inadequate to the steep incline of tasks awaiting her.

The first of which is obtaining — with only her mediocre French, an Arabic phrase book, and a Visa at hand — a car that will take her to Merzouga, to Stéphane Michaud's hotel. The guy at the rental agency is young with the thickly handsome features and receding hairline common to the men around here. He speaks some English, which is a relief, but wields it in a confrontational, sparring way. She had intended to get an ordinary car, but he scoffs at her choice. To get to the dunes past Erfoud, he tells her, she will need four-wheel drive, a Land Rover, which will be more expensive, of course, and more difficult to drive. He peers at her as though sizing up her worthiness to rent such a daunting vehicle. Which makes her feel teenage, as though she is borrowing the jeep rather than renting it, taking it on her driver's training certificate and a note forged with her mother's signature. He so intimidates her that she neglects to check the price against the exchange rate. It is only as he is filling out a seemingly endless sequence of carbon forms that she begins to worry that the bill will translate out of dirham into hundreds and hundreds of dollars, a figure closer to a fair purchase price for the car.

Although an unlikely ally in her venture, he is so far her only acquaintance in Ouarzazate and so she asks if he knows a good hotel. He looks up from his form-filling, and she can see a whole new assessment taking place behind his eyes. American equals money. T-shirt and jeans equal young and penniless. Age cancels out youth but doesn't compute with the jeans. After a prolonged moment, these calculations add and subtract to a recommendation of the Berbere Palace. He pens a small map on some scratch paper.

"It is very near," he says, and she worries for a moment that the Berber in question is his brother-in-law and that the hotel will be above a tannery, its rooms smelling of DDT, the breakfast porridge squirming with weevils, like those in the hotel dining rooms in *The Sheltering Sky*, but she takes the slip anyway, her options in this and everything else in the moment severely limited.

The Land Rover turns out to be a total beater of wartime vintage. Some war, some way other time. Its color appears to have once been tan, now faded and sandblasted to a mottled white. The seats are cracked leather, a match for the bomber jacket she tosses into the back along with her duffel. The ignition, although it unpromisingly yields only a series of blank clicks with the first turns of the key, finally catches spark to gas, and she is off with a lurch of gears.

Even with shades on, she has to visor her eyes to look up into the kiln of blue noontime sky, bleached pale and translucent by a dominating sun. As she drives through it, Ouarzazate appears both timeless and at the same time devoid of any human history. The main drag appears jerry-built, prefab, its architecture utilitarian, mostly one-story buildings, some with a second floor, but often this part is roof- and windowless, unfinished in a permanent way.

At this siesta hour, there is little activity. A bit of car repair. Turbaned vendors leaning against the doorframes of their shops, the entrances hung with kilims bleaching in the relentless light of this African summer, the rugs displayed to attract the tourists who are in scant supply in the middle of summer. There's a small grocery, a bank. A café, the tables in front filled entirely with men.

Contrary to everything she expected, the hotel, up a winding drive into the foothills, is absurdly luxurious. A doorman takes the Land Rover outside and she enters. Huge and pink, the Berbere Palace's vast lobbies are peach-colored with terra-cotta floors overlaid with thick antique carpets, indoor potted trees, high French doors opening onto an enormous pool, white tables.

A uniformed bellhop walks through ringing a bell, carrying a blackboard that silently pages, in chalk, "M. Dustand. Chambre 322." In a small way, this is thrilling, a scene out of a forties movie coming into real life, except that nothing about life here feels at all real.

She checks in at the reception desk, handing over her Visa card and passport, and is taken down an abundantly landscaped path to one of a sequence of small villas. Her room is up a short flight of tile stairs, possesses a small terrace, a TV on which, after the bellhop has left, she flips through the channels of cartoonish Italian variety shows and English weather maps to find the Cleveland Indians playing the Detroit Tigers. She swoops up and out in her imagination, like Cecil B. DeMille on the set of some biblical epic, rising high above the action. In this mode, she sees the whole world as a map. On it, she is one dot, the Cleveland Indians another.

It takes some doing to get hold of Jacques Aumont at the film lab. Chris is first cut off, then the woman who answers says she thinks he is not there, but she will check, and then there is a pause until an extension begins ringing, and he answers, "Aumont."

She takes his breath away when she announces herself, her presence here. She can't remember ever having effected this cliché literally.

When he recovers, it is to ask if there is any news. She sees he has taken her call to mean something, something conclusive. Something bad. That she is bearing tidings.

"No," she says. "There is nothing. I'm here empty-handed, just making my own search."

"You understand I am as saddened as you. I received a call from your friend Leigh. And then I asked some questions around here. Places Taylor might be. I found nothing. She has not been back here, I am confident in telling you this."

She doesn't want to bother with this line of conversation. She has never thought Taylor was here in Morocco, takes as further corroboration the fact that she can't feel her anywhere in the air, no presence vibrating its hard ground. Having such thoughts, she knows, means she has become a person who puts stock in notions so evanescent she would have found them laughable a few months ago.

"It's another matter I've come on," she tells Jacques Aumont, then waits a bit to see if he says anything. When he doesn't, she says, "I'd be more comfortable speaking with you in person."

"Ah," he says, stalling, she can sense it. "But I am not much of an in-person sort of person, I'm afraid." He punctuates this comment with a giggle.

"Well, but, it would be a terrible disappointment, coming all this way and only talking on the phone. You were her friend. It would mean a great deal to me to meet you."

"*Alors*, I am flattered, of course," he says, but offers no invitation. She can't be sure what's behind his reluctance. Perhaps he is only being coy. There is a coyness to everything he says. She is losing patience and would like that not to show.

"Please," she says.

From all Taylor's talk about what an ascetic he is, Chris expects Jacques to be wraithlike, in a loincloth, sitting in front of a small bowl of rice. And so she is quite taken aback when he greets her at the door of his nondescript house, yet another mud-and-straw bungalow with wrought-iron grates over its small windows. He is huge, well over three hundred pounds. He looks like a typecast old-fashioned homosexual villain with thinning, slicked-back hair, an overgroomed mustache. The crooked art dealer who has enemies casually garroted and, for a hobby, keeps tarantulas, strokes their fur as he holds them in his lap, gives them pet names.

He is wearing a white djellaba, which, although it seems an affectation for a European, must, she admits, be more comfortable, less constraining, than western clothing. The decor of the living room he ushers her into is spare. A low, sagging sofa, a patchwork of kilims on the concrete floor. Bookcases line one wall. There is no stereo or TV; the phone is an old rotary dial model, dull black and heavy-looking, its receiver like a dumbbell. The dining alcove has a table, but is set up for work with a small manual typewriter, stacks of folders.

The profile she assembles is of a person who doesn't entertain much, has little social life. Maybe a sexual life, she thinks, then immediately pictures this revolving around eccentric pornography. Paid encounters with extremely specific delineations. A shrink's tic, conjuring up the most private aspects of the newly met.

What, she wonders, did Taylor find so charming about this guy? He seems merely to be a sad anachronism, a kind of gay guy everyone else has gotten beyond. But there must be hidden attractions; Taylor is very fussy about who she spends time with, has far fewer friends than Chris.

But Chris will never ferret out the charms of Jacques Aumont. This brief meeting, she knows, will be the only intersection of their lives. She is not interested in hearing any of the Blossom Dearie records she notices stacked next to an old portable record player. They won't be sitting together into the night sharing Taylor with mutual affection. She needs to be ruthless. She has three more days before she has to be back to her clients, so she has to make tracks. She is not here seeking camaraderie or alliance, only a small piece of information. Which she is determined to obtain.

"Please," he says, gesturing toward an armchair as he settles himself deeply into the sofa. "Sit. I'm afraid I have little to offer in the way of refreshments. I take my meals at the café." He waits, appears comfortable in this posture. She gets the feeling he could sit there for an hour, patiently waiting her out.

"The thing is, I want to meet her." She is afraid he'll be coy or fatuous in his response, pretend he doesn't know who she means.

Instead he remains silent, although no longer waiting. Finally he says, "To what point?"

"Well, that's a tricky question, isn't it? I'm not sure. I'm trying to put together a picture, a puzzle. I think I'm having trouble because there are still too many pieces missing. She's one."

"Stéphane, she is a very private person."

"I'm not interviewing her for a tabloid," Chris says, then tries to pull around to a less confrontational tone. "I'm private, too. We share the same private matter."

"She may not agree to a rendezvous."

"I'm not asking for an introduction, only an address. If she doesn't want to talk, she can tell me that herself. You needn't mention that I'm coming," she adds, although of course, as he sighs and goes over to the table, finds a pen, and bends to write out directions, she can already see herself outside his door on the way to the car, already see him picking up the dumbbell receiver of the ancient phone, putting through a call to the auberge in Merzouga.

The next morning Chris is awakened early, before dawn, by a haunted song wafting through the easing darkness — the muezzin chanting from the minaret of the mosque the first call to prayer, piped out in this town on a public address system so tinny that the chanting sounds as though it is being played on a scratchy 78 rpm record, as though it is floating up from the past, drifting in from the thirties or forties, a call to prayers long since heard by Allah.

She pulls on her bathing suit, takes the terry robe provided by the hotel, and goes out to the pool, breaking with her shallow dive the surface of its utterly still, heavily chlorinated water. She feels powerful once in motion, as though she is a much better swimmer than she really is. She pushed through her exhaustion the day before, managing to stay awake until eight, dropping off easily in spite of a nearby din set up by the drums and trilling of a folkloric show outside the hotel dining room. Her reward was sleeping through the night, this morning feeling full of the potential of the day, her body clock reset to the local time.

Afterward, she is ravenous. Breakfast is a panoramic buffet, designed to appeal to foreign tourists with cereals, chafing dishes of watery scrambled eggs, pocked crepes, croissants. Here and there, though, she finds what look to be African specialties. Thick, chewy pancakes, smoky from grilling. She wants to ask what they're called; she has become fascinated with the details of this place but has to fight down her curiosity, hold the bulk of her questions unasked. There will be no time to steep in all this differentness, acquire it in any way. She has to pass through here without getting snagged. It will be a full day's drive to Merzouga without stopping for sights, wayside attractions, souvenirs.

The highway out of town is eerily new and smooth, lunar, anthracite black cutting through pale, crushed eggshell sand, an endless rubble of rocks punctuated here and there by a Kasbah off to the side of the road, human-scale sand castles, their turrets stuffed with giant stork nests. Occasionally along the vast stretches of nearly nothing, she passes a black, low-to-the-ground, batlike tent, or a solitary figure will appear, walking across the open earth, on his or her way from somewhere to somewhere else, with neither point apparent.

The morning heat gathers and the black of the highway turns liquid, absorbing the sun and shimmering with it, connected with the vast sky by a field of wavy air that looks as though it could vaporize anything, easily a hunk of tin as rickety as the ancient, wheezing Land Rover in which Chris is spinning across the Dadès Valley, along the lip of the Sahara. Although there are dials for air-conditioning on the dash, nothing but a hot, dusty wind rushes from the vents.

She passes Skoura, the first palm oasis out of Ouarzazate, which would be startling anywhere, but seems miraculous and miragelike in the middle of this barren landscape further bleached and dusted by nearly two years of drought. There are lush palms, thousands of trees heavy with young dates, almond and olive trees as well. In the distance, beyond the oasis, is a crumbly, centuries-old Kasbah. From there, she passes through El Kelâa des M'gouna, improbably the site of fields of pink Persian roses. Small roadside shops advertise "eau de rose" for sale. Outside the one she stops at, boys at rickety stands sell fossils, trilobites and ammonites; she recognizes these from a childhood geology book. Also packets of playing cards. She buys one, opens the thin paper wrap on the slim deck. The cards are tarotlike but clearly intended for play. She wants to know the games.

By the third or fourth hour on the highway, Chris feels burned and dusty and slightly hardened, also a little exhilarated, having shed her cloak of troubles, having received a temporary dispensation to make this absurd run. She is fearless, unthreatened by the guys slouched outside the cafés where she stops for almost cold, fiercely sweet Cokes, or by the forbidding terrain of the pre-Sahara.

What is there left to jump at, after all? What bogeyman could still spring from beneath the stairs? She is a woman alone in a place extremely foreign to her, a woman whose lover has disappeared, someone for whom the bottom has fallen out. She has canceled fourteen appointments and boarded her dog, postponed dinner with her mother, and left messages on the phone machines of her friends. The uniform message was that she was going away for a few days, but she did not say where. Daniel will call Leigh, who will have already figured it out.

In these ways, the doors of her life have been closing behind her. The slightest wind could push them shut for good and she would be as gone as Taylor. These recent events have made her aware of the ephemeral nature of existence, how much closer to liquid or vapor it is than to anything solid. Understanding has made her less cautious. There is no real security, no effective ballast, so why not just leave the hatches unbattened and set out traveling light?

Just past Tinerhir, she stops at a Berber market of maybe a thousand people, half as many donkeys crowding a vast field. She needs bottled water, and although she finds it right off at a stand near the front, she is drawn in by the tides of the crowd, by the voluptuous displays of olives — pyramids of black and green and pink. High formed cones of spices and powders — deep brown and coral and yellow, dark red. Milling currents of shopping women in chador. Donkeys burdened with crushing loads, an entire sofa in one instance. Some of what is being sold is plain, recognizable, like bar soap, plastic dishpans. Meat, albeit not the cuts found in American supermarkets. Fly-specked carcasses hang from hooks. Sheep heads replete with hair and eyes are arranged in a row on a counter, along with the forelegs of some animal not readily identifiable. Much else is simply mystery, and extremely seductive. What's one to make of the man sitting behind a card table covered with human teeth and a pair of pliers? Or the one kneeling on a blanket, scooping out the powdery insides of a large (ostrich? stork?) egg, then mixing these crumbs with brilliant and dully colored powders from jars at his side, folding the mix into newspaper packets for which there is a surging consumer demand, perhaps two dozen people thronging around him, waiting their turn?

Instead of alienated, Chris feels absorbed into the mystery. Instead of being at odds with the normal, as she has been lately at home — everyone else going on in a usual, predictable way while her own life has come to a dead halt — here she understands that she is but a small oddity, one element in a much larger, deeper pool.

Until this moment she has been — along with her terrible fears for Taylor — nettled that this disappearance has turned her into an eccentric. She should be granted an exemption, a dispensation. Having escaped the peculiarity of her childhood, the fates should have allowed her to step through the rest of her life in a regular, one-foot-in-front-of-the-other way. She should not have had to try so hard for so long to obtain some measure of control over her circumstances, only to be tossed into this centrifuge where she has none. Now is the time in her life when she should have been allowed to be regular, to move into a pleasantly dull middle age. Her troubles, when they came along, should have been like everyone else's, the predictable sorrows of gradual decline — knee problems and memory loss. Hot flashes. Eventually, the bad biopsy or sudden stroke in a restaurant. Not an event so dreadfully out of the ordinary, so into the realm of the "Sunday Night Movie," where husbands are stalkers or serial killers from another state, where children are kidnapped, and where everyone needs a private detective. A hard landscape in which the central characters are powerless against the malevolent caprice of the fates.

Here, though, is a respite, an emotional oasis where the fates hold the deck and often deal off the bottom. In a culture so veiled, a scheme in which so much is occult and filled with hardship, with people of small possibilities, a woman who has lost her lover, it would seem, can be easily accommodated.

In the late afternoon, Chris stops at a roadside restaurant and eats a tagine of chicken and olives, drinks three Cokes in rapid succession. Although she is the sole patron at this off-hour, service is still slow. Yet there is nothing to be done, there is no McDonald's here. No service plaza. Earlier, when she pulled into a gas station, a donkey stood, inexplicably, at the pump. She had to wait for its owner to emerge and lead it away.

The heat by now is beyond any in her experience. Her baseball cap is a joke as protection against this fierce element, the work of the overbearing sun. When it finally passes from the sky and she drives through dusk into night, the air thins out and chills down dramatically. She stops to pull her jacket out of the back.

She slows down through Erfoud, another desultory gateway to the desert beyond, then takes a turnoff southward toward Merzouga. At first she's driving on an actual road, but within half an hour it has given way to an unbordered route, and Chris has to negotiate deep sandy tracks. Beyond these, any semblance of a single road gives way to wildly free-form parallel tracks created by vehicles that have preceded her, and she has to follow the telephone poles to keep on course. At one point, even the oversize tires of the Land Rover fail her and bury themselves. She fights down a wash of panic, rocks the car into forward, then reverse, until it comes loose and she is on her way again. Soon, the massive, splendid dunes — the Erg Chebbi — appear, blotting out the horizon and night sky beyond them.

She passes a strip of small hotels glowing with light from within, a café, a sandswept town (more sand than town, really), and then just outside it, a sign for the Auberge Lyons and then the hotel itself, as though flung all the way out here from the middle of provincial France. Two stories, its walls a pale blue with white shutters at the small windows, a child's toy lost on a vast beach. She tries to imagine Taylor here, imagine who she was, who she became when she arrived here again and again.

It is nearly ten when Chris herself arrives. She worries first that such a small hotel will be locked for the night, or full, leaving her in the middle of the desert with no place to stay.

Instead, the lobby is dimly lit, a concierge does accounts at a desk behind the counter, inducing a clipped whir from an electronic calculator. This is the only sound in the sleeping lobby. He is quite handsome, she sees as she approaches, with thick gray curls, expensive tortoiseshell glasses, a linen suit in a pale gray that almost matches the hair.

"Ah," he says, standing up with a charming smile cultivated, she guesses, through years of greeting strangers. "You have finally arrived. We have set aside a room for you." So. Jacques Aumont did call ahead. Of course.

"Is Madame Michaud here, then?" she says.

"My wife has retired for the evening, I'm afraid," he says. So this is the husband. Chris hadn't gotten so far as imagining an actual person. "She must accompany a small group of our guests to the Erg Chebbi at dawn. If you wish, she would like you to come also. These dunes are the reason people come out here." He pauses, then adds, nodding slightly toward her, "Ordinarily, that is." She has no idea how much he knows about his wife and Taylor.

"What time is dawn?" Chris says, looking at her watch. She is exhausted, can't imagine being up to any activity, much less tricky emotional interaction, before sunrise.

"Well, of course, they will be leaving before dawn. The point of the excursion is to view the sunrise. If you could be down here at four-thirty."

Chris nods, unable to come up with a countersuggestion. She will just have to take the meeting on Madame Michaud's terms.

"We will call your room to awaken you."

The room is small, a nun's cell with white linens draping a single bed. A plain armoire. Heavy lace curtains at the window, a pitcher and bowl on the nightstand. She *could* be in Lyons.

She showers the long day off herself, changes into fresh underwear and a T-shirt, and lies in the dark with the curtains tied back, the shutters open to the desert night. She slides into a bad patch as she waits for sleep to overtake her. Until now her short time here has been a reprieve from impotence. With the sole of her foot vibrating on the accelerator, barreling through a thrillingly alien landscape, she was operating from the premise that finding this woman was crucial, was going to yield up significant information. The hours heading toward the auberge were the first time since Taylor disappeared that Chris has felt like an actor in her own drama. She was traveling within the soft folds of the delusion that she was, either physically or metaphysically, rushing headlong toward Taylor.

Now, though, she is once again powerless, without a course of action to take, on the edge of this great desert, Rommel yanked out of her jeep. Now all she can do is wait for tomorrow. With the windows open, the indoorness of the hotel room is so insubstantial that in Chris's transparent dreams, she is lying not in a narrow bed, but on the eddying sands beyond, tidal without any adherence to the moon, alive with the skittering life of hard-shelled creatures.

She wakes a couple of hours later, equal parts exhausted and wired, rummages around for a cigarette, then lights up and sits in the dark, on the floor, leaning back against the wall across from the bed, trying to prepare herself to meet her lover's lover. There are a few obvious tones she would like to avoid taking. Jealous would be one, confrontational another. If Taylor has found something compelling in this woman, Chris needs to give credence to it as a way of under-

standing her partner, who, it is beginning to seem, she rather criti-
cally misapprehended. Taylor came here the first time, to this hotel,
to take photographs of the dunes beyond. She and Chris were still
new enough with each other then — a year or so into being together
— that the separation felt like harsh punishment to Chris, a particularly bleak February, followed by the heady, breathless reappearance
of Taylor, which Chris marks as the beginning of her slipping away.

• • •

"You look as though you've found religion," Chris says.

"Something," Taylor admits. They are in bed. Taylor is working on the nail on the big toe of her left foot. She picked up a
fungus in it a while back, before Morocco, shooting rain forest
pictures along the Amazon.

"This is a toe with a goal," she says, rubbing back and forth
over the surface of the nail with an industrial-strength emery
board. "It wants to be an inch thick. It wants to be a hoof. With a
lot of work, I can thin it down and shape it to look almost
normal, but in the night it just starts up again." She looks up and
grins goofily. She is radiant.

"Religion or sex," Chris says, continuing down the conversational track that interests her more than Taylor's toe. "Like
you've just discovered sex."

"Not sex. I found sex with you. I was just playing post office
with those other girls."

"I think you were playing doctor with some of them. But tell
me. Tell me what happened over there. You're like a person with
a happy secret."

"I'm not sure what to say," Taylor says. "It's as though, knowing they're there — those dunes — that they'll always be there, I
can rest easier. Now I have something in reserve."

• • •

When Chris walks into the still dim lobby, Madame Michaud is
already busy, sorting tourists into groups for the ride into the desert in
Range Rovers. When she is finished, without appearing to have even
noticed Chris, she comes over to meet her.

She walks with a limp, a slight drag of her left leg, which somehow
makes her more rather than less attractive. There is a sexual quality to
the weariness of her body. The photographs, it turns out, were flatter-

ing in a way; she is older than Chris was expecting, perhaps fifty, maybe a dozen years older than the husband in the lobby, a decade older than Taylor. But the photos were also bland, almost insipid in how little they captured of her aura, a heavy musk wafting through the air around her. She is large for a French woman, lean but big-boned. Her heavy hair, brown verging on black, falls in a drape across one side of her face, is brushed back, falls again. She's geared down for an upscale, colonial version of desert travel — jeans narrow at the ankle, silk shirt, buttery leather jacket and soft boots.

Oh, honey, Chris thinks. Not that the woman is beautiful; it's not that easy. Even the ways in which she is striking are not entirely attractive. Her nose is too heavy, her high cheekbones only point up the hollows beneath them. Her eyes are large and tired. Her androgyny and age and makeup combine to create the effect of casual drag, extremely, if oddly sensual, and heightened for being slightly faded, as though implying glamour, experience, knowledge she must bear up under. Chris finds herself daunted and turned on at the same time. An image flashes across the fresh white screen of her mind. Taylor in bed with this woman, responding to some command for service.

Nothing about her is Taylor's type. That is, she is not like any of the women Chris knows who have all fallen before Taylor, in a petal path. This woman is of quite another order, a seducer's seducer. Whomever she wanted, she would probably get.

As she approaches, there is an immense amount of activity at the back of her eyes; she is immediately interesting. Also, it is clear she recognizes Chris, which Chris wasn't quite prepared for.

"Madame Michaud," Chris says, expecting to be told to call her Stéphane, but she isn't. Instead, Madame merely nods, silently appraising.

"So. You have made a very long journey. I'm afraid you will be disappointed, though, to not find what you are looking for," she says, her voice roughed up, as Chris imagined it, doubtless by a long past of cigarettes. Her scent is a tumble of smoke and sylvan cologne, the fabric of her clothing, mint. There's more, but Chris can't sort it all out in the moment. "But you will join us anyway? You really should have this experience, as long as you have come so far."

With Madame Michaud leading the way, they go together into the blue-black night. There is no city here throwing its lights up to the sky, to be reflected down by the clouds. There are no clouds, only cold, distant stars. Madame Michaud turns, and says, "You look exactly as I expected."

They are alone together in Stéphane's Range Rover, following the pack of tourists in the others. Conversation is impossible over the engine, the heater blasting. As they bump through the darkness, small desert animals scuttle out of the way of their headlights. When they reach the base of the dunes, Chris instantly recognizes the small, funky café as the backdrop of the photos she printed in Taylor's darkroom. Outside, camels rest, their legs folded neatly under their bodies, like huge furry card tables.

Stéphane does a little negotiating with the Berber guides, matches tourists with camels, then indicates that Chris should mount one of the animals herself, and gets on behind her, putting a casual arm around Chris's waist as the camel lurches to its feet. Chris feels a flash of heat, just short of arousal. She realizes, with the next heartbeat, that what she is feeling is Taylor as she must have felt as the recipient of this same gesture.

It takes maybe half an hour through the darkness, up the slight, early incline of the dunes. When the going gets too steep, the guides help them dismount, then take the women each by a hand, up the rest of the way to the top. The pack of tourists have different guides, are being led up the next dune, away from Stéphane and Chris. Whether their seclusion is accidental, or by Stéphane's design, Chris can't tell. At any rate, gradually, a situation affording privacy is achieved, a situation in which a conversation will occur.

When they get to a narrow sand plain at the top of the dune, Stéphane tells Chris, "And now we wait. For the sun." She points into the distance. "It will rise there. Over the Algerian border."

The guides, dismissed, sit off at a distance. Chris sits silent. Madame Michaud has called the game; she can deal out the hand they'll play.

She pauses, as if summoning up a rehearsed line. "First I must tell you, I cannot be involved in any police business or searching. I am sorry there is a problem that requires intervention, but I really cannot help. Also I am sure I do not know anything that would enlighten. I knew her in such a limited way. What we had was a private affair. An *affaire d'amour*, do you understand?"

Until now, Chris has been cool about this woman. She seemed so remote, on a different continent from Taylor's real life, which, of course, was with Chris. Now, though, now that Chris is on Madame Michaud's continent, close enough to inhale her perfume, and hear the tone in her voice, which is condescending, she finds herself suddenly considering a little mid-desert violence.

She tries to tamp her emotions back into place. "I have to ask. You haven't talked with her since she was over here?"

"Once. A brief phone conversation. Just after she went back."

"What did she say?"

Stéphane gives her a look that is some French equivalent of "get real," then says, "Well, I am sure you can imagine. The usual particulars of such talking. Long pauses and careful remarks, very careful. On both sides. No one is her best self at the end. You see, the last time she was here I was forced to put a stop to what had been between us. My husband, I think, began to tire of this interlude. He finds this type of thing amusing only to a certain point. What began as a light affair was becoming heavy, a weight on me. Taylor was not seeing that she was becoming this weight."

Chris winces as she tries to accommodate the image before her now: Taylor in a puppy dog position vis-à-vis this self-infatuated French jerk. She tacks around onto another course. "Did you get any sense, in the phone call or when she was over here, of where she was in a more general way, of what was happening with her in the rest of her life? Maybe she knew people I didn't know about. Maybe some trouble she could have gotten into. I don't know."

"But what are you saying?"

"Well, I'm only wondering where could she have been whisked off to?"

Madame Michaud seems startled. "But what do you mean about these others? I think this is of course all within Taylor. She is in some hiding, to protect herself. Or . . . or, I don't want to upset you, but surely you must be thinking along these lines. I am saying that it is not so unlikely she has gone off somewhere, to end things for herself."

"No," Chris says emphatically. Although she has come all this way in hopes of disclosure, there are still areas of speculation that will have to be off-limits.

After a long time, she says, "Protect herself from what?"

Madame Michaud fills up with herself. "I have told you she was disappointed about us, that we were at an impasse, but also she was sad before this. From the beginning. At first this sadness was appealing. I think maybe she seduced me with it." Here she allows herself a rueful little French laugh. "But surely I am telling you nothing. You must know all about this *tristesse*. Being her lover, also a *psychologue*."

Chris considers that the opposite might actually be the case, that it is possible the slump-shouldered parade of woes that passes through her office every week set up a barrier that kept her from seeing the suffering of her own lover. But she does not want to investigate her failings now. And so, to jump tracks, she says, "You put this crisis down entirely to her being brokenhearted? Over you?" She really doesn't mean to be insulting, although that would certainly be a little bonus.

"Well, and of course her age. She did not have a European view on these matters. For Taylor, aging was like a death. The powers she holds are youth and beauty. Having whoever she wants quickly, through little coded messages. Now she will have to work harder. Later, harder still. She could see what lay ahead. The codes, they would have to become more complicated. She would have to work where once it was all play. You see?" She punctuates this point by pressing the butt of her hand into the sugary sand, then dotting with a finger in front of the mark, then repeating the motion, making false footprints of some nonexistent desert animal. An idle child's game.

Stéphane sighs, then looks up. "Desperation," she says, "never shows anyone at her best." She adds a small smile of regret for not having been able to love Taylor quite so much as Taylor loved her. Which in turn, implicitly, is not quite so much as Chris loves Taylor.

Already disadvantaged, Chris is resistant to making herself vulnerable to this woman, but then thinks what does it matter if she tips her hand on this rise of sand in the dead middle of nowhere? Particularly if it will get her a critical piece of information.

"How did she speak of me, could you tell me? How did I fit into all of this?"

"Oh," Stéphane Michaud says, suddenly quite earnest, as though she has straightened up, squared her shoulders, when in fact she hasn't moved a muscle, "you were so very important. An aspiration. She said what she most hoped was to be the person who would deserve you."

"But meanwhile, while she was working her way up the food chain, she'd have an affair with you."

Madame Michaud shrugs. "She was Taylor."

The conversation has angled slightly. Stéphane has taken Taylor and set her gently on a shelf for the moment. At first Chris can't see why, can't see what she would be replaced with. And then a flicker passes inside Madame Michaud's eyes, and Chris inhales sharply, involuntarily. Aha. There is already someone else on Madame's horizon. Chris doesn't want to know anything more. Already she is experiencing a caustic sadness, lye flushing through her veins, on reflecting that Taylor could have been laid so low by the rejection of someone whose sentiments for her were so vague, so easily siphoned off.

"Ah," Madame Michaud says suddenly, as though they are nothing more to each other than tourist and guide. "Look." The sun has swelled over the horizon, dividing the world sharply in two, black sand and orange sky — all there is of the universe in this moment, and the two of them, tourist and guide alike, are subsumed into it.

Chris hits her lowest ebb in the Casablanca airport, where she must change planes and has too many hours to dispose of. Where she sits is the ultimate point in the concept of neither here nor there, a duty-free gauntlet of chocolates and liquor, restaurants and shoeshine stands, all catering to a horde of the transient, held exactly between where they are coming from and where they are going to. Chris sits in a molded plastic chair in an empty waiting area at the farthest end of a concourse.

How could she have seen so little of Taylor, ignored so much? If Taylor cast a shadow so apparent to others, but was always presenting herself to Chris only when the sun was high overhead, with no darkness visible around her, then what real resolution can lie ahead? Now, even if Taylor comes back to her, Chris realizes she will still be alone.

"NICE TAN," Myra says, deadpan. Chris didn't tell her she was heading off for Morocco, just skipped last week's session without calling.

"I couldn't let you know," Chris says. "I didn't want anyone talking me out of going."

"Awfully long way to go to talk to a jerk."

"Well, it was enlightening. And deflating."

"You might want to take this woman's information — what is it but her self-serving impressions, really? — take what she told you with a large grain of salt. Factor in a little that she *is* a jerk. Probably didn't mind pointing out to you her privileged position."

Chris brushes this aside. "But what she told me was cautionary, instructive. What I was doing, I can see, was assembling who I wanted Taylor to be, based on what she gave me of herself. I can see now that her presentation was extremely selective rhetoric. And beyond that, I was selective in what I chose to notice. Now it's like the lights are going on. I should have seen that she was out of whack, that she didn't care in the appropriate spots, the proper proportions. Like, she was great at what she did — taking pictures — but she mostly just blew that off. I'd encourage her to put a show together; she has friends who run galleries. But she was never interested enough to go to the bother. She could have been any kind of photographer. I think she got into the travel stuff not because it particularly attracted her, but simply because those were pictures she could take somewhere else, away from her life, from me, from Diane before me. It gave her some kind of relief.

"Relationships — the same thing. She was living with me; we were partners, but I wonder how much space I took up in the larger scheme of things for her. Now I think it was more that I served some particular function for her, made her think of herself as a regular girl with a regular girlfriend, not a lone figure in the desert wandering along a path between nowhere and nowhere."

Myra doesn't say anything, but follows Chris with her gaze when Chris turns away. She doesn't let the client out of her clutches for a second.

"What a trapdoor," Chris says. "I thought what we had held weight and reality, and where it veered into fantasy, that it was a mutual concoction. From the beginning, we pumped each other up, I see that in hindsight. We were giddy with our potential. Underneath, though, I was taking it all pretty seriously. Everything just seemed to augur — you know, all of it seemed to imply huge rooms we were walking into."

• • •

Sitting in Taylor's Cherokee, parked along a deserted stretch of lakefront north of the city, out of reach, they hope, of Diane's radar.

They have conducted a large part of their clandestine courtship in these diagonal postures, at oblique angles to each other, legs draped across the divide, running nervous fingers along the seams of each other's Levi's, baggy khaki shorts. Talking, or not. Talking about them, the dilemma that is them. Other times about everything but. A lot of fooling around with straight faces, but it feels great and they indulge themselves.

"One of the things I love about you is that you can be dramatic with me, that you get it — that it's ridiculous, but important, too," Taylor tells her. "And with you, it's so seriously dramatic, and at the same time trashy and voodoo. And I want more. I want all the stuff I longed for when I was, like, seventeen. Mooning around up in my bedroom. You know, exchanges of significant jewelry. Codes only we understand."

"Blood rituals," Chris says.

"Definitely blood rituals. And matching tattoos we give each other in the bathroom with India ink." She reaches over and wraps a hand around the back of Chris's neck, applies pressure. "I want to write you terrible poems, embarrass myself. If I get famous and there's a biography of me, I want it to say, this is the woman she lost her mind over."

. . .

Myra studies her now, from across a professional divide. "Once you were off and running, after all the fooling around with your importance, what did Taylor give you that made you so desperate to hold on? Can you articulate that?"

Chris thinks. She has never asked herself this question, although it is precisely what she would ask any client in a troubled relationship.

"I think it was the opposite of holding on. It was never being able to get her in the first place. Even after she left Diane for me — maybe because she left Diane for me — I thought I was there on a trial basis. That she had her doubts and was hanging on to them, a little stack of poker chips by her right hand, visible so I'd always be aware she was still considering cashing them in. And even after I got her, I got only pieces. She kept on withholding herself, and I guess that made me think there was so much more there to tap into, and that it was a sign of how much she loved me every time she let me in a little more.

"And then in bursts, she'd come at me with such ferocity. Crawl on top of me, grab my T-shirt in her fist, stare hard into my eyes. She yanked me out, forced me to show up. And when that would happen — I know it sounds like not that big a deal, but it was as though I'd been waiting my whole life for the release.

"What a terrible discrepancy, though — her boring into me while keeping me at such arm's length from her. I'd met my match. I'm so very good at not tipping my hand, at knowing what's happening on all sides of the table. When you're cheating, of course, you have a nice edge on the action. But sometimes you wind up in a situation, at a table where there's more than one sharp, and things can get quite treacherous, and exciting. You can't be sure what mischief is afoot. There's too much withheld from normal play for you to have your usual control. There's always the possibility of the palmed ace sitting up inside someone else's sleeve, throwing everything out of whack — harrowing, but also exhilarating. And that was it, I guess. She was the other sharp."

Tiffany the cockatiel screeches through the air above them, wrapped up in some private bird drama. They wait until she settles on top of a bookcase.

"I'd like to stop the pain," Chris says, suddenly tired of analysis. "What I want is even one day of feeling normal, a morning where I don't wake up feeling as though I'm being slammed into an abutment."

"If you want, I can send you to see Ralph McPherson about getting on antidepressants. There's no shame in that. It might bring you up a level or two, for the short run."

Chris considers Myra's proposal. "I don't know. Maybe I should. I guess my instinct, though, is to try to keep driving through the middle, see where these emotions take me. If I lay a fog over them, I'll be able to see only as far as my headlights. If I can tough it out, then when I get there — wherever there is — maybe I'll be better acquainted with who I am."

"That's my girl," Myra says.

Chris is desperate for signs of progress. She hoped Morocco signified a break, and that getting back home to a regular routine, to her schedule of clients, fixing small meals, taking in her dry cleaning, would be an antidote to her relentless turmoil. But she is still so off balance, and growing so weary of tragedy, of being tragic, of watching, as though from a free space just next to her, as her emotions reduce to the banal. She sees that her extremely particular, her dazzling and brilliant, grief has been greatly co-opted by the soaps. Living in the midst of all this mystery and suffering has turned out to be a lot like playing a substantial role on "All My Children." Her small epiphanies and crying jags alternating with steely dry-eyed days make her feel like someone named Blair, someone with longer hair and a makeup person.

She doesn't want the attention the situation is bringing her. The messages pile up on the phone tape, friends concerned, of course, about Taylor, but they also want to know how Chris is faring, and she understands that underneath there is a desire to know, through her, how they would do if their own worlds came crashing down around them. She doesn't want to be a test case, the canary in everyone's disaster.

The phone rings. Chris has been letting the machine field calls for her, but it is late Saturday, a night she and Taylor used to set aside for each other, and as sometimes happens, hope makes a small leap in her chest. The image of Taylor always comes up as clear as a movie; always she is standing at a pay phone by the side of a gas station on an anonymous highway. Semis whip the air, putting her inside an ersatz wind, running ghostly fingers through her great hair. She pulls it back with one hand, then covers the exposed ear to better hear the connection when it is made, Chris picking up, saying,

"Hello?"

Hope takes a nosedive; it is only Audrey. The baby wails in the near background.

"Horace is keeping me up anyway so I thought I'd check in, see how things are going." Audrey and her husband have named their baby after his father. The new Horace has relentless, red-faced colic; so far this alone defines him. Audrey has admitted to Chris that she has had a few fleeting, immediately regretted impulses — usually coming over her when she has been operating on two hours sleep in three nights — when she has thought of throwing him out the bedroom window.

"Not much new," Chris says. She's getting good at saying this, no matter what is really going on. Nothing about her situation seems easily relatable to others. She fears that whatever she says will sound foreign, will drop peculiarly between her and whomever, will widen the chasm rather than bridging it. She has acquired a life that absorbs all her energies, fascinates her, but makes for deadly conversation with anyone outside the grip of her obsession.

As it turns out, Audrey is easily deflected. She doesn't really want to talk about Chris; she is too absorbed in her own drama. She is sick with love.

"I wasn't looking for cataclysm. I was looking for something easy and on the side. She already had a girlfriend, so I figured it was, well . . . safe. But then things between us got heavy and they broke up and now she wants this whole life with me. She can describe it exactly, like it's already there and we just have to walk into it."

"Except for the small problem that you already have a life," Chris says.

"Oh, honey, I'm just so scared. I'm not at all prepared to blow everything sky-high."

"So you're going to back off."

"No. The unbelievable thing is I think I'm going to do it. I'm going to give up everything because she's going to walk if I don't, and I can't stand the idea of not having her."

"Boy," Chris says. She's not often surprised by what anyone tells her, but she would never have expected such abandon from Audrey, who she had neatly slotted as a chickenshit.

"Can't talk more," Audrey says in a scrunched voice, indicating that her husband has come into range. His sudden arrival interrupts so many of their calls that Chris has begun to wonder if he creeps around intentionally, suspicious.

"What about you? Are you eating?" Audrey asks. She stopped by Chris's office the other day on her way to the pediatrician and noticed that Chris has lost weight.

"When I remember," Chris says. Another thing she finds she doesn't mind lately is a little self-dramatizing.

"Avocados," Audrey says. "They're appealing even when nothing else is. I remember that from the early days of my pregnancy."

Chris doesn't hear whatever else Audrey goes on to say.

"You're not listening to a thing I'm telling you," she finally says, but with no real exasperation. She is the most endlessly kind person of Chris's acquaintance.

"But I'm happy you called," Chris says, and there's even a little truth to this. "I know I'm not easy these days. But I am appreciative. Honestly." She flips open the tinny top of the dollar butane Elvis lighter she picked up at the 7-Eleven and fires up a cigarette.

"You're not *smoking?*" Audrey says.

"Just lighting a votive candle."

"Oh, darlin'."

Chris needs to hang up. She is pushed up against the battery of pillows that formerly were both hers and Taylor's but have gradually regrouped on her side of the bed. She is looking the short distance across the room toward the open door of Taylor's closet, which suddenly presents itself as a portal.

She ends the call; she's pretty sure she has said goodbye to Audrey before putting the receiver down. She hops off the edge of the bed, nearly stepping on Bud, who is wheezing away through his ancient dog sleep, one paw on a rubber mailman toy.

She opens the door and drops to her knees and picks up a pair of jeans, some underwear, a sock, finally the sweatshirt Taylor wore when she ran, then hardly ever bothered to wash. Pressing her face into the inside fleece, Chris is thrilled; little oiled BBs of pleasure roll through her. She has found an untapped source. And here it was all the time, waiting for her discovery. Here, still here, microcosmically, in this atomic residue, is a shadow presence. She can still have this shot of Taylor.

At about three in the morning, Bud wakes her with a bit of pacing. A storm is coming up, its heralding winds already whipping through the blinds at the window. Soon rain crashes onto the aging roof, sluices down the windows around her. By five, Chris is standing at the top of the basement stairs, looking down into two feet of water. Various items from her past and present float into, then out of view. Her winter boots. A copper teakettle she doesn't recall ever having seen before.

She is on hold, waiting for Clyde, with AA-Open Drain Sewage, flattening her nerves with a cigarette. She has had to concede that she is smoking again. The evidence is pretty irrefutable. The ruses of bumming and buying the occasional pack have given way. She now owns a lighter. The inside of her car has a slight ashtray aura. She joined right in with Myra during their last session.

She used to smoke only in moments of crisis, but now crisis seems to have turned into a state of being. She pushes into the background the knowledge that she is eventually going to have to quit again — wear a patch, sit in a wheezy, confessional quitters group watching the "Your Lungs" video, and carry her butts around dissolving in a jar of water as aversion therapy. For one thing, Taylor is allergic to smoke. When she gets back, Chris will have to put an end to this nonsense.

Lightning and thunder collide like fists directly overhead. Bud leaps into the air, throws back his head, and howls. Chris looks down the stairs, sees one of her photo albums float by, and flips out. She shouts "No!" at the tides, and at Taylor, who hasn't just left her, but abandoned her to the small, steady sequence of dilemmas that were barely manageable between the two of them. She is never going to be able to handle everything on her own.

Clyde finally comes back on the line. She and Taylor initially got him, as they have most of their workpeople, from a card stuck in their mailbox. They have had to call on him twice since to pull from their drains and catch basin great masses of hair and grease belonging to them and also to the Herbsts, who practiced an extremely minimalist brand of maintenance on this house. (They had no shower, only a tub. When an electrician who Taylor hired went into the walls to upgrade the wiring, he found that in places, gaps had been bridged with extension cords.) It will be a couple of hours before he can stop by.

"Christine," he says. He pronounces it as though she spells it Krysteen and they both hail from the same part of Texarkana. "When it rains like this and the whole city backs up, you're gonna get a little water."

"It's not a little. I could ride a motorboat around down there. Plus there's stuff coming through the wall in the back corner. Like the wall's a little fountain. That can't be right."

"I'll be over. Meantime, just wait 'til it's over, then start bailing."

He shows up much faster than he promised but won't be able to fix the leak in the foundation until the water subsides. He pulls large clots of leaves from the drain just outside the basement door, which helps everything start to ebb, but the water leaves behind a terrible mess. She tries to decide how soon is late enough on a Sunday morning to call Daniel. She looks at the kitchen clock; it's 6:32. Nearly seven. Only a few hours shy of noon, really, when she thinks about it.

Of course he'll be sleeping the deep, peaceful sleep of the dry. He lives in a condo on the seventeenth floor of an apartment building overlooking the lake near Belmont. Any technical crises he has are dispatched with a fast phone call to the janitor, Ulf, a rail-thin, stubbled guy who lives in the basement in a feral situation and looks as though he has a social life conducted primarily through 900 numbers. If there is flooding in Daniel's basement, it's Ulf who gets wet.

When, early into their rather one-sided conversation, Chris mentions the "storm," and Daniel says "What storm?" she wants to kill him, but ignores the urge in order to be able to project through the line the spirit of friendship and need that will bring him over to help her. Which it quickly does.

"Boy, flooding. I don't have any experience with that, but I'll be right over. Camille's with me this weekend. I'll bring her along. We'll bring some sponges."

She's not sure if he's kidding.

The rain finally gives up and they can begin salvaging, which takes them the better part of the morning. There are some satisfactions to this enforced housekeeping, like tossing out Taylor's stacks of magazines, which are hopelessly waterlogged. ("We had to make decisions for you. You weren't here.") But boxes of Chris's childhood games have to go too, which makes her mopey.

"Oh, come on," Daniel says. "Try to imagine the day when things would be dismal enough for you that you'd get a hankering to play Rich Uncle."

Chris nods. Camille, a notorious pack rat, looks the game over, puts the soggy box in a small pile of stuff she is setting aside for herself. Bud sniffs around this stack for some time, as though it harbors a long-forgotten cheeseburger.

Earlier, Daniel went to the Ace and bought a shop vac, which is speeding their progress. Slowly, a light follow-up rain — like the stuff that mists lettuce at the Jewel — starts sifting down on everything they've set out to dry on board and crate shelves propped around the backyard. They throw paint tarps on top and a couple of old shower curtains Chris digs up. Daniel and Chris go inside to forage for a belated breakfast while Camille takes her treasures out to their car.

While Chris is bent over, head in the refrigerator, Daniel makes a comment about last night with Rachel, the woman he met at his mother's nursing home, and it suddenly dawns on Chris.

"I didn't interrupt anything this morning, did I?" The possibility hadn't occurred to her until this moment. She is so used to thinking of Daniel as single, or as a single parent, watching "Saturday Night Live" with Camille, fixing air-popped corn, interruptible on a twenty-four-hour basis.

"No. We went to see a dance performance last night and I dropped her off afterward." Daniel, she has noticed before, has many of the interests of a gay guy — dance, particularly ballet, and obscure, aged cabaret singers. He hates spectator sports. "It's her idea — not being sexual just yet. She thinks people approach intimacy too fast."

"She's probably right," Chris says, wondering how old the eggs are in the carton she has found in the refrigerator's outback. "When I think of all the great women I could be having fascinating, intellectually stimulating lunches with now if only I hadn't sailed right past friendship, waving merrily as I took the exit ramp off to sleeping with them. But are you completely chaste with each other? I mean, do you make out?"

"That's kind of a personal question."

"Oh, come on. I've given you gruesome details for years. Don't you dare try to duck me. Do you kiss at least?"

"Sort of."

She tries to think what this could mean, then quickly decides to reverse course and let the subject drop. She doesn't want to run into anything really grim.

"I'd like to meet her," she says instead, and it's true. She doesn't mention that she has quite a bit of attitude already built up, and would like to meet Rachel mostly to confirm the worst of her suspicions. She knows from Daniel that Rachel is "statuesque," which Chris has translated into a tall sort of fat. She is in software sales and so, Chris imagines, has a personality that's been molded in peppy seminars. She probably first-names people a lot when she talks to them. She is active in her church, some bland denomination. Presbyterian. Methodist. She plays the piano, but to be considerate to her neighbors, she uses an electronic keyboard with headphones. Chris enjoys imagining her, bulky on her piano bench, pounding out a silent "Für Elise." She knows she is being horrible.

"You look good since you've been back," Daniel says.

"If you think that suggests I'm feeling better, I'm not. I'm like Hans Castorp just in from the terrace, ruddy but still with a fever, and still at the sanatorium."

"What does Sikora say?"

"Nothing. There's nothing. Nothing on her charge cards. No tickets on her license. No calls on her phone card. She hasn't applied for any jobs. As he put it, there's no paper on her paper trail."

"What does that mean? I mean, I wonder, is that good or bad?"

"They don't say anything, but what can it mean that's good?"

Later, while Daniel is answering a call on his beeper, Camille sits down next to Chris on the back steps.

"I've never lost anybody," she says. "Even all my grandparents are still around. I had a sad experience with our class gerbil in the fifth grade, but I guess it's not the same, not nearly."

"I'll still let you talk to me," Chris says, putting an arm around Camille's shoulders. "Even though you're short on misery."

"Still. It's like, it would be better in a way if I could offer you some big tragic item that happened to me."

"This could still have a happy ending."

"Like what?" Camille seems truly bewildered, as if she hasn't understood.

"Well, on the docudrama shows, they've always got some poor soul with amnesia who's been living in Baltimore for years, but they've no idea who they are or how they got there, and meanwhile their family is in Seattle going nuts. But at the end of the show, everyone is reunited and happy again. Kind of."

A long time goes by while Camille, clearly embarrassed for Chris, looks away, in the direction of nothing in particular, then finally fades off with, "I'd better get some paper towels to wrap around those magazines, to blot them."

She watches Camille walk through the gate, her girlish figure padded slightly in the same, squared-off hips that her father has, a microscopic quirk in their DNA.

Chris wonders where she will go to find understanding now that she has parted ways with the strictly rational. Where will she find a peer group of people who won't walk out in the crucial middle of her conversations? She has always taken pride in being hardheaded, grounded. Now will she have to start hanging out at the Discovery Center, taking weekend miniseminars in determining the color of her personality? Casting about for other slightly off-center types who approach life at a steeper-than-average angle? Or will she settle in with Bud, cooking him special chicken-liver dinners, and taking him out in inclement weather in a plaid dog raincoat and paw boots?

After Daniel and Camille have gone, Chris sits alone at the dining room table and checks to make sure there's enough in their joint household account to cover the check she wrote out to Clyde this morning. She goes through the square forties ceramic serving dish they keep on the sideboard to hold their bills, and digs out the latest statement from the bank and the small calculator Taylor uses to balance the account every month, yet another task Chris will have to take on.

She never looks at these statements, just gives Taylor a check for her share of the expenses at the beginning of the month, then writes another if they're short toward the end. She has always assumed Taylor did the same, that the account filled and drained on a monthly basis. And so she is startled to see the balance at nearly eight thousand dollars. She scans down the credit column and sees that, after the initial monthly deposit on the third, which was fifteen hundred dollars, there was another, subsequent deposit of sixty-two hundred dollars, on April 28, the day after Taylor got back from Morocco.

Chris at first doesn't know how to process this information. For a brief moment she gets a crook's rush. Surely this amount must signify one of those impossibly rare computer errors working in her, rather than the bank's, favor. Quickly, though, she sees it is a transfer, doesn't recognize the account number, but understands immediately it must be Taylor's savings. She stares at the hard numbers on the page until they go spongy under her gaze. This patch of ink surely holds meaning, though she isn't sure what the meaning is. As far as she knows, Taylor has the finances of a fairly successful, modestly commercial artist, which is to say they're just shy of dismal. Six thousand dollars probably represents the bulk of whatever money she had put by. And so this transfer might represent the guilty offering of a woman who has left her partner saddled with what had been a shared burden. But then she realizes with a sweep of nausea that it could also be a final settling of accounts by someone who doesn't foresee a future, and won't be in need of funds to support one. The statement does almost certainly eliminate the worst possibility, the Taylor-in-a-car-trunk possibility. She has left on her own steam, prepared for her departure. Now it is only her destination that remains veiled.

There doesn't seem to be anywhere to go with this information. She should tell Sikora for sure. Daniel and Leigh. But for the time being she needs to huddle by herself. She lies avalanched on the sofa. Bud is in the backyard so she doesn't have to be accountable even to him.

She stares through the blinds at the sky outside as the afternoon turns absurdly sunny in the wake of the morning's storms. Just as it is graying down to dusk, the doorbell rings. She looks at the clock, sees it's five-thirty. Her memory jolts into retrieval.

Her mother. Their date for *Tommy*. Chris can't imagine being able to get through the musical without running, screaming, for an exit. Even at her best, this evening would be a challenge, and she is a long way from her best. She lies stock-still on the sofa while she considers as a possibility simply not answering.

"You're not ready." Her mother stands in the doorway, assessing the situation.

"We flooded out," Chris says, hoping this will do as an explanation for standing here in old tennis shoes, long shorts, and a sweatshirt over another sweatshirt. Un-*Tommy* wear. Her mother, armored in a taupe suit, holding a leather purse shaped like a miniature suitcase, is, on the other hand, absolutely appropriate to the occasion.

"I can change in a sec," Chris says. "Let me get you a glass of wine to keep you company while you wait." She goes toward the kitchen, getting as quickly as possible out of her mother's perfume range, which is about four feet.

142

Her mother, she reminds herself, thinks she is walking into an ordinary, if rained-out Sunday in Chris's life. Chris has not told her about Taylor's disappearance. Taylor and Chris's mother, by casual avoidance on her mother's part, have never even met, so what would be the point? Her mother has no real interest in Chris's personal life, having instead created, Chris suspects, a fictional, negatively exoticized version, along the lines of *Cabaret*. Something set in nightclubs and involving gender fluidity abetted by costuming. To avoid running into seamy details, her mother has also created a cover persona for Chris composed of equal parts social worker and jaunty single gal. Someone employed and unpartnered, so conversation must cling to her work, her activities. Chris figures, given this artificial zone in which her lover is nonexistent, what does it matter if she is present or absent?

It is not that she and her mother are antagonists. They are just so very different from each other that they long ago had to give up the search for common ground, can only blink at each other from opposite horizons. Her mother, years back, remarried, a lawyer who was in estate planning before he retired. She is Jewish now; she converted for Maury. She lives in Highland Park and goes to sculpture classes and tries to keep up culturally.

The two of them are reminders to each other of their failure to achieve family. After the divorce, Chris and her mother led a life of quiet hardship, of waiting for a man to come along and rescue them. But when Maury finally showed up, there turned out to be no room for Chris in the lifeboat. He was finished raising children; his were already off in marriages of their own. Chris was gently set aside in boarding school.

There is no picture of Chris anywhere in her mother's house amid the many photos of these sons and their wives. Chris has been swept under the rug of propriety, part of her mother's less-than-successful first start out of the gate in life, the practice marriage and child she had before she got this whole business right.

Chris's mother would say she took her only opportunity, that she gave Chris what she could, then took what was left for herself. She refuses Chris's resentment. Rather she thinks it is Chris who betrayed her, taking after Tom Snow, choosing a reckless life lived on the margins, although she sees the margins as her daughter's lesbianism.

Her awareness of the gambling Chris was doing on those school breaks and summer vacations is minimal. She doesn't want to know any more than she does. And so she has no understanding of the hard trek Chris made back in from the lightly seductive criminal world that exists just over the line from lawful and polite society.

Chris had to make this journey alone. Her grades were good enough to get her into a small liberal arts college in Minnesota. She majored in classics. When she returned to Chicago, it was to get a doctorate in psychology at the U. of C. Her notion of becoming a therapist was an impulse of restitution, a way to give back some rough equivalent of what she and her father had stolen.

Chris's clients come through, one after another, trying to sort themselves out through the discovery of just what kind of villains or heroes their parents really were in their earliest dramas. Her own parents present a more subtle problem. To be sure, her father stole the last of her childhood by bringing her to the green felt tables, but also gave her an early shot of glamour. Her mother, beyond having sold Chris out for a husband and never having shown her much affection, seems not very interestingly villainous. Rather she seems to be who she is on the face of it — wife to Maury, formally maternal toward his two sons and their nearly adult children. This seems to be a rich enough landscape in her view, where she sits content, shadowless.

On a practical level, the genial alienation between Chris and her mother makes sense. These evenings, which they force themselves through maybe two or three times a year, are a trial for both of them. Seeing more of her mother would mean much more of the deadly small talk that lies on the restaurant table between them, like dusty domino tiles. Getting closer would necessitate being brought into Maury's large, warmhearted, golf-crazy family, which would be the sixth or seventh circle of hell in Chris's personal version of the Inferno.

Of course, emotions know no practicality, and Chris goes through periods during which her dream life is thick with cheesy fulfillment scenes. She is at a regular high school, a prom queen, a hostess at pajama parties. Or younger, and her mother is bringing her to tap class, where she is immediately a tiny star. In other dreams, her mother beckons her onto a large, velvet divan, folding her up in arms that have plumped up from reality in order to accomplish the dream's blatant purpose. She used to be embarrassed dragging this flotsam in to Myra.

Alternately, her fantasies would expel her parents entirely, smooth over her embarrassment at having come from so little. She would concoct a bland, kindly couple, devoted to her development, encouraging her prosperity in life. Later, these longings receded, transforming themselves into efforts to recreate herself as the person she might have been with all the tap lessons and the doting. Until these past weeks, the model on which she based this more dashing version of herself was Taylor.

Tonight, as usual, she and her mother have come to Un Grand Café. The energy of the restaurant goes some distance in filling the inert air that hangs between them.

Chris is preoccupied, trying to figure out what the bank deposit means, and what she would prefer it meant. First she thinks it would be worse if Taylor considerately moved this money over before she did herself in, pushed it silently into Chris's coffers to avoid any posthumous legal wrangling that might set up between her and the Heyeses. But then she plays out the other scenario — that the money is Taylor's attempt to buy off guilt at having left Chris in such a ruthless way. At least, Chris thinks (so childishly that she is immediately covered with shame), if Taylor has taken her life, she has rejected the whole of it, not merely Chris.

Chris goes through the motions of the dinner, an actor in a play. She talks about her plans for the garden, about Bud and his recuperation from knee surgery last year. In turn, her mother talks about her own dogs — small, irritating terriers — and about the low-fat, low-cholesterol diet she keeps Maury on since his bypass surgery, about their exercise regime, which this winter has meant mostly brisk walks through a shopping mall in their neighborhood.

"We both wear Walkmans," she says over a stylish salad that looks like vegetation foraged in hardship conditions, above the tree line. "I put in duplicate tapes. *Tony Bennett: Unplugged.* Julio Iglesias. Like that. So we're marching to the same drummer."

While they are waiting for dessert to arrive, Chris begins to fake a migraine, which will peak around the time they finish their coffee.

"You shouldn't have had that bleu cheese thing," her mother says. "Or red wine. They're both terrible for migraines."

"I have some medicine at home," Chris lies. "I wonder if we have time before *Tommy?*"

"Oh, don't be ridiculous. You can't go to a musical with a migraine," her mother says (bless her heart), as though musicals are in the same category as veiny cheese and cabernet. Chris is pretty sure she sees something pass beneath her mother's concerned expression. Of course. She, too, is relieved that the evening is being cut short.

When she is inside her front door, her back pressed against it as she listens to her mother's Camry pull away from the curb, North Shore–bound, Chris reaches into a few pockets of coats and jackets hanging on the hall tree until she finds it in the left inside pocket of her leather bomber — the phone number of the nice, unsurprisable woman at Berlin the night Chris was out scouting for Taylor.

"I'm sure you don't remember me," Chris says when, a few minutes later, she has her on the line.

"I remember fine," the woman says. She's Loretta, according to the writing above the number. "I don't give out my number but about a couple of times a decade. So, did that girlfriend of yours ever turn up?"

"Well, the thing is, she hasn't."

She lives in a renovated factory on Racine, what the ads call a "soft loft" because it has a large, high-ceilinged living room with tall windows and pillars breaking the space here and there, but it also has a real kitchen and bedroom and a bath with walls rounded at the corners. There are cats lurking on the premises. Chris can tell by the faint scent of their urine and then by a glimpse of one darting into the bedroom. She is allergic, which has turned out to be a fairly serious dating liability since lesbians are great cat lovers by and large, usually owning several if they own one.

Loretta gives her a tour, showing off the apartment.

"I wound up lucking into this great divorce lawyer. I would've settled for just being out of my dismal marriage, but she shook some real change out of his pockets. It was kind of a high."

"I'm supposed to be at *Tommy: The Rock Opera,* with my mother

146

tonight," Chris tells Loretta, who is prettier than Chris remembers her from that night at Berlin.

Loretta nods, as though weighing several factors or considerations. "This will be more fun" is what she finally says.

As Chris follows her around, it becomes clear that the loft part of the apartment's design — the notion, promoted by the decorating magazines, of sparse furnishings and large artwork — has been lost on Loretta. She has instead filled the place with small, rickety, cheery things — a chintz loveseat and matching recliner in the living room area, a rag rug. The dining table is colonial. Everywhere there are small framed prints of mountain lion cubs and beach sunsets, the sort of decor sold at Target, designed to cover in a fell swoop the fresh walls of recently revised lives.

Chris thinks, about half an hour into the visit, that Loretta is probably one of the women in the lesbian personals ads who list long walks in the rain and cuddling in front of a fire as favorite activities. She has that sort of softness to her, of manner and expectation of life. There are no edges to snag.

Sometimes Chris wishes lesbians were a little more like gay guys, more into sexual expedience. Which is, at base, what Chris is longing for tonight. She finds this woman attractive, thinks it might be nice to get naked with her in the bedroom at the other end of the loft. Instead she is sitting on one end of the chintz loveseat, having given Loretta a vague summary of the work she does with her clients. In exchange, she has been shown around the loft, heard a bit about Loretta's travels to all fifty states. Now Chris is trying to pay attention through a chronicling of the complex personal dynamics of the office where Loretta is a supervisor.

". . . and she rides me constantly, mercilessly, gives me piles of work on her way out at five, and the thing is she knows she can get away with all of it because she's sleeping with Bill and he'll always come down on her side in the crunch."

Chris tries to hold an expression of interest, but she sees she must be failing when Loretta smiles sheepishly, and says, "I'm sorry. I realize this is probably about one one-hundredth as interesting to someone who's not in that centrifuge forty hours a week."

"To which you're going to have to return in just a few hours. I should go and let you get some sleep."

Loretta stares at the wound ropes of the rag rug beneath her feet and nods. Then says in a voice much smaller than the one in which she was relating the politics of her office, "Or you could stay."

Chris's immediate response is a fit of sneezing. She has been feeling for the better part of an hour, the hallmark of cat dander — a nasal tickling, as though she has inhaled paprika.

"Do you have any antihistamines around?" Chris says.

"I have Contac, I think."

"If I take that, I can stay."

Chris knows what she is doing here is trying to elbow her way back into the crowd of everyone else in the regular, lucky world. All her concerned friends, Taylor's hyperactive relations, the police who want to close this file, have been no real comfort to Chris, only pushed her further out, made her realize how alone she is. But this woman, Loretta, with her rec-vee vacations and absorption in office politics, doesn't know any details of Chris's troubles and has politely asked not so much as one question on the subject through the entire evening. And so, with her, Chris thought, she could for a few hours take pleasure in being naked against someone in a way that wouldn't really amount to intimacy.

It doesn't work, though. She almost immediately begins weeping against the bare shoulder of someone who shouldn't be required to comfort her.

"I'm sorry," she says, probably a few too many times before she finally gets dressed in the dark, a cat winding around her ankles. "I guess it's too soon."

"You need it to be her," Loretta guesses.

"It's not even that. You'd think it would be that, but it isn't. It's that I've fallen too far into myself, and at the moment I don't seem to be capable of climbing out."

"I don't mean to sound harsh," Loretta says, not getting out of bed to see Chris to the door, "but I think it would be better if you didn't call again. This place you're in, the whole thing, really, is a little too heavy for me."

S I K O R A looks as though Chris's sofa makes him itch. He is asser-
tively not the kind of guy who would be caught dead in therapy.
Chris can tell that being in her office is too close to the process for
comfort, as though he is worried that whatever he says here will be
interpreted to mean he hates his mother.

Chris sits down next to him and hands over the bank statement.
She was oblique when she called. "I'd rather not do this on the
phone," she told him. She wanted to get him over here. She wanted
to be able to see his reaction. Now, she watches him as he looks over
the printout. Time passes heavily. Clouds shift in front of the sun
outside and the quick darkening of the room seems like a change,
not merely of light, but of season. Chris looks away, into her vast,
formless future.

"It's not good, is it?" she says.

"Probably not. Wherever she went, if she was planning to go somewhere, she would need money. Especially if she was starting fresh. So it's more likely she was anticipating her . . . her demise." When Chris doesn't say anything, he says, "I'm sorry."

"But isn't it possible she was feeling guilty, dumping everything on me, and wanted to smooth things over, that the money was a gift to assuage me?"

"Anything's possible. I don't know her. I don't know how things were with the two of you. I barely understand how things go between men and women, and I really don't understand how they go between ladies together." He clears his throat. Now he's really itchy. He taps a few mints into his palm, as though relating all this bad news will have tinged his breath with some sorrowful smell. The silence in the office creates a vacuum in which she can hear him grinding the pellets with his back teeth.

"So what do I do?"

"Do?" He shifts uncomfortably in his leather jacket. Because she is sitting close to him, and because it is a little too warm to be wearing leather, she can smell, in small gusts, a shadowy scent of the animal the garment was fashioned from.

"Do I just give up?" she says. "Do I go on hoping? I see those people on TV, holding photos of their kid who disappeared at a rest area. Or their husband who hasn't been heard from since Vietnam. Or those people in Oklahoma City, waiting weeks later for those last hunks of concrete to be dragged out, trying to work up a version of reality in which their person wasn't smithereens within the first split seconds of the blast. And I always think they're pitiful with their little handful of hope, like dust in their palm. And now I'm one of them, aren't I?"

"More will come to light." He speaks as if chipping each word out of stone. For a guy who has been doing this his whole professional life — being the messenger of a thousand bad tidings — he is remarkably awkward at it. "Few people disappear in a complete puff of smoke like Jimmy Hoffa. We'll probably find her car, for instance. We'll probably eventually find her. And there's still — you're right — a chance she'll turn up alive. But you might try getting on with your life a little. Waiting is probably not the only thing you should be doing anymore."

Chris nods. And listens to the creaking of his jacket. And hates him.

When he is gone, she tries to gather herself up, but there doesn't seem enough raw material to work with. She has become almost purely reactive to immediate circumstance. She can only wait for what happens, or doesn't. She is incapable of independently creating days to walk through comfortably. Time stretches before her as a tricky enemy, vast slicks of pain to be steered around with sleep, which now often needs to be augmented with Xanax from a bottle she found in the medicine cabinet — a prescription Taylor used for getting sleep on transoceanic flights. Chris tries to be cautious, holds the pills in reserve for the worst of her nights, when the harrowing dreams precede and preclude any real sleep. She holds herself to half a blue tablet, then lies in the dark and waits for the flannel rush.

The sleep she really wants is the deep cryonic coma Sigourney sleeps through in her gray *Alien* underwear as the spaceship travels for years, getting her to the next mission. Chris wants out of this phase, into some next one, whatever it is.

She looks to her work for salvation, for distraction in the sorrows of her clients. If she keeps her focus narrowed, laserlike, perhaps she can force her own concerns to the periphery.

Tonight Jerome Pratt is troubling her. He seems to be losing ground. The meds are holding his obsessive-compulsive symptoms in check. The hand washing and window adjustment have completely abated, but the relief he initially felt in their absence — not to mention the free time their departure opened up — has allowed other demons to surface. But these are somewhat amorphous, and Chris is having a hard time getting him to articulate. Furthermore, the boyfriend turned out to be temporary and Jerome is taking the breakup much harder than such a brief alliance would seem to warrant.

He met Keith on a sexual bulletin board on the Internet. Keith is a bear, which is to say he is a large man with a surplus of body hair, the type Jerome goes for. Jerome's broken heart has left him in a crisis of confidence with no handwashing to take the edge off. Chris can see, maybe a little too late, that she misread his troubles, their nature and degree, and will have to backtrack. She is energized by the challenge, though, ready to grapple with the real, underlying Jerome now that she is beginning to see who he is. She might be muzzy in her own sorry life at the moment, but she is still there — incredibly tuned in — for her clients.

"What about your friends?" she asks him. "Is there anyone you can lean on in your moments of missing Keith? Do you feel you can turn to Evelyn, for instance, and she'll give you meaningful support?"

Jerome blinks, then says, politely, as though he hates to bother Chris with the question, "Who's Evelyn?"

The phone is ringing as she comes through the door, trying to side-step Bud, who is doing figure eights of welcome, tangling up her footwork. Sometimes the ring has a more distinct Taylor cast to it and she is led against her better judgment into picking up. It's Audrey again. The thought passes through Chris's mind that maybe Audrey has a phone karma similar to Taylor's. Then she stops herself, realizing this sort of thinking is about a half step shy of consulting numerologists, that Rosario Delacruz probably has an aunt who deals in interpretation of phone rings.

"I didn't know if you knew" is how Audrey starts off. "About the TV thing."

"What TV thing?"

"They're advertising it for the ten o'clock news. A special report on missing persons. Taylor's picture was one of the ones they showed so I'm assuming she's part of it."

"Is this by any chance on Channel 5?" Chris says, smelling Leigh lurking around the corner.

"Here it is, it's starting," Audrey says. "Go turn it on."

Chris approaches the TV with trepidation. The news frightens her lately. She doesn't want to see reports on this or that body unearthed in a forest preserve or discovered alongside I-55. The missing, even when they're not Taylor, are the population to which she now belongs, her neighbors in limbo. Chris doesn't want any of them being found in bad circumstances.

Carol Marin is introducing the segment, which is catchily called "Into Thin Air." The camera opens tight in on Leigh's face. She is wearing some red-framed glasses Chris hasn't seen before. They make her look a little like a Sally Jessy Raphael. She has an expression of terrible gravity, as though she has just been told by the oncologist that the tumor is inoperable.

"While the Chicago police, with their limited staff and resources, prioritize by putting the bulk of their energies into the search for children who have disappeared, the sad fact is that hundreds of files on missing adults stay open — unsolved — for months, years, sometimes forever."

Leigh's face is replaced by a Christmas snapshot of a beefy union electrician who has yet to return from a Michigan ice fishing trip in February, then by the smiling face of a woman in a birthday party hat, a Winnetka mother of two who was last seen in March buying a slip in the lingerie department of Marshall Field's at Oakbrook. When Taylor's picture comes up, it is the one that was to go on her book jacket. Hair in controlled disarray, casually crumpled khaki field vest.

"Over a month has passed since the mysterious disappearance of Taylor Heyes, Chicago photographer . . ."

Chris wants to turn the set off, wants to be able to say she clicked this stupidity into oblivion as soon as she saw it coming, but she can't. She's a gaper at the sight of her own accident. She watches with an eerie detachment for the few minutes it takes the television to compress the large, shapeless problem of Taylor into a neat flip of photogenic flash cards.

She's not familiar with the rest of the pictures on the screen; they must belong to Leigh. Taylor in wide-smile close-up, then in long-shot hilarity at a cookout. (Was Chris there? She can't place the occasion.) Then Taylor on camelback on the pre-Saharan dunes, her teeth brilliant against her darkened skin. Missing since late April, disappeared into the middle of a seemingly ordinary day. Without a trace. Into thin air. No cliché goes unstruck. Friends and family are terribly worried. Chris is not singled out in this prime-time piece.

Nonetheless, the phone begins ringing almost immediately. Within half an hour, there are — she counts them as they come in — seventeen messages from the curious and well-wishing. One of whom is Renny.

"I just got wind of your troubles. I'd like to help if I can." Like the vulture wants to help the wounded antelope on the desert highway, Chris thinks, but takes down the number. Sometimes she can still surprise herself.

As the phone starts up again, she nods to Bud, grabs her keys, and they're out the door.

"How could you?" she shouts into Leigh's intercom. "How fucking could you?"

The answer is a low, humming buzz emanating from the front door. Chris and Bud scoot into the foyer, up the stairs. Leigh is standing in the open doorway to the apartment. It looks as though she was in bed; all she has on is a T-shirt and underpants. Tiff is nowhere in evidence. Bud slips past her into the living room, always up for a little visit.

"You didn't even have the nerve to tell me," Chris says.

"I suspected you'd be obstructionist."

"You knew I'd be dead against it is what you knew, you terrible coward. You wanted to exploit your best friend for some sweeps week feature and you didn't have the nerve to tell me. I was just telling the cop I can't stand being thought of as a victim or survivor or whatever. I hate this. I want my regular self back. And I can't have that while everyone's feeling so fucking sorry for me. I thought you understood."

"You're being, if you'll pardon my frankness, a selfish shit. Think of Taylor for a minute, if you can spare it. Do you have any idea of the reach that little segment will have? Do you know how much response we're going to get from it?"

"But from whom? I can tell you. Amateur psychics and some housewife in Harvey who discovers Taylor's face on her screen door, or a trucker who saw Taylor sharing a peanut butter and jelly sandwich with Elvis at a roadside diner in Indiana. Meanwhile, instead of merely hiding from the people I know, I'm also going to have to start hiding from everyone else who's ringing my phone off the hook even as we speak. And none of it is going to help find Taylor."

Chris is crying now, puts a hand against Leigh's chest to steady herself as she tells her about the bank statement.

"Oh boy" is all Leigh says, wrapping Chris up in her arms. Bud stands at their feet, looking up with the smile he uses when he's trying to turn human events around.

Later, in bed, Chris sits cross-legged against the pillows and fiddles with the slip of paper that holds Renny's phone number, trying to figure the odds on whether this call will make her feel better or worse. She is looking for anything that will make her feel better, even a long shot, even a little better for a small piece of time.

If she calls, it will be the first conversation they'll have had in the years since they broke up, that is, since Renny dumped her for a large-breasted, pouting Xerox assistant at Kinko's. This was an expensive lesson for Chris. She learned the hard way that in love it can be the very set of dazzling attributes you are polishing that work against you in the end. Renny didn't, in their particular end, want Chris's jokes and the great sex and all the huge, battling power struggles Chris thought were bringing them into a new territory. She wanted pouting and busty and adept at spiral binding.

The only time Chris has seen her since was at a party Chris left within minutes of discovering Renny's presence. If you'd asked her even a couple of months ago, she would have said it would be another several years at least before she was ready for any contact. But with all that has happened in these past weeks, what untouched place on Chris could Renny find to wound? From the far remove of suffering Chris occupies, Renny's devices seem almost innocuous, small, shabby, obvious tricks. Tricks that could only have worked on a more naive Chris — a Chris who hadn't yet experienced Taylor, or for that matter, a Chris who hadn't yet experienced Renny herself.

The number on the slip, she notices as she begins punching it in, is one she has actually never forgotten. She gets Renny's tape, leaves a message. When they finally connect after a bit more phone tag, Renny says she thinks it's time they talked, directly instead of through the friend pipeline.

"What kind of talk?" Chris says. She's tough. She has had this line ready for years.

"If you can't handle it, I understand," Renny says, and Chris realizes she doesn't have a second line prepared. She can't bear the thought that Renny might think Chris is still too unsettled by her to meet face to face, that she still holds this kind of power over Chris (although, of course, she does).

Chris worries that she has hesitated a beat too long, and so quickly and, she hopes, casually, suggests the next night and a kind of hip coffeehouse; Renny counters with the night after next and a bar-restaurant called the Commodore Club in the west part of the Loop, near where she works. She is dismissive of places that are trendy; her idea of atmosphere is a bar with low lights. She would gag on a mocha latte. Her hatred of pretension was initially one of the most endearing, in the long run one of the most tiresome, things about her.

As soon as Chris has pushed open the leather-tufted front door of the Commodore Club, she is plunged into a cavernous dimness, the hallmark of anachronistic rendezvous joints catering to executives romancing their secretaries. One of those places where the drinks are incredibly strong and the food incredibly bad, but who cares? There are no chairs, only semicircular booths with flickering votive candles on the tables. Where does Renny dig up these dinosaur palaces? But even as she wants to laugh out loud, Chris gets a cheesy thrill as she walks into the overconditioned air.

Renny is in a booth toward the back. She has changed out of her work clothes and is wearing jeans and a white shirt with the sleeves rolled up. (She is insanely vain about her arms.) If she's freezing in the polar air-conditioning, she probably won't admit it. Her cowboy-booted feet stick out from under the table, her long, callused hands are wrapped around a vodka tonic.

Chris takes the hit in a couple of places — heart and knees, both of which buckle. The moment is a whirl of guilt and power. On the way over, she knew her elevated pulse had nothing to do with the anxiousness she has been suffering all these weeks. This was a new set of nerves laid over a familiar one. Taylor hated Renny, or rather — as they never met — hated the idea of her, hated that anyone else ever held Chris in thrall. By coming here tonight, Chris is executing the ultimate betrayal, putting herself in the range of the temptation that is always Renny, paying Taylor back for leaving, not just this time, but for the leaving always implicit in her never having been able to come to Chris and stay.

Renny looks both the same and quite different after all this time.

Her hairstyle is new, a longish, minky crew cut. And the years have done some work on her, allowing her to grow into her toughness. Her face is creased from tanning, the smoking she used to do. The androgyny of her youth has reduced to pure butch now that she has passed forty.

Renny is from an earlier period of Chris's emotional life, when she was hitting the bars, going home with a wide assortment of women, the width of the assortment providing part of the charge. A period during which she remembers telling Daniel, "It's not politics, it's *bed* that makes for strange bedfellows."

Now Chris has most recently been with Taylor, who is nicely professional, a more conventionally suitable match. They both speak a little college French, diminished over time. They spent their junior years abroad, two years apart, in Montpellier. They belong to professional associations, are on the boards of a couple of gay and lesbian organizations. They get the *New York Times* delivered, talk sometimes about issues. They are longtime liberals in the voting booth. Between them they have a pretty good grounding in the classics. They know a little about wines, gourmet cooking. Although they liked to think themselves unique, they are also, Chris knows, girls of a particular class and place.

Renny is from another place. She is a FedEx driver. She has a tricky back, soaks in a hot bath when she gets home from her day on the route. She has never been to a health club, especially enjoyed hearing Chris describe the StairMaster. "Hey, my whole day is a health club and I never realized it. They should charge me to come to work."

In the tub she would read long biographies of everybody — Mother Teresa, Alexander Graham Bell, Elvis, Gramsci — and drink red wine from the current year, a holdover from her days as an ironworker (instant courage for walking I beams). On her days off, she went to the track. She slept, in the days when Chris was sleeping with her, with a .38 on the floor next to her water bed.

Although their relationship went on for nearly a year and a half, she and Chris never lived together. Renny likes to keep enough room around her to stretch a bit. She is serially monogamous, but some women appear in only one or two episodes of the series. When an attachment begins to chafe or confine her, she looks for someone new along her route, which is, in fact, how Chris met her. Renny stopped by Chris's office with some software Chris had ordered for her computer. Chris opened her office door and found Renny in the hallway, a nonreligious apparition bearing a small package. Tan from a booth, several dangly feathered earrings in her left ear and Giorgio pumping up in wafts from her cleavage, which was just visible within the undone, flipped-up collar of her deep blue uniform shirt. Chris remembers her knees going fluid.

On that first visit and on subsequent deliveries to Chris (who started doing a lot more overnight mail-ordering), Renny smiled in a way that was not precisely professional, leaning in a little farther than was absolutely necessary to steady the clipboard while Chris signed for the delivery. Chris has come to suspect that this is her standard m.o. And if the object of Renny's interest is interested back — and she probably quite often is — things might heat up right there in the office (as they did on about the fifth or sixth delivery with Chris), the empty boardroom, or a little later, after work. And if the women she pursues are not interested, or if they develop hang-ups later on, or undue attachment, then Renny is on her merry way again, with other packages to deliver.

Renny is best at beginnings, which she has worked into an art form. Actually trying to be in a long-run relationship with her is trickier, and quite a bit more exhausting. A typical assignation would start with a call from Renny in the afternoon, was Chris free for dinner? And before Chris understood the drill she would say sure, what about six-thirty, then shower and dress and sit until seven or seven-fifteen on her sofa overlooking the little plate of goat cheese and wheat crackers she'd set out.

And then Renny would call from a pay phone, something inconsequential but unavoidable (and never specified) had come up and she was going to be a little late. And then there would be a follow-up call, maybe they should just meet at the restaurant. Where Chris would wait until the exact moment before exasperation set in, when Renny, a master of timing, would rush in, breathless and sweating slightly from all her sure-to-be-underappreciated effort at arrival.

There were endless variations on this theme. Dates made and canceled at the last minute. Intimate dinners for two at which she would show up with another friend unexpectedly in tow, or her niece visiting from New Jersey, whom she'd forgotten to mention.

The absolute best days would inevitably be followed by ones in which Renny wouldn't return Chris's call. There was never any ambient light, spillover, afterglow — only backlash. It was like living on a cheese grater, and it got so that even as she was being dragged along in the smooth direction, Chris was already filling with dread about being dragged back the other way.

Chris still isn't sure what was at the root of Renny's ambivalence. She grew weary trying to puzzle it out, and in the process found she was turning into a worse version of herself. She could hear the tremor in her own voice when she called, never certain which Renny would be on the other end of the line. She felt like someone with a mild, unseemly malady, a vague disturbance of the inner ear that kept her always a little off-balance, stumbling, unable to get any sure footing. Another symptom was a tendency to bleed profusely on any of her friends willing to listen to the latest particulars of Renny's ardent (and inventive) declarations of love followed almost immediately by her going incommunicado for a week. Yet another was Chris's queer jumpiness around her telephone, a hyperactive sixth sense that it was about to ring, of course with Renny on the other end of the line. (Now it's Taylor holding back the ring.)

Renny happened to Chris when she was already into her thirties, past the time when she would have thought she was eligible for firsts. But, loony as it was, their relationship was undeniably an altering experience for her, changing the configuration of connection possible between her and another person.

Until then she had pretty much been cruising down an easy street of women — brief, slipknotted affairs alternating with longer, manageable relationships, tidy portionings of her emotions, situations where she always felt more or less in control. Until then she had thought passion was fleeting and primarily about sex, commitment largely about comfort. But then, even as Chris was dismissing her as not smart enough or right enough, and of course way too crazy, there was Renny, stomping straight into Chris's heart, beating on its walls with her fists.

And looking back, Chris suspects she let Taylor in only because it would allow her to jump once again off the same stupid cliff, to feel all that air rushing past her in the plummet, an exhilaration she apparently had become addicted to during that first swift drop with Renny. In this indirect way, Renny is responsible for not only the straits Chris was in after their breakup, but the straits she is in now. Which is probably why, as she slides into the booth opposite her, Chris's first flush of thrill at seeing her after all this time is nonetheless tinged with fury.

"You look great," Renny says by way of disarmament. Other people have noted this recently. She figures it must be the fading Moroccan tan, the weight she has lost.

"I'm just faking everybody out."

Chris doesn't want to give her much. Renny doesn't always make the best use of information.

"When I thought you were out there and okay, it was one thing. But when I heard you had bad troubles, I thought you might need someone who really understands you."

Objectively, Chris can see that Renny is calling her bluff, manipulating her into a position of vulnerability, leveraging with the relationship they once had. None of her dispassionate observation, however, has any effect on her emotions, which are tumbling around like socks in a dryer. She begins biting her lower lip to stop the tears working up at the back of her eyes, but it's no use. Within moments, she is sitting in this ridiculous restaurant — across from a woman with D A N G E R - E X P L O S I V E written all over her — crying.

"You really love her," Renny says, as though she is the friend she never was.

"I really love her, *and* it was complicated between us," Chris clarifies.

Renny nods, her wide shoulders dropping slightly under the accumulated weight of years of women. "I'm getting old, I guess. I'm getting tired of how it's all so complicated."

"What about . . . ?" Chris blows her nose in the cocktail napkin she tugs from under Renny's glass and scrambles around in her memory for the name of the Xeroxing girlfriend.

"Melanie? Well, you know, the thing is she and I will always be important to each other . . ."

Chris doesn't bother listening to the rest, which will only be colorful wrapping around the only interesting piece of information, which is that Renny has broken up with the girl and is on the loose, which suits Chris's immediate and specific needs. They are, she sees, in testing these waters of girlfriends gone and girlfriends missed, negotiating. When this realization hits Chris, it is so sudden it makes her smile, which, she then sees from a flicker in Renny's eye, has lost her some measure of advantage, the advantage of surprise.

"It's freezing in here, don't you think?" Renny says, rubbing down the thick cords of her triceps. "Maybe I could pay up and we could go someplace?"

"That would be someplace like your place?" Chris guesses.

"Only if you want," Renny says, creating the illusion that she is lobbing the ball into Chris's court, when in fact she already has her answer.

The apartment starts with a long hallway. As soon as they are inside the door, Chris is slammed by nostalgia, by the smell of what is old and familiar. A base coat of Giorgio layered over with the kitchen smells of steaks and spaghetti sauces past. Paste wax on the old wooden floors, lemon Pledge on the table surfaces. (Renny is a girl out of the blue-collar South Side; she keeps a nice house.) And, as always, fresh-cut flowers in vases in the living room and bedrooms, a touch that surprised Chris at first.

Renny has lived here for years. By now her smells are worn into the grooves of the place. These smells are erotically nostalgic for Chris because, although she did eat steaks broiled in Renny's kitchen and watched videos in the living room and once even played canasta at the dining room table, what she mostly did here was have big sex. She once tried to describe to Myra what transpired between her and Renny, but grew quickly embarrassed and inarticulate. And anyway it wasn't really the specifics of what occurred in Renny's bedroom (which she can make out at the end of the hall by slices of streetlight coming through the blinds), the "what" of whatever they did. Rather it was that Renny afforded Chris a narrowly defined version of safety. If only in the hours they were naked together, Chris could always let herself go with the certainty she would be caught. She longs to feel this safety again, especially now, and so she doesn't trouble herself wondering whether she's doing the right thing. With Renny it's never the right thing. The only question in Chris's mind at the moment has nothing to do with reason, only with how much prelude she will have to go through to get back to where the two of them left off.

She gets her answer when she begins patting around in the dark, along the wall for the light switch.

"I remember it's right around here somewhere," she says, then feels a hand over her own, pressing down.

"I don't think we'll be needing that," Renny says, kicking the door closed behind them, then bringing the same foot around Chris's calf, locking her in place as she pulls her in and Chris experiences the whole length of her at once, and a switch does get flipped on, though not one that produces light.

"Oh," Chris says, blushing in the dark, where it's worthless currency. "I'm so — "

"We should take care of that," Renny says, helpfully, and leads Chris by the hand through the darkened apartment, into the bedroom. The advantage of past acquaintance: without having to ask or fumble around, Renny knows what Chris wants from her.

"So you still enjoy this," she says a little while later, at a crucial moment. "That's a nice girl."

CHRIS'S FATHER often calls late at night. "I saw that TV thing," he says this time. "They didn't get into it, but the thing is, people can buy new lives." He wants to remind her about Fred Bonner, some hustler they knew from the cruise ship days who got into debt to the Mob and took what he had left and got a topflight ID man and a good, quiet plastic surgeon and a lease on a duplex in Toledo.

"That's part of the deal. They pick a city they'd never think anyone would move to," he says. She can see he's trying to be of help, bringing in a voice from a world where disappearing is a career move as frequently as it's a tragedy.

"Thanks for calling, Dad," she says, and turns the phone off for the night as she crawls into bed.

"You don't look so good," Rosario says, casting a scrutinizing eye up and down Chris, looking beneath the tan that has been fooling the less discerning. She pauses after passing this judgment, allowing Chris an opening to unburden herself. Rosario frequently indicates to Chris that she considers their association a friendship, albeit one in which Chris is often disappointingly less than forthcoming.

Chris's policy with clients is to offer them basic information about herself, should they get curious. That she is a lesbian, lives with a lover, unnamed. When she goes on vacation, she lets them know where she's going (and calls them from there if they leave a message and need her). Larger, more private matters, such as Taylor's disappearance, or smaller ones, such as the minimal sleep she has had these past nights in Renny's bed, lie on the other side of the curtain.

Typically with clients, an understanding of these limits takes over and wards off further probes. Rosario, however, enjoys lifting a corner of the drape, as though Chris is a nun and Rosario is trying to peek under her wimple to find out the color of her hair. This curiosity has a naughty quality, as though she is pushing for beloved bad girl–favored student status.

Chris doesn't respond to this particular foray, instead tries to turn Rosario's scrutiny in a more therapeutic direction. "You, on the other hand," she tells Rosario, "look good. No bruises. Radiating health, I'd say." Which is true. She is settling into her spot on Chris's sofa, today wearing a hooker's version of a business suit — red, with a skirt so short Chris is put in mind of Sharon Stone in that movie where she's driving a room full of interrogating cops nuts by crossing and uncrossing her legs.

Chris averts her eyes; she doesn't want to be caught looking. Rosario is already a little too fascinated by Chris's sexual orientation, which she takes as a kind of sideshow oddity. Before Chris, she never knew any lesbians except a distant cousin who apparently wears men's suits and sideburns. Rosario couldn't squeeze Chris into this pigeonhole and so at first conceptualized her as a woman in transit. "Someday," she told Chris once, "a real man might come along and make you see things differently. Not that men are so great, I have to admit. Still I don't think I could ever be a lesbian. For me, with women, there is no —" To illustrate, she licked a finger and made a *tssst* sound of electrical charge.

"And I can't get that with men," Chris explained.

"Ah," Rosario said, getting it, and since then the issue has been neatly closed.

Now Rosario considers Chris's compliment on her appearance, which she both accepts and rejects. "But then I am only fooling you. The truth is I am really miserable." She has sent Tony, the pummeling lover, away, but it is a couple of weeks into the silence that has followed, and she is slowly filling with regret.

"But perhaps you are discovering some things about yourself, now that you're not so focused on him?"

Rosario mulls over this suggestion. "I would say that mostly I am discovering he is seeing someone else. A piece of garbage named Luz with dyed blond hair. Maria saw them together at a club Saturday, putting coke up their little noses in the back hallway. She was rubbing against his leg, you know . . ." She lowers her head and looks up with Chris to share a glance of shared sexual understanding. "I get *morada* — purple — with rage when I picture this scene."

"Then," Chris says, "think of poor Luz getting beaten to a pulp later that night. Which is almost surely what happened."

Rosario looks at her but doesn't nod or say anything to indicate that she concurs. Chris hunkers down within herself, trying to find a way to come around and pry Rosario's tentacles off the dead issue of her relationship with Tony. A lot of what she does in this room is work of this sort, getting her clients off what is not the problem, onto what might be.

"Try to think about protecting yourself from all this anxiety, positioning yourself —"

"She should think about protecting *her*self, this Luz bitch. I took needlenose pliers and pulled the pins on all four of her tires. She should think twice about parking on the street for a while is what I'm saying." And Chris thinks, Well, another great moment in psychotherapy.

When she wakes up these mornings on the soft tides of Renny's water bed, Chris feels like a compliant hostage. Her limbs ache, her chest is weak, her breathing shallow. Her neck is tender when she presses her fingertips against it, and so she knows before she even gets to a mirror that the capillaries have burst into a hickey.

It's early, barely dawn, not even six yet, but Renny is already late getting started on her day's route. The alarm, which Chris recalls going off in a middle-distant past, has been silenced, and Renny is proceeding to ignore the hard realities of the many anxious, irritable businesspeople awaiting overnight envelopes, documents and contracts, boxes of architectural plans and new product samples, while she lies on her side, dragging the rough knuckles of her hand over Chris's exposed shoulder, arm, hip, thigh. Chris opens her eyes to take in the foreground figure of Renny. Bud scuttles in the background as he paces the perimeter of this still unfamiliar bed. She pulls on jeans and takes him down the back stairs into Renny's alley so he can pee. When she comes back, Renny reaches out to undo Chris's jeans, then pulls her onto the bed, covers Chris's mouth with one hand, restrains a wrist with the other.

"Two things I'm going to need to do to you," she says, mouth at Chris's ear. "They won't take long."

At home, Chris pulls on some shorts and a T-shirt and takes out of her Walkman one of the tapes Taylor made for her early on, this one a mix of songs configuring her obsession with Chris. A few weeks back, she rummaged it out of her glove compartment and has been playing it in reciprocal, if belated, obsession, looking for any way at all to keep Taylor around. This morning she replaces it with Bonnie Raitt.

She drives over to the lake for a run, to be a part of whoever is out there, one of the girls in the park. Sometimes it is not a particular woman who excites her. In fact any one particular woman — even Renny, even this morning — would be beside the point; there is always this or that particular woman. In these moments she is celebrating something larger and more pervasive — her connection to all women, the notion of them as a species — like caribou on the plains, the thrill held by them in their accumulation, their exhalations clouding the northern dawn, hooves scraping the icy snow in anticipation.

When she gets back, Leigh is there, making coffee in the kitchen. Leigh has a key now, stops by when she can to help with Bud, to help maintain the rhythms of what is supposed to be a two-person household. The two haven't spoken since the TV incident, which has not — as Chris predicted — produced Taylor, only a lot of unanswered calls on Chris's phone tape and a slight increase in market share for Leigh's station.

Chris can tell from the new bag of coffee beans and the bagels and lox on the kitchen counter that Leigh has come by to make amends. But these amends are on Leigh's terms.

"Nice," she says when she looks up from grinding the beans and notices Chris's neck.

Chris doesn't have a ready comeback, and so silently asserts herself by putting on a kettle to boil water for a solitary cup of tea.

"So we've decided the period of grieving is over? We can go from wearing black to purple? Who can it even be? Are you dating now, taking fix-ups from friends, hitting the bars? Someone from your health club? Really, I want to know how this goes."

Chris is guilty enough to let Leigh work her over; besides, there's no point trying to stop her. Her relentless, hectoring manner is a well-developed job skill. Once she interviewed a hysterical woman whose child had been run over by an old guy in an ancient car who'd had a coronary entering the school crossing. The wreckage of the boy's body had just been taken away in the ambulance. After five minutes of concerned questions and sob-choked responses, Leigh's camerawoman realized there was no tape in the videocam. And Leigh was able to slide past this awkward juncture by asking the mother if she'd mind doing the entire interview over.

"Come on. Who?"

"It's Renny," Chris says. There's no use trying to hold out. Coyness would only prolong the interrogation. As soon as she has confessed, they both stand still for a moment, silenced, considering from different angles the ridiculousness of everything. "Is it awful of me?" Chris says finally. "I really don't know. I was thinking about that while I was out running. All these weeks. Most of this whole time I've been waiting by the phone, calling the home tape, checking my voice mail at the office. Going through every drawer in the house for a possible note. Looking for her in every store and restaurant we've ever been to. I've slept about four hours a night, and those thanks mostly to Xanax. I've called everyone she has ever known, looking for anything that might be an explanation. I went to Morocco to be humiliated by a French asshole."

"*Con*," Leigh says helpfully. "That's French for asshole."

"I've probably given short shrift to my clients, although I think I'm gradually getting back on top of that. I've cut off most of my friends. Now I've found something that gives me a little bit of comfort through the night, and in some moments I think I get to do that, and in others I'm on your side thinking that it's rotten and faithless to Taylor, that I should still be doing nothing but sitting on the front porch, rocking in my chair and looking down the road for her." She knows she is soft-pedaling Renny, casting what she is doing with her in a benign light, but she can't bring herself to admit to Leigh that she is also in some measure taking revenge on Taylor as well as trying to gain some distance from her. Her impulses have become so conflicted that she can't explain them to herself, much less to someone else, much less to Taylor's best friend.

Who is already exasperated with her, at the moment lifting off the kitchen counter, as evidence, an ashtray holding a few butts. "You're fucking a woman who just about put you in the asylum. *And* you're smoking. Honey, nobody smokes anymore. Get a grip. Smoking is over. And you're getting too thin. You know that Duchess of Windsor thing — no woman can be too rich or too thin? I think you can't be too thin only if you're already too rich. If you're middle-aged and middle-class, you look bony and peculiar."

For the first time, Chris considers the notion that she might be middle-aged. But, technically, she supposes it's true. Twice thirty-nine would be seventy-eight, quite a reasonable life expectancy.

"What's going on, really?" she says to Leigh. "Are you pissed off about something else, so you're taking potshots at me to bleed a little of it?"

"Maybe. It's just everything lately. Taylor. And now Frank's gotten this major job offer." She's talking about Frank Weiss, her cover boyfriend. "From a bank in Texas. It's the right move for him. I can't really stop it from happening."

"Can't he live somewhere else and still be your beard? Can't you say the two of you are having a long-distance relationship?"

"I guess. For a while. But the main point of him is his boring physical presence. He's so straight and three-piece-suited, he squelches any questions about my personal life. People look at him and suddenly they don't care. He's a giant bucket of water to dump on their curiosity. If I start showing up at dinners and parties alone, I'm afraid it'll give everybody room to start thinking."

"Couldn't you let this all go?" Chris says. "I mean, they wouldn't fire you or anything, would they? I don't mean come out exactly . . ."

Leigh looks at her as though she is dealing with a hopeless bonehead. The two of them, Chris sees, are poles apart. Chris inhabits some midpoint along the peninsula of outness. Which is to say that while she doesn't march bare-breasted with the Lesbian Avengers contingent in the pride parade, she is openly gay to whomever might be interested enough in who she is to want that piece of information. From where she is, she loses track of the fact that the closet still exists in such an important way for some of her friends. Audrey. Leigh. It's a wholly different life that involves not only hiding, but also exoticizing their gayness. Leigh is always asking if whoever they're gossiping about is "a sister" or "on our team." She knows how many apartments in her building are "gay-owned." She keeps her copy of *Outlines* tucked away in case any friends from work drop by, or the Thought Police come to confiscate it. It's as though she belongs to a secret society with a clubhouse beneath the stairs. All of this subterfuge allows her to remain continuously fascinated by her sexual orientation; by never coming out, she always has the live wire of her lesbianism to touch for a little buzz. While Chris has so subsumed being a dyke into whatever larger notion she has of herself — along with the way she is nearsighted and tries to be kind and has spiritual elements to her thinking without exactly having a religion — that she no longer gets to think of being gay as an aspect of herself that is particularly dramatic or interesting.

"I'm going to have to scout up another guy with a tux and no girlfriend or job transfer in sight. Maybe someone on our team. Someone who needs a little protective coloration himself." Leigh sighs. "It's that kind of time. Everything collapsing quietly around me. My infrastructure is eroding. Like Venice."

Chris has listened to clients for long enough that she is able to spot what she has come to think of as "lead-in complaints," nettles that are easy to talk about and serve as ground cover for whatever is really on their minds.

"What's going on with Tiffany?" Chris says, her best guess.

Leigh puts down the knife, unfolds the bagel she has split. Chris can smell its burnt bits of onion. Bud is down on the linoleum, but hugging the counter, enhancing his opportunities for handouts.

"Oh, she says she loves me," Leigh says, "but what does that even mean to her? I always forget to ask that on the way in, for a definition of terms. She says she's going to call, and sometimes she does, but more often lately she doesn't. And when I do, of course she was just about to call, which means she wasn't. And it's so good to hear from me, which I suppose means it isn't. What I don't know, even after all these girls, is, well, do you think they deliberately torture me by not calling, or have I truly flown out of their minds, a thought they had yesterday but today they're thinking about something else? In my whole life, I'm never the one who doesn't call. And this setup just seems like a problem that'll only get worse. When I want to get really morose, I think about the women who won't be calling me when I'm sixty. You're a shrink. What do I do?"

"See a shrink. See Myra. She's a genius."

"I went a couple of times, years back. Remember? After that Francine thing. And you're right, she's smart, I guess. But all that smoke, and those bird droppings."

"Maybe," Chris says, "you're investing too much in the wrong people. Staking too much on them before you have all the crucial clues." Chris worries that her advice sounds stock, like a line out of a book for teens. But Leigh nods deeply, as though Chris is offering dazzling new information, as though she is an oracle, her words bathed in light.

"Wow. I can really see how that was true the other times. I can see the pattern so clearly now that you point it out. But this is different. Tiff and I connect in such a deep way. I feel sometimes we're children together in a secret garden, speaking to each other in our own private language."

"Then maybe she's telling you something in your little language that you don't want to hear."

She sees that she has stung Leigh, and is immediately contrite. She knows the human heart shouldn't be held up to some rigorous set of standards, be required to pass tests of logic and dexterity. The heart is a dope. In love, everyone is a moron. She once read Einstein's love letters and he was a total goofball. So why is she being tough on

Leigh? What does it matter that Tiffany is vain and shallow and almost an exact replica of Leigh's last girlfriend? Or that Leigh will, in a few months, have forgotten her and be enmeshed in another, equally futile liaison? What matters is that at this exact moment in this particular kitchen in Chicago, Leigh's pain has its own absolute legitimacy. And, because Leigh has dedicated herself to Chris's sorrows through these past weeks, Chris must reciprocate.

"Let's give her a call" is what she suggests.

"No. She sits in the morning. You know. Meditation."

"But maybe she isn't sitting this morning. I kind of feel she isn't. I kind of see her up and about. What's her number?" Chris prompts, picking up the phone. Leigh reaches over and punches it in and Chris hands her the receiver.

And a few minutes later, Leigh is happy again. It's that easy.

"How did you know?" Leigh says when she has hung up.

The truth is that in Chris's experience, they always want you to call, even when they don't really want you. Plus, Leigh and Tiffany seem at that stage where things are unraveling, but there are probably still a few more loops to go through, and one of them might as well happen today, when Leigh is so in need of it. What Chris says in lieu of saying all this is, "Just a hunch."

When they're settled at the kitchen table and all three of them, Bud included, have their bagels, Chris says, "Tell me. A while back, when you said Taylor was always trying to make herself feel better — "

"Well, you must have sensed she operated out of a dark place."

"I think I saw and didn't see. Didn't want to see."

Leigh doesn't say anything for a while. Chris waits and watches her, fascinated, as she spreads cream cheese on a bagel half, making an incredibly small amount go an incredibly long way, as though they are snowbound in a cabin and will have to make this container last until the spring thaw.

"She hid the worst from you," Leigh finally says. "Some of her sadness had to do with her attractiveness, her desirability, that she was losing it. The problem in Morocco was the most recent incident, but it wasn't the only one. She was as faithful to you as she could have been to anyone, I'd say more than she'd ever been to anyone before, but there was always going to be this testing thing, which meant there

171

would always have to be new test markets. And how could she bring that piece to you?

"Plus that was all part of some larger hopelessness. Everything was on a downhill slide for her. Tomorrow was doomed to be worse than today. Honey, I don't totally understand how this all rattled around inside her. But she could let me in on a little more of it, I guess, because I was someone she put on her own level. A lot of what we talked about I'm sure you would have found pretty shallow.

"You, on the other hand, she set up as a kind of ideal, someone living in a more important way. I think she was embarrassed by her despair, that she was foundering on issues she rationally knew were slightly ridiculous. Even her career. There she was, out shooting pictures of jolly vacationers while you were nursing people back to mental health."

"But the feminist guidebooks, that was a serious project."

"The publisher canceled it. Last year."

"But . . . then what was she doing in Morocco?"

"Oh, honey," Leigh says, and takes Chris's hand across the table.

"What were we then, roommates?"

"I know I'm going to sound cracked, but I think in a way it was a testament to what she did feel for you. I think to be close to you she needed for you to not really know her. I think the person she liked best was the Taylor you thought she was."

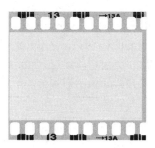

It's late, after eight at night, although it is still light outside her office windows on this long June day. Daniel is perched on the arm of her client couch. She guesses he has waited until her last client left before drifting in. He's nervous about something.

She herself is nervous about him being here. Renny may be stopping by. She has an uncanny way of knowing when Chris is done with clients for the day. Or maybe she has copied Chris's schedule into the electronic pocket datebook she carries. It's hard to know exactly how calculating Renny is beneath her cultivated veneer of nonchalance.

She likes to come by here and get Chris onto the couch. Taylor used to enjoy these cheesy scenes, too. Chris figures it must be a cheap thrill, like fucking someone in uniform. ("Could you keep the gun on?" Chris remembers asking a girl cop once, somebody who wrote her up for a U-turn, then took down her number and called later that night.)

She doesn't particularly want Renny and Daniel running into each other, which would force her to account for Renny's presence in her life. She doesn't quite occupy the girlfriend slot. After all the anguish Chris suffered in her wake, the emotions she has for Renny in this installment are oddly muted and hazy. For her part, Renny seems to have lost a good measure of her signature bravado, acts almost shy with Chris this time around.

"I've done a lot of thinking since we split up," she told Chris the other night, as though these intervening years have been merely a hiatus. Although she has parsed this particular sentence of Renny's quite a few times in spare moments, Chris is still not sure what to do with the information.

More than anything else, Renny seems like a passageway. Starting up with anyone else would be shutting a door on Taylor, but this interlude can be passed off as a settling of scores, a revisitation of the past while waiting for the present to come into focus again.

Something about Daniel, Chris now notices, looks different.

"Did you dye your hair or something?" she says.

"Something," he says, as if this will close down the subject.

"It's your face."

"Eyebrows."

"What could you do to your eyebrows?"

"At the electrolysis place. It was her suggestion. Isolde's. To clear the bridge of my nose. Give me a lighter look."

Chris doesn't think "clear" used in this way is Daniel talking; he is acquiring, she sees, the vocabulary of professional hair removal.

He has another surprise in store.

"I know a really good psychic." He reveals that he has consulted her on several occasions. Chris is at first astonished, then she begins trying to mesh the information into who she thinks Daniel is, imagining him sitting earnestly in a carnival tent with a caftaned woman in a trance.

"She's told me amazing things about myself. Things she couldn't possibly know."

Chris gives him a nod, to say, Like?

"Like she knew I have two sisters, and that I get along with one but not the other. And that I had bad allergies when I was a kid. She saw me in the hospital with a little oxygen tent. She could see both my marriages. She knows Camille is going through a tough time."

"But those are all things you already know."

He blinks, then doesn't say anything, then says, "Still, you have to admit it's pretty amazing."

"Maybe," Chris says, trying to be polite.

"She says I'm going to come into money."

"Well, that's great," Chris says, but she knows he can hear her, building a wall around herself on this subject.

"Look," he says. "I've made an appointment."

"Yes?"

"For you."

"Oh," she says, getting the picture. She pretends she doesn't. "To what point?"

"I think she might be able to tell you . . . I don't know . . . something."

"About Taylor?"

"Well . . ."

"Like what? She's joined the Ice Capades? She's a telephone operator in Albuquerque? Or maybe she'll see her on a little cloud playing a harp. And then I can begin to let go?"

"Stop."

"Okay," she says, but knows she will be dismissive for however many times this psychic business comes up between now and the appointment. Also that she will, in the end, keep it. Daniel is the closest friend she has. He is trying to help, to make an offering he feels has value. She will have to go.

The psychic turns out to be neither caftaned, nor operating out of a tent. She lives in a tan brick ranch-style house out in Bolingbrook, near the edge of the metropolitan map. It takes them over an hour to get there at the tail end of rush hour. Her name is Sheila and she answers the door wearing a modest cotton dress with a small print to it. Chris saw this dress on a rack at Lord & Taylor a few weeks back, as part of the American Woman Collection. It's an Amish look, a buckboard riding look, an egg candling look from a simpler time.

Sheila has long, light brown hair, pulled back in a clip at the neck.

She leads them through a paneled family room loaded with bowling trophies, so Chris imagines a husband outside the frame. Sheila herself doesn't seem like a bowler.

Daniel takes a seat on a leatherette sofa and opens one of the professional journals he has brought along to occupy himself. "Don't hurry on my account," he says, patting the periodical, settling in. Chris feels she could start crying at any second over his kindness.

The room Sheila brings her into, down a narrow hallway, muffled with sculptured carpeting, is a home office. There's an old computer under a yellowed plastic computer cozy, a few overflow trophies on the windowsill. Sheila sits behind the desk and gestures for Chris to take one of the armchairs in front of it.

There's no small talk. She closes her eyes as if to gather herself up internally, then jumps right in. Chris is told that she is an only child, her parents a disappointment to her. She watches Sheila work from a professional remove. They are, after all, competitors of a sort, working the same territory of hope and despair.

"I see people coming to you, their hearts heavy in their hands," Sheila says, as if reading Chris's mind as well as her future. "I see cards, spades and hearts, aces and jacks, shuffles and deals. Money and secrets."

In spite of her reservations, Chris is drawn in. She tries not to let her interest show. "But you must know I already know these things," she says.

"I'm opening the door," Sheila says. "Establishing connection. To make you understand there is one. Daniel has told me a person you love is missing to you, and that you are troubled."

"Yes."

"But I see trouble before. This sorrow is only an extension, a bridge out from earlier sorrows."

"It's true."

"The letter T. Does that mean anything?"

"Taylor."

"Just tell me yes or no. You don't have to tell me names. They'll eventually come to me."

"But the name's not what's important."

"It is for me, in making the pictures come up."

"What pictures?" Chris says. "What do you see?"

"Trees. Woods. Do you understand? A wooded place? And water. Small. Not a sea, a lake perhaps."

"And you can see her there?"

"Not really. I feel her presence in this place. The place is very clear, but she is not. She's there, but obscured."

"What does that mean?" Chris says.

Sheila refocuses, from within herself, outward, toward Chris. She shakes her head. "What I see comes only in pictures. There isn't any bigger context. Sometimes the meaning isn't immediately clear."

Later, at the door to the room, Sheila reaches behind Chris to keep her from opening the door, on the other side of which waits Daniel and the rest of Chris's evening and, beyond that, all of life outside this room.

"If I could make the pictures I see into pictures you could see, into, say, snapshots, you might recognize this place. Sometimes this happens. I'm seeing something familiar the client would recognize if they could see it along with me."

A question begins to form in Chris's mind, but now Sheila has let go of Chris's hand, allowing her to open the door, and then they are on the other side, walking down the hall toward Daniel and the trophies, and the question evaporates.

He has apparently paid for the session; money doesn't come up. In the car Chris sits silent beside him until he clears his throat, and says, "I don't want to pry — "

"No," Chris says. "It's okay. It was pretty surprising, but you say you trust her."

"I do. Really."

"Well, she said one of the Rolling Stones — she thinks Keith Richards, but she's not sure — is going to quit the band and they're going to ask me to join up."

He stares ahead and keeps on driving.

"It'll be an adjustment in lifestyle," she presses on, "but I'll just have to handle it."

He refuses to say anything, not even that he hates her in this moment. They drive in a vapor lock of silence, past strip malls and the garish Chinese restaurant they picked out on the way here, planning to stop afterward for terrible egg rolls. Instead, he keeps going and gets on the expressway.

She knows she is being a jerk, but can't stop. To stop would require apology, which would in turn require revelation, and she doesn't want to give over the pictures of the lake. They make her feel, so far into this long stretch of uncontrollable emptiness, that she is finally holding a hand with possibilities.

Desta is on the tape when she gets home. Jon Folan has discovered the funds transfer by requesting Taylor's bank records. Chris resents the invasion, but so what, really? She's way ahead of them. The bank account is old news. Now Chris knows about the lake.

The picture she calls up is Taylor in the Adirondack chair at the lake where they vacationed those couple of weeks early on together. Taylor is reading some brooding novel. Not Sylvia Plath this time, maybe *The Magic Mountain*. She's boring her way through it and will call when she's finished. From the pay phone on the empty highway. All of Chris's visions will come to pass; she'll turn out to be minorly psychic herself.

Of course, it could be another lake. During their time together, they've been to several, visiting friends with summer places. It could, of course, be any of these, or some lake from Taylor's past, or some entirely new one she has found on her own. But in Chris's private vision, it is Deer Lake up in Wisconsin, where Taylor sat in the Adirondack chair.

She would go there straightaway but for her schedule of clients. She can't abandon them again so soon. But it really doesn't matter. *The Magic Mountain* is a big book.

She doesn't want to tell anyone about this vision yet, not even Daniel. She understands that while it makes her feel calm and sane to be in possession of this picture, it might seem a little untethered to someone else. It is reassuring to her that she realizes this much. Understanding that she's a little insane probably means she is sane underneath it all. And there are other good signs along these lines.

She is pulling herself together, gathering up the loosened cords of control. She's showering every day again, washing her hair, remembering to floss. She got groceries this week and has everything all ready in the refrigerator. Soon she'll start cooking; she just hasn't found the time yet. She's a long way, though, from the night a couple of weeks back when she ate what was left of a cold can of Bud's food, thinking it was really terrible corned beef hash. She's miles from there.

SHE PLANS to go up to Deer Lake over the weekend. She is compelled to gather up a collection of physical elements — her human self, the dog panting out the window, the steel and rubber and road — take these tangible realities and hurtle northward toward a phantom vision, the freeze-frame of Taylor waiting in a chair. Connect one plane of reality with another, for the fact is that the image is grounded in its own way, given weight by its elaborate detail. Taylor is tan. She's wearing baggy black shorts. There's a cabin in the background. Inside, an old iron bed covered in quilts. They go in and make love wordlessly. Nothing will have to be said.

Of course, under the clarity of this vision she has trouble denying its essential lack of logic. That is, Chris is not sure anymore who it is she's searching for. Now that the person she loved turns out to have been in great part concocted for her approval, who she is missing and who she might find are quite different people.

Now when she flips through memories, they have an ersatz quality, the sort of tint applied to enhance photos — rose on the cheeks of the sallow graduate, blue on the muddy lake of the dilapidated resort. While it is both charming and pathetic that Taylor created this colorized version of herself, it is mostly just scary. It means that the person who is gone from her — a supposedly deeply flawed woman of superficial but overwhelming concerns — might well have much greater reality than the one who was her partner. If Taylor walked through the door now, she and Chris would have to shuffle into their reunion embrace through the stack of lies and misunderstandings littering the floor between them. There is no going back to what they were before. Before has become unavailable. Perhaps — more frightening — what Chris thinks of as "before" was unavailable even as it was happening.

· · ·

There is nothing about performance or technique when Chris and Taylor are in bed together, little brought to bear from their prior experience. Rather, they tumble together down a sluice of surrender. Often, something Chris would find invasive, if done to her by someone other than Taylor, instead makes her happy, precisely for the feeling of having been invaded. Taylor seems intent on giving Chris everything, while at the same time taking everything out of her. The exchange is quite powerful, like swapping blood with a vampire, and Chris is often affected for days afterward. She has begun to notice, though, that Taylor, for her part, puts borders on her surrender. At the moment, Chris is watching her do this.

A long Sunday afternoon they've burrowed into is ending; they have to meet friends at a restaurant and are already late. Chris stays in the bed a moment longer while Taylor leaves it, as she invariably gets up afterward, from bed or floor or sofa. Years of tai chi behind her, she co-opts these graceful moves of containment each time she turns away from Chris, staring at the wall, out the window — without seeing, Chris assumes — as she pulls on her clothes, stands stock-still, folding back into an envelope of self.

· · ·

Maybe Chris is only using this Wisconsin pilgrimage to give her some sensation of forward momentum, the wind rushing over her hand as it dangles out the car window, gas stations and rest areas whipping by, the rural landscape blurred by her acceleration through it.

She buys a road map, as though Taylor is an invisible dot on the page, an unmarked destination. To further ground the enterprise, she gets her tires pumped up, her oil changed, buys a pint of chicken salad, a bag of chips. She forages in the cupboard for a thermos for Bud's water. She's ready, set.

And almost immediately thwarted. On Friday afternoon she comes home to find a message on the machine, her mother using her tight voice, never a good sign. "We have a small problem. Give me a call when you can. I'm having my hair highlighted, but I'll be done by three." If she's going to the beauty parlor, then it's nothing too grave, not her husband's bypass bursting.

"Let me go to the kitchen phone" is what she says when Chris calls back, which means the problem is one she would rather keep away from Maury and his fragile ventricles and auricles and highly pressured blood. "It's your father," she tells Chris against the open background of the living room phone left off the hook. Across the room, she can hear Maury's cable stock report, which runs all day, a ticker-tape undercurrent to their life together in retirement. "Apparently he's been up to some mischief at a golf club. Do you know anything about this?"

Chris tells her no. It's an easy lie.

"Well, it's in Glen Ellyn. Forest Glen. Somewhere west. I have it written down. They're not really interested in pressing charges, they don't want the publicity, but there's a bit of money involved. If they could recover that and be rid of him, they'd be happy enough."

"How much?"

"Well, of course they can't say exactly. They've had meetings among themselves and tried to figure up and round off and, well, they're willing to call it a day at twelve thousand."

"Oh, my."

"I can help," her mother says. She has bailed him out of other jams. Chris doesn't think this charity can be about love, suspects rather that her mother merely wants to avoid any embarrassment he might slip into her now orderly life. "Not the whole thing, though.

Maury would notice that much gone out of my account. I don't know exactly what your situation is at the moment . . ."

She leaves the sentence hanging and Chris fills in the gap by suggesting they split the amount, and says she'll go out and settle matters with the golfers. It'll mean peeling off a bit of her secret stash, but she supposes it's only appropriate that some of this money her father taught her how to make should go back to him in the end. Of course, there's another part of her that would like to let him hang, but she overrides the sentiment and goes to the bank for a cashier's check, which is how the golfers — once burned, twice shy — want their restitution.

Trouble, by conventional wisdom, is supposed to come in threes, she knows, but for her it usually arrives in pairs, and so she's only half surprised when the other shoe drops.

In bed that night, at Chris's, Renny is draped diagonally across her, sleeping with the dead weight of arduous sex on top of a long day of many packages delivered. It's nearly two in the morning, but Chris is still wide awake. This sudden seizure of nerves happens too often lately. She takes a quick tumble into someplace black and bottomless. In this particular moment, she is trying, unsuccessfully, to call up Taylor's voice, what she sounded like, and the inability to hear anything sends her spiraling downward.

Sliding out and onto the floor next to the bed, she tries her standard dewigging technique, a wordless mantra, a litany of okayness. She is doing pretty well considering, she tells herself, then tries not to consider too much, reaching instead for some easy successes, some signs of progress. She'll get her father off the hook, charm the golfers; it'll be a breeze. Her clients are making small strides. Nida Louis has moved out on her oppressive husband and not (yet, anyway) in with her oppressive girlfriend. Clarissa Sims has begun talking about her razor marks, which turn out to be self-inflicted — a definite problem, but one that they can now at least address together. Alma Alvarez, a referral from Rosario, has gone two weeks without buying any more Diane Von Fürstenburg outfits from QVC. (Her problem is not the spending, but her inability to cope with real stores and other places where crowds must be negotiated.)

All this self-congratulation turns out to be like skiing merrily down a mountain, thinking how lucky she is never to have run into a tree. The phone starts ringing. She gropes around the floor through three rings until she finds the receiver under a FedEx uniform puddle on Renny's side of the bed.

It's Grant Hospital, reporting Jerome Pratt's emergency admission. His broken heart overwhelmed him and he has tried to do himself in.

He's in a slot in the ICU, looking ghastly, like one of the undead who wander shopping malls in B movies. His skin is a greenish ocher, as if everything essential to thriving has been drained out of him through the tubes snaking from his nostrils, and out from under the thin sheet covering him, already stained with blood, while artificial support is pumped in through other tubes snaking into his nostrils. An IV board is slammed onto the fragile inside of his forearm. It is as if, through all this intake and outflow, he is being held in a translucent state just to the side of actual life.

No one bearish is present. His friend Veronica (the friend who is not Evelyn; since that unfortunate moment, Chris keeps more detailed notes with lists of the people in her clients' lives) is hovering over the bed, deliberate in her uselessness.

"He's resting more easily, finally" is what she says after introducing herself, then proprietarily running a vein-roped hand through his damp hair. She is decades older than Jerome, a small, brittle woman with lipstick askew, her French twist coming unraveled.

Chris nods, hoping more information will be forthcoming without having to ask for it directly. She still has no idea what has happened. When Veronica settles, with a stagy sigh, into the vinyl-upholstered armchair next to the bed, Chris relents.

"I'm his therapist," she says. "They called me over, but I still don't really know the nature of the . . . the problem."

"Well, I guess you could say our boy," Veronica pauses, twisting her mouth a little before going on, "is a rather spectacularly unsuccessful suicide."

The facts, which Chris has to drag out piece by piece — Veronica clearly wants to prolong her speaking part in this drama — are that Jerome downed a Drano cocktail earlier in the evening, then, for good measure, jumped out the window of his high-rise apartment.

The window was apparently the sort that tilts open, and his foot caught on the lower pane, leaving him dangling for more than an hour while his stomach and a good part of his upper intestine were being chemically eaten away until a passerby looked up and called the paramedics. His prognosis is iffy.

She stares down at him and sees the result of all the clues she missed while she let his concerns drift past her narrowed peripheral vision. She was looking at the sweetness of his Internet connection, at Keith's bearness (four-inch chest hairs, Jerome once brought one in to show her, pressed like a relic between the pages of a book), at the two of them as though they were characters in some merry, butt-fucking fairy tale — completely missing the fact that this romantic encounter was too serious for someone as fragile, as newly released from his other obsessions, as Jerome. She wants to reel him backward in time, like a film in reverse, the tubes coming out, the sheet coming off, Jerome rising off the bed like Lazarus, pulling on his nerdy white jeans and plaid shirt, going back into the library stacks to one of his initial encounters with Keith, which a more focused Chris might have examined in a harsher light and gotten him to look at more closely, cautioned him to take this new relationship a little more slowly.

"I'll be back," she tells Veronica, not at all sure she'll be able to bring herself here again, into the shallow-pulsed presence of her utter failure.

How can she meet with these guys at the golf club today, when she's not really up to anything. But she has to, has to sit behind the wheel with a Flashmap on her lap, trying to find this far-flung suburb, which is near the one where the psychic lives. More and more lately, she stands outside herself; it's now often the only way she can get herself to operate, by remote control. Stand back, push a button, and make herself move this way or that, then watch. Or consider herself in the way she would a client, trying to predict how she will respond to a given situation, often finding herself slightly off the mark. She cries when she least expects it, the other day, for instance, while running. Once she woke up crying, and had no dream to account for her tears, only the terrible, undefinable sorrow of the oncoming day. In the same way, she will suddenly be grabbed by fear. Cutting through an alley behind the Federal Building downtown last week on the way to get her driver's license renewed, she suddenly became sure there would be another bombing, that one of the several trucks parked at the loading docks belonged to some militia group that was about to blow her into a thousand flying pieces. Standing in line at the bank to get the cashier's check, she felt like clawing her way out of herself. These moments are absolutely unpredictable; even afterward she can't find their triggers.

The 8 Ball has become an obsession, even as it has been getting more and more evasive. CONCENTRATE AND ASK AGAIN, it tells her. Or BETTER NOT TELL YOU NOW. Once, a completely new piece of advice floats up into the window when she asks if Taylor is coming back: ASK ANOTHER QUESTION. She is convinced, although the thought falls outside all rational bounds, that the ball has extended itself, coming up with a message especially for her.

She has changed, is changing, although not superficially. When she inspects herself in the mirror, she seems the same, maybe a little wearier, her hair a little longer, that's about it. But deeper down, on the molecular level, there are subtle but interesting shifts occurring. Her taste, for instance. There are whole categories of food she used to enjoy that seem vaguely repugnant to her now. Chocolate. Pastas with cream sauce. Too heavy. Even coffee, which used to be a central pleasure of her mornings, suddenly seems unpleasantly intense; she has switched to black tea. She eats the frond and fern salad mix from Whole Foods straight out of the bag, grazing as she drives. And then amid all this spartan foraging, she will suddenly and urgently require a cheeseburger. She will sit at a small Formica table on an attached chair, alone in a McDonald's next to an unruly birthday party of children not entirely entertained by the hired Ronald clown. She devours a Quarter Pounder with Cheese, then, gorged, will head like an lioness back out onto the Serengeti Plain.

Her relationship to bathing is also undergoing a transformation. After her brief alienation from it, she has returned with a peculiar fervor. She who used to shower expeditiously, with grocery store soap and two-dollar shampoo, whatever was on sale, now frequents places like the Body Shop and H_2O Plus and brings home seaweed and birch shampoo. White musk shower gel. Papaya and sea salt body scrub. Uses a nubby Irish linen mitt to get rid of unessential layers of herself, shedding old skins like a snake.

She is turning into someone interesting, a curiosity, a case for close study, someone to keep a sharp eye on. Chris watches these odd shifts in herself, which seem to have the air of preparation about them, but preparation for what she's not at all sure.

Some of the rare moments when she feels truly unselfconscious are those she spends in bed with Renny, an old, familiar territory, an enclosed world of their creation.

Renny ferrets out what Chris wants, then taunts her lightly. "Oh, I think you'd have to say 'please' for that."

And Chris will inhabit fully the long moment before she is able to begin begging.

In this way, for spans of an hour or two or three, within the circum-scribed rectangle of the bed, the terms well defined, Chris at least knows who she is. None of what happens in this white space has any reverb into real life, and so these are moments she can occupy squarely.

They never talk about the possibility of Taylor's return. Maybe Renny has already dismissed it. Or, Chris supposes, this silence could be their way of tacitly not owning up to any sort of continuing rela-tionship. Renny never presses about Chris's tangled-up feelings; Tay-lor's name never comes into the space between them.

At the same time, neither of them shines a light into any shared future. If Renny wants to get together, she calls that day. When they part, she never says "I'll call" or "We'll talk." They are only a collec-tion of their moments together, without linkage. They don't talk about taking a vacation together, don't set up dinners with mutual friends. When they eat, it's usually just the two of them, at a restau-rant or at Renny's. Renny fixes them dinners from a couple of dec-ades past, a couple of states deeper into the Midwest. She fries up pork chops, makes spaghetti (as opposed to pasta) with large, lumpy meatballs. These she molds casually out of hamburger and bread crumbs and solid shakes from a jar labeled "Italian Seasoning," as though the country has only this single flavor, then sets them on a sheet of waxed paper on the counter until she's ready to brown them. She's a butch version of Harriet Nelson, Donna Reed.

Chris never reciprocates; they've concurred that she's not yet up to cooking. Renny treats her gently, as though she is the sufferer of a great breakdown, progressing out of an asylum, with only lawn privileges as yet. Sometimes Chris thinks all Renny is doing here, with hands and mouth and the pressure of her body, is nursing Chris back to recovery from an industrial-strength emotional accident.

She doesn't know what else Renny is getting out of their affair. Maybe she is between new things and this reconnection provides a temporary comfy chair. Maybe there was some way in which she wasn't quite through with Chris. For Chris's part, this second installment has pulled Renny off the pedestal Chris now can't believe she had her on. Not that she belches, or repeats boring jokes. But, in the absence of the urgency of Chris's passion for her, Renny seems like a sexually compelling, otherwise only mildly interesting, middle-aged woman at the moment absorbed in expanding her benefits package. Whatever Renny might be, she is certainly not The Person Someone Couldn't Talk About. Apparently time has, beneath Chris's notice, done a terrific amount of work.

The scene at the country club is worse than she imagined, spinning fantasy versions on the drive out. The boardroom is filled with blond wood. The smell of lawn is pervasive. The five guys waiting for her are straight in a way she seldom has to confront. Their pants are green, raspberry. Their hair is barber-cut rather than styled. Their glasses have stern steel rims.

She sees herself through these lenses. She imagines their own women as softened by life out here, provided for, deferent. She sees immediately that in her T-shirt and jeans (she hasn't bothered costuming herself as an urban professional), her untamed hair and shades (she doesn't want to remove them and give anyone the advantage of seeing her eyes), the three rings in her left ear, she must appear to them like an animal in from outside. Not from some wilder, romantic place, not from a veldt, just something scratching around in the backyard at night, more irritating than menacing. They'd rather not have to consider her existence, reckon with her in any, even the smallest, way.

And so they don't prolong the transaction. She hands over her mother's check, and her own, and the guy who is serving as their spokesman gets in a few licks about tighter membership policies being set up to keep out "your father's kind." From the way he stares hard across at her as he speaks, it's clear he isn't addressing her as though she is a respectable person with an errant relative. Rather he decides that she and her father are cut from the same cloth, which, as it turns out, they are. She begins to enjoy the rush of being an outsider among men of this age and class, their full wallets and nice lines of credit. An alien in their midst, particularly around a table, she imagines them holding hands of cards, stacks of chips, ready to be siphoned off. She wonders if she could have gone her father a little better, done them out of more than a paltry twelve thousand.

In his apartment, Tom Snow is doing his impersonation of truly contrite, the best Chris will get out of him. The only sincere aspect of his emotional makeup at the moment is gratitude that she has paid off the guys at the club and kept him out of jail, where, although he does win at cards, he also tends to get beaten up quite a bit. A slight man with a foppish accent and a droll wit does not go down too well among the general penitentiary population. During his last stay, he became known as the Queen of England.

She visits him here as little as possible. He is living out her worst nightmare of her own old age. The Majestic is a residence hotel, a decrepit building filled with small, dark apartments, but also with the trappings of service — an emaciated concierge, a coffee shop off the lobby, a small newsstand. As her father is quick to point out, there is also a quite lovely pool in the basement, and it is actually a fascinating relic, ancient and bathwater-warm in deference to the aged residents who swim back and forth so slowly they appear to be pushing against strong currents.

Her father's apartment, on the third floor, overlooking a row of Dumpsters that seem to be getting hoisted and emptied and slammed around every time Chris is there, is what the Majestic bills as a convertible studio, because it has a small nook off the living room in which a bed can fit snugly. His is covered in tan chenille. In the living room there is a brown nubby sofa provided by the building and an armchair Chris recognizes from her mother's house before she redecorated. There is a small dining table compressed out of synthetic fiber mulch into something not unlike wood, laminated with a hilariously phony grain. Three chairs sit around this piece, but these have been rendered unusable under stacks of yellowing *Tribunes* and racing forms. Every foot of available space, along with some unavailable space, is occupied with the crucial detritus of someone living alone and well outside any concern for convention. Dirty clothes are piled everywhere. Everything in the kitchen is opened or unwashed or used up but not yet thrown away. The building offers maid service, which Chris has suggested on previous visits, but her father doesn't want his disorder disturbed.

"I could make us some tea," he's telling her from the kitchen, which is one wall of the living room, inset with a stove, an under-counter refrigerator, a sink, some shelves. The counter is cluttered with cups of half-drunk tea (which have been present on other visits). Those with the longest tenure on the counter, she knows without looking, will have developed floating islands of milk evolved to some beyond-food form.

"That's okay," she says. "I don't want to get in the way of scientific progress."

"I'm a little behind in my housekeeping this week," he says, ignoring her refusal, opening the freezer door, revealing about four inches of free space between the upper and lower glaciers that have formed over the years of his occupancy.

He himself looks a little better than when she last saw him. He's wearing good slacks and an old Banlon polo shirt, the kind now considered a retro look, only his is the real item. His closets are filled with clothes, usually expensive, dating back to the fifties. Although his habitat is a mess, he himself manages to emerge crisp, his own version of dapper, stylish without that style adhering to what's in fashion this particular season, or year, or decade.

"What did you do with the twelve grand?" she says, sitting down on the sofa after pushing a few dozen magazines aside. "Why aren't I at least standing here furious with you in a better apartment?"

"Ah, well," he says, pulling out a frosty Baggie jammed with cookies, probably left over from Christmas. "I'm afraid this was a matter of robbing Peter to pay Paul. I seem to have become as bad at playing the horses as I am good at playing cards."

"Not that good, apparently," she says, pulling out from underneath her a crinkly mystery item that turns out to be an opened bag of barbeque chips. "How'd you get caught?" If she can't shame him about his living circumstances, she'll go for the jugular — his professional pride.

When he stops fiddling with the cookies, arranging them on a small plate, putting the kettle on for the tea — and doesn't speak — she knows she has succeeded in humiliating him. She waits while he turns and carefully arranges his expression into wry and self-deprecating.

"I'm perhaps getting a bit old for my line of work. I forgot the order of the little setup under my cuff, and wound up laying down the second ace of clubs on the table at that moment."

An instant passes in which they acknowledge the tragic element of this slipshod, rank beginner's flub.

"This is the last time I can help," she says, and he nods seriously as though accepting this, when in fact they both know she will continue to bail him out, perhaps with greater frequency as time goes on and he starts losing it in other ways, like not being able to keep a count of what's been bid and played. Not being able to pick up on bluffs. Losing his spectacular sense of when to fold. It is quite possible to lose at cards even while cheating — the sharp's greatest disgrace.

"How's the search going?" he says, ducking away from his troubles, into hers. He called a couple of weeks back offering to put a friend onto the matter of retrieving Taylor. Chris declined politely, touched by his concern, while at the same time not wanting someone named Vinny turning up out of the shadows of her friends' garages when they came home at night, asking them murky questions.

"I think I may have a lead," she says, but remains oblique. She both doesn't want his solicitousness at the moment, and doesn't want to reveal that this lead is a vision drawn from a psychic's reading. "What're you going to do now?" she asks him instead.

He shrugs and sets the cookie plate and teacups down on a pileup of *TV Guides*. The cup designated for Chris has a creamy violet lipstick print around its rim, undisturbed by his cursory wash. She tries to conjure up a woman wearing this peculiar shade, a visitor to this sad place. She quickly arrives at the sex part and shuts off the picture, shrinking it down to a tiny white dot, like on an old black-and-white TV.

"I've got a few party gigs," he says. "Back into the old clown suit, I guess."

She nods, but doesn't believe him. Two calls in rapid succession have come in while she has been here, both absorbed with a click into the answering machine on the nightstand. Bad company he doesn't want her to know he is keeping. Schemes being set up, she suspects. The nervous, excited planning stages of a job he'd rather keep from her.

His dreary belief in some next big score, along with his easy defeat, eddies around her, laps at the edges of her careful self-construction. In his presence, she is yanked back into all the other small rooms they have inhabited together, counting their winnings or balming their losses with revised strategies. With her father, she is always more accomplice than daughter, and invariably gets dragged out of the solid confines of legitimate society onto its warping margins, a geography that makes her nervous in its familiarity.

"Do you have anything I could use for an ashtray?" she asks. She expects a sticky saucer, but he comes back from the kitchen cabinets with a legitimate ashtray, black ceramic with STORK CLUB in raised white letters around its rim.

"This is probably worth a pretty penny on the junk shop circuit," she says.

He nods, then gestures at her lit cigarette. "They seem to think smoking's not all that good for you anymore," he says politely, admonishing her in his extremely gentle way. She would be tickled by the understatement if it came from anyone else, but she has carefully built up an immunity to her father's charm, works at resisting its pull. Their kinship, their affinity, affects her too strongly. Her father must be kept safely pocketed. He has to stay a character, a discreet part of a past she has put away. She takes a drag off her cigarette and exhales the smoke into the space between them, trying to sit in this room and not let their history overtake her.

She sees that, for all her current troubles, she is not going to be cut much slack. Her father is going to continue to be thinly tragic, a reminder of the folly she came out of. In the same way, her clients are not going to considerately improve themselves to soothe her fragile ego. They are going to hold danger and mayhem in the folds of their damaged psyches. Life will continue to be treacherous in its unpredictability, granting no concession to her diminished capacity to manage it. She is simply going to have to grab on, or risk sliding off.

MYRA HAS four rules for living a life:

1. Show up.
2. Pay attention.
3. Speak the truth.
4. Don't be attached to results.

"I've fallen down on Number Four, I'm afraid," Chris says now.

"You might also have paid a little more attention along the way," says Myra, never one to mince words.

"Oh, but I did. Though I took the information as challenge instead of warning. I was so sure I could get her, keep her. It wasn't my attention that was the problem, it was my terrible arrogance."

"So where does that leave you, saying — for the sake of argument — that she might have slipped away from you, for good?"

"You think the relationship was folly, don't you? Folly I dressed up as something more important?"

"I think you could start to think about how you occupy your emotions. Can you begin to imagine another way, can you project yourself into any future that doesn't look like the past?"

But Chris can't come up with anything. "I know I should be able to. I know there's a correct answer. I should be able to at least tell you I can imagine some sequence of small steps. Absorbing myself with work until I meet some likely person. That's what I'd hope to hear from a client. But I can't get there from here. I'm too weighted with all my failure and faulty assumptions. I don't trust that any moves I might make would lead to any happiness, or even relief."

"Now," Myra says. "You're stuck in how you feel *now*. But the thing is, now is always — sometimes mercifully — a fleeting state."

"Oh, Myra, you can't possibly see. Now is huge."

Myra waits. She is the high priestess of waiting.

"Everything's flying apart" is what Chris is finally able to say. "Inside me. And it's not just Taylor. She's the monkey wrench thrown into the works, but now all the gears are jammed and pieces are flying off in all directions."

Tiffany lands on her knee, digs tiny talons into the denim. Chris scratches the plump bird chest, says, "And the thing is I can't afford for everything to be going kaflooey. I can't tolerate disarray, I've pulled my whole life out of disarray. If I lose the structure, I'm sunk. Already I'm on shaky ground with my clients, not just Jerome. I couldn't see what was happening in my own relationship, so how can I presume to be worth anything in my analysis of their troubles? And how can I be back with Renny? I mean, really. How can that be constructed as any kind of step forward? And in the midst of everything, what do I think about? It's so pathetic. I can't even tell you."

"Tell me." Myra taps her hearing aid, as though the lapsed sentence is a mechanical glitch.

"I think about Vegas a lot. A cheap flight, a quick check-in at the Four Queens. All I want is to get to a poker table, breathe in a little stale air, open a fresh hand, and find a tiny space where I still know what I'm doing."

"A good sign," Myra says. "You can imagine something that would make you feel better. That's not nothing."

"No, Vegas is going backward. Renny is backward. To get to anything good, I have to go back. With Taylor, too, of course, since there's no here and now. I go back to the most ordinary moments. Some night I fixed dinner. It wasn't perfect. Maybe the spaghetti was overcooked. There was a small problem with Bud, a rheumy eye. One of us was going to have to take him to the vet and we were power-struggling a little over that. We rented a video, but it wasn't good enough and so we shut it off. That sort of night. What I'm trying to say is that it's not some distilled, perfect moment I find refuge in, but the most dreadfully ordinary ones."

• • •

Chris puts down the lid on the toilet, sits and gets comfortable with her feet up on the washbowl, so she can keep cozy company with Taylor, who is in the tub.

"Ah," Taylor says, sliding beneath a fizzing bank of bubbles. "Everywhere I go, every hotel no matter how flea-bitten, I try to get a room with a tub. Chase out the spiders, or worse. Fill it up hot, sink in for a soak. Can I say water grounds me? Is that a contradiction or a paradox?"

Chris doesn't respond, taking advantage of the luxury of ignoring her lover, a payoff for the long months of courting attentiveness, the further time of waiting anxiously for Taylor to remove herself from the relationship with Diane, the early days of worrying that one thing or another was going to topple their tenuous union. Now they share a lease on this apartment, have a few months of domestic routine under their belt. She can relax, take Taylor a little bit for granted. And so she stands up to look in the mirror above the washbowl and runs a hand through the longer top part of her hair. "Maybe I should do something totally different with this."

"Get it cut short," Taylor says.

"It's already short."

"Really short. Short and weird. Bleach it white-blond, go a little nuts. I always think how conservative you are, really."

Chris stops fussing with her hair for a split second, the space of a flinch — thrown slightly off -balance once again.

• • •

Her Sunday lunch plan with Daniel and his girlfriend has Chris dragging her feet, stopping to look at wares in the dusty shop windows along this stretch of Belmont around the El stop, a furthest commercial point from Middle America. The dry cleaner that also sells leather items — gauntlets and studded wristbands — accessories of sexual menace. The tailor with a sign hailing WE WELCOME CROSS-DRESSERS. The wedding invitation and wig shop.

She is purely killing time, not up to meeting Rachel, which she was supposed to be doing starting twenty minutes ago. She should have shown up early; she's trying to atone to Daniel for her bad behavior at the psychic's. Earlier, at home, her anxiety displaced itself into an attempt to find an appropriate rhetoric of style. She changed clothes three times before leaving for the India Palace, which has oilcloth on the tables and plastic flowers in bud vases, the occasional roach waltzing its way up the wall, and is not, all in all, the kind of restaurant that requires wardrobe decisions.

The lovebirds are already there when she finally arrives, nearly half an hour late; they look ensconced rather than merely seated, as though they're in their living room and she has entered without knocking. They've taken seats on the same side of a table for four, have already drunk what look, from the pale foamy orange dregs in the glasses, to be a pair of mango shakes. Now they are just holding hands under the table and, against a light background of sitar music, gazing at each other without speaking, as though conversation were a rough-hewn form of communication for those with less developed telepathic mechanisms.

Chris has a hard time looking at them, with all their implications of happiness. She's not ready to emerge into their terribly bright light. Now that the blade of her pain has turned and flattened, become dull and spatulate, she is perversely reluctant to let it go. It has become what she knows and anything beyond it, healing or even happiness, would require more change, which she's not ready to take on just yet.

Rachel turns out to be surprisingly attractive and sociable. After all this time of listening to Daniel's dating trials, Chris had concocted a last-ditch candidate at the end of a long line of fatally flawed women. Instead she turns out to be a perfectly pleasant person, nice-looking in an upscale peasant way reminiscent of Carole King on the cover of her "Tapestry" album. She has bright green eyes and hair long in a way it seems hardly anyone wears anymore. Reddish blond and crinkly, fanning down her back like a show horse's mane.

She seems heartily interested in Chris. Which, of course, is more than Chris can bear.

"I want you to tell me all about you," she says brightly. "I've been looking forward to meeting you all this time Dan has been talking about you."

Dan? Chris lets this stop her for only a beat before ducking Rachel's interest and tacking around to interviewing her. (Years in her profession have given her certain skills that also sometimes prove socially useful.) Rachel is amenable to a recitation of her own interests, which are numerous and upbeat. Language study, folk arts, gamelan music.

In response, Chris tries not liking Rachel. She thinks she has a real leg up when she notices that Rachel eats one food at a time, finishing the first before starting in on the next. This method has a certain degree of difficulty at an Indian buffet, where one saucy blob of curry runs into another of vindaloo, which in turn is awash in yogurt raita.

But all her bad intentions are eroded; through the course of the meal she is won over by Rachel's manifest affection for Daniel, who has been transformed, backlit by her attentions in a flattering way. He seems more handsome, more confident and relaxed in her presence, than Chris has ever seen him.

Rachel is a little bossy with him, which also seems to go down well. He basks in her directive to hail the waiter for a fresh pitcher of ice water, her reminder that he pay up on the parking tickets that litter the back seat of his car. She is good for him, Chris sees, and after all his loneliness and hair removal and dating rigors, how can she begrudge him?

So she behaves herself. In turn, Daniel, who has seen her in a few situations where she hasn't behaved, is grateful. Then she is ashamed, the gratitude implying that he was afraid she would be unkind to Rachel, and went ahead and planned this lunch anyway, in hopes her good will would triumph.

By the time they are sitting in front of little dishes of cloyingly saccharine, torpedo-shaped pastries afloat in sweetened milk (the only dessert offered with the buffet), Chris feels enough at ease to mention her plan for the trip to Wisconsin. She tries to pitch it in a solid way, talking first about drive time and getting a AAA listing of motels that take dogs.

She thinks she has them with her. They are nodding lightly as if all three of them are in sync. That is, until Rachel says brightly, "Getting away from it all for a few days might do you a world of good."

Forcing Chris to clarify. "I wasn't talking about getting away. I'm hoping to find her."

She releases her secret, tells them about the vision, how vivid it is in its detail. "I think she may well be up there. Waiting for me to find her."

The two of them sit silent across from her, uncoupling their hands under the table, blinking a little, like rabbits. When Daniel wipes his mouth with a saffron-smeared paper napkin and breaks the silence, saying, "Maybe we could talk a little more before you go, maybe at the office," Chris sees she has made a tactical error. Either Daniel and Rachel are not the right audience, or her plan is not one to tell anybody. She's not sure which. She's not sure, either, when she started drawing lines between inside and out, creating an us and a them, then drawing the string tight around the us to include only herself and Taylor (who can't, she realizes, really be considered a wholly active agent at the moment) and Bud, who has become the one friend she can count on to accept her decisions.

She hopes Daniel will just forget the matter, but he doesn't. He's lying in wait for her on his client couch when she gets into the office on Monday. She's running late for having stopped at the hospital to visit Jerome, who is out of the ICU, awaiting further surgery tomorrow. He'll live, it appears, but minus a significant portion of his digestive tract. The new surgery is to insert a feeding tube.

"I don't suppose you think he was quite worth all this bother" is what he told Chris in a small, terrible voice after the nurse and orderly had left.

"I only wish we could have headed this off together," she said.

"Don't take this on yourself," he said. "You couldn't have headed me off. I was determined to make a grand gesture."

Now Chris tells Daniel, "Remember how you felt like Charles Manson's shrink? Well, now I feel like Judy Garland's."

"Hey. We've both had these confidence busters before. You can't have forgotten that time I had Mr. and Mrs. Rayner in couples therapy and was about to graduate them as a big success in resolving their issues and then she put a fork in his eye."

"A fork with tuna salad on it," Chris reminds him.

"Yes. I mean the thing is, these sorts of failures are the hard part of the deal, but I think they're unavoidable. You can't find anybody who's been in practice any length of time who doesn't have a short litany of them."

"But I worry this one was true negligence on my part. Would I have picked up on how far he was sliding if I hadn't been steeping in my own troubles?"

"Christine. No one could have tried harder, done better, under the circumstances."

"From inside here" — she taps her breastbone — "it seems like I'm punting like mad, always running to keep up with them."

"Listen. If I thought you'd been slipping off the track, I would have said something."

"Okay," she says.

"Which I'm about to do now. About this expedition of yours."

"Yes?"

"I'm frightened about you going up there."

"Hey. You brought me to that psychic. So she gives me this piece of information and now you want me to disregard it."

"You don't know what she meant. You don't know if it's the same lake. And even if it is, you don't know what form of Taylor's presence she saw. You're envisioning her alive and maybe that's not what Sheila saw. And even if she is alive — I don't want to sound harsh, but you can't still imagine any sort of happy, carefree reunion, can you? Something where the two of you dash across some field of wildflowers toward each other, into a mad embrace and all is forgiven. No harm, no foul. Forgive and forget."

Chris considers for a moment, then says, "I want an end. A happy ending would certainly be preferable, but at this point I'll take what I can get."

That night, for a treat, Renny takes Chris to one of their old favorite haunts, the Asian ladies spa out on Montrose. Chris suspects that something is up.

They shower and scrub themselves pink in the Western-style stalls.

Further along the wall, the Asian women sit on tiny plastic stools and lather themselves and each other, then rinse off with handheld hoses. In the far corner, a woman lying face-down on an ancient leather-topped massage table is being scrubbed with a heavy brush by a Korean attendant, a small woman with overdeveloped arms.

Chris and Renny watch while they sit, sequentially, first in the massive whirlpool, then the hot bath, then the cold one, Renny positioning herself so the bladelike waterfall beats an icy guillotine of pleasure on the knotted muscles in the back of her neck. Then she continues to watch the scrubbing while Chris watches her, her all-over booth tan lightened a few shades under the surface of the water, her still nearly perfect body enhanced by this sybaritic setting, where Renny can languidly display herself in an indirectly sexual way, which makes her presence all the more arousing to Chris.

It's not until they're alone together in the steam room, flattened by the oppressive wet heat, pressing like a hand down from the dripping ceiling, that Renny finally works up to her subject. There's someone she's been seeing. As she listens to Renny's confession, Chris hazily realizes that the frequency of nights they've been spending together has tapered off a bit.

This new woman might really be important, she tells Chris. It has the look of "something kind of possibly big." Which doesn't mean she and Chris have to stop seeing each other altogether, nothing that drastic.

Chris jolts with a little surge of atavistic jealousy, but then can gradually tell from Renny's tone that this announcement isn't really serious, only a little test. Renny wants to gauge Chris's response. If she demonstrates enough interest, Renny's insecurities will be assuaged and this new woman will disappear. She won't have to even be given a name, she will simply be absent from future conversations and Renny will resume stopping by and calling with her previous frequency. It is in Chris's power in this particular moment to make this woman vanish. She stops to consider if this is what she wants. Knowing there's no real future for her and Renny, she should gracefully let her go, to whomever. It's only fair. But she has become ruthless, she knows it. Fair is far behind her now. Better times still a ways off, she thinks, around a sharp, obscured corner. And so just now she would like to keep Renny around, close by, part of the small present tense she has constructed. With this understanding, and seeing that they are alone and enveloped in thick vapors, that it is late and they are probably the last customers of the evening and will probably not be disturbed here, Chris rolls over and extends a foot, running a row of toes casually between Renny's thighs.

She still wakes every day before dawn. Even though the days are moving toward the longest of the year, she still manages to beat the light. When Taylor first disappeared, all those weeks back, Chris was hurled into the darkness by dreams of fire or flight which slammed her heart against the inside wall of her chest. Now she is just suddenly completely awake, okay enough, but in the middle of everyone else's night. Knowing the clinical signs of a restless soul, she worries. When she mentions her sleeplessness to Audrey, though, she is peppily dismissive. They're on the phone; their friendship — because of geography and the general harried quality of both their lives — has devolved to one conducted almost entirely through phone calls.

"You just have to roll with insomnia," Audrey tells her. "I'm up all the time. I wake from dreams about explosives, so obvious and boring."

"I know I'm practically the chairperson for the Committee for Everyone in the World to Come Out, but, gender aside, do you think maybe you ought to wait a bit before you throw everything up for grabs, at least until you two are out of heat? You know, see what you are to each other when your temperatures go back to normal."

"No, even when the dust settles, I'm still going to love her. I can tell. She's the one. It's like I've been waiting my whole life for her and didn't know it until she showed up. It's not a piece of information I can back away from."

Chris doesn't say anything.

"At any rate, one thing I can help you with is getting through the nights. I've got it down to a science. Here's where cable really comes through for you. I see tons of Deborah Kerr movies, William Holden movies. Movies no one saw even when they came out forty years ago. You know — she thinks they're supposed to meet under the big clock and he thinks she said by the rose garden and they just miss each other, and then spend the rest of their lives feeling totally rejected.

You can watch, too. Or you can listen to Marianne Faithfull CDs. I'll lend you a couple. Or you can call me. Anytime. I'm probably up."

After this conversation, Chris is okay with being awake before the rest of the world joins her. She takes Bud out for long walks in the waning moonlight, smokes and drinks Snapple and ruminates, reads Jane Austen.

This morning, though, there is an urgency to the waking. At 4:31 her eyes were closed and she was sound asleep; at 4:32, her eyes are open, her thoughts laser-focused. Taylor must have left some documentation behind. Chris has just overlooked it. If she was troubled in the way Leigh described, she must have set her thoughts down somewhere. But there's no journal; Chris looked everywhere, all through Taylor's drawers and shelves here and down at her *Transit* darkroom. All she found were ledgers and paid bills, a few unilluminating letters and postcards from vacationing friends having a wonderful time, wishing she were there — the generic dust of an unexamined life.

But this morning, in this predawn epiphany, it comes to her with a soft click. She pulls on jeans and a T-shirt, tells Bud, "Come on. We're going for a ride."

The darkroom, having languished vacant these past months — held in suspension for Taylor's return by a surprisingly generous and optimistic MarySarah — has gathered up a musty accumulation of airlessness and neglect. Lower, more occult life forms — spores and motes — have taken over in the absence of a human constantly pushing them back, tamping them down. Coming in, she thinks of anthropologists moving away the stone, entering the chamber of a pyramid.

Everything is as it appeared when she came here weeks back, and discovered the negatives of Stéphane. Now she is certain there's another discovery to be made. Taylor's laptop, gray and folded down like a flat tool case, but still plugged in, sits squarely in the middle of the old Formica dinette table Taylor used as a desk. It's been here all the time, in full view. Chris just wasn't seeing it properly. She flips it open and toggles the power switch in the back, then watches the screen as the computer boots itself to life.

Taylor's files are a mess, but pretty straightforward — "Accounts

P," "Accounts R," "Neg Directory," "Games." What she is looking for turns out to be amazingly easy to find. Amid these folders is a floating document titled "Real Life." The document, when it's opened, scrolls down to nearly sixty pages. Only when it is laid open before her does Chris pause, hesitant in the face of making such a major invasion. Still, she doesn't bother making excuses to herself before beginning to read.

She sees after only a few entries, which start late last year, that, like most journals, this one is a sad and tortured chronicle, a downhill run, embarrassing for the raw, unprocessed quality of its material, a catalogue of internal roiling dumped wholesale onto the hard drive.

Some of the concerns are almost adolescent. Taylor (who Chris always thought was just naturally thin, didn't care much about food) seems to have been obsessed with her weight.

> 11.28
> 137. Chips. Chocolate.

Later,

> 12.12
> 131. Thighs.

Leigh seems to have been right, about Taylor constantly testing her attractiveness.

> 1.7
> Hit on N at dinner. So stupid. Totally obvious. Totally shot down. I must have come off as totally drooling. Some hag at an old-dyke bar, Sansabelt slacks/white shoes, asking does she want to slow-dance to Frank Sinatra?

Who, Chris wonders, is N? What dinner? Chris combs her memories for dinners in January, for Nancys or Nells, but can't come up with anything.

A few pages on, she spots herself in the text. She is not referred to as Chris or Christine, or C, but as Snow. As though she is a colleague of Taylor's in some college history department, a fellow explorer on a Himalayan expedition.

2.10

> Snow distant. I wanted to make love. She pretended not to
> notice. Turned away. Wrapped up in herself, her Important
> Work.

Again, Chris scrambles around in her memory for this instance,
but can't find it. This entry seems so foreign to her experience of
them as a couple. If anything, she thought she was always the pur-
suer, Taylor only by turns receptive. She punches in F I N D and asks
for Snow. Some of the entries are maddeningly opaque.

3.6

> Snow unexpectedly kind.

The most notable aspect of the entries about Chris, though, is
their scarcity. They make up a minimal shadow text to a frenetic life
Taylor was apparently living in some universe parallel to the one they
inhabited together. With Snow and her infrequent, unexpected kind-
nesses. This tandem life seems to have had some actual, real-world
elements — some nettling professional interactions, but mostly personal ones, and these were mostly passes and failed passes. Which are
laid out in blunt, pulp-novel terms.

2.12

> Went with P to her new condo, still under construction.
> Drywall and plywood flooring. Against the wall. She wanted
> it, so . . .

Further on, there's a list of women's names, just first names, some
Chris doesn't recognize, others who, alarmingly, seem to be friends
of theirs, girlfriends of friends. One, Mandy, is a therapist colleague
of Chris's who stayed with them for a weekend when she was in for a
conference. After each name there is a mark — an asterisk, a check.
She supposes this tally can only be a score sheet, and ponders the
code briefly before deciding she probably doesn't really want to
crack it.

The person delineated by this journal isn't a total stranger. The
language and self-deprecating tone are Taylor's in spades. And it
wasn't as though Chris didn't suspect the womanizing (although

she couldn't have guessed at its range). But the compulsion behind it, the ferocious insecurity and relentless self-testing are pretty astonishing.

The rhetoric of journals — she knows from those clients have brought into therapy with them — seldom paints anyone to her best advantage. Almost no one fills these sorts of pages out of elation or triumph, or out of a need to express global hopes for peace or disease cures. Rather they are typically the small endless broodings of the depressed. Collections of petty grievances, slights perceived. Most typically they follow bad love affairs and end abruptly when the breach is mended, or the writer becomes involved with someone new.

Chris tries to factor this understanding into her appraisal of the creator of this particular journal, to consider that what she has pried open is the lid to Taylor's very private can of worms. She tries to not sit in judgment of someone she loves on the basis of a document its author assumed no one would ever see. Still, it is hard not to rue a little all the hours she spent trying to puzzle out a partner whose silences she assumed held volumes, while it appears they mostly held worries about getting heavy and not making every woman she met.

And while it appears that Taylor did love Chris, it seems to have been, as Leigh made clear, in an idealized, abstract way held aloft and separate from her constant struggles in an inner landscape of harsh elements. If the journal were reconstructed as a Renaissance religious painting, Chris would be the Madonna, standing benevolently in the middle of a wide azure sky, arms outstretched over the hunched martyr figure of a flayed Taylor.

No real partnership, she realizes from what she's reading here, was happening between them, or was ever going to. The house, the dog, the friends, the plans, were all just an obscuring gloss over the truth implicit in these on-screen pages. Chris has been sharing a life with someone who was going it determinedly alone.

This realization affects her less than she would have expected. As she scrolls through the journal, the clinician in her moves forward in the chair, observing Taylor's decline as though she were a case history rather than an actual person. It seems even the gone Taylor, even the ghost she has left behind, is growing fainter, more transparent.

She sees now that Taylor's disappearance began before she left.

Even when they were still together, she was already beginning to vaporize.

• • •

Taylor is late tonight, not just a few minutes, or half an hour. It's nearly eight by the time she gets home, feigning fatigue, but looking exhilarated even under the weight of her camera equipment; she has a side job on a fashion shoot for Carson's this week — winter coats for the fall catalogue, the weather not cooperating. It is in the eighties and the models are wilting is all she has told Chris.

This morning, Chris offered to fix dinner, and when she got home she started, then, somehow sensing that Taylor wasn't yet in the channel of arrival, turned off the flame under the garlic bits, allowing them to grow cold and oil-saturated in the pan, the chicken breast limp and translucent, filming over on the cutting board.

When Taylor finally comes through the door, she offers no excuses and Chris asks no questions, doesn't beg an apology. They have moved beyond these mechanisms of defusing.

"Do you want me to help?" Taylor says instead of saying anything of consequence. She nods toward the counter.

"Are you hungry?" Chris says.

"Not really. You?"

"I made a sandwich a while ago so I'm okay," Chris says.

"I'll cook the chicken up for Bud, then," Taylor says coolly. They are both so very cool at this by now. Chris would never be so uncool as to press Taylor, who would only come up with excuses about how late the shoot ran, how there wasn't a pay phone in sight, how she forgot to wear her watch today and wasn't even really aware of the time. Instead Chris adds this piece to the slag heap of all the missed dinners, forgotten events on their social calendar, all the cartons of milk or bunches of broccoli Taylor promised to pick up on her way home but which remained unbought in the supermarkets Taylor never got to. She's not terrible all the time, just often enough that Chris has begun to think there's a message being telegraphed.

In return, Chris will shower, then leave a wet towel on the

207

bed, on Taylor's side if she can arrange it. Park her car just a little too far over in the garage so Taylor won't be able to squeeze in her Cherokee. Small, pathetic maneuvers, really. And she is only getting back. Taylor does all the real getting; the war has been defined by her conventions. Chris remembers from high school that if the quiz asked a cause for whatever dispute or skirmish between whatever countries, "ice-free port" was your best shot at a correct answer. She can't see now, where their ice-free port is located. But something is being fought over, and though she can't see what it is, she suspects she's losing.

For her, winning would be having Taylor back as she was in the beginning, when Chris was the prize, the ice-free port Taylor had to fight for. Now Chris has been moved to another position, but she can't see where that might be, and can't ask Taylor, who she suspects doesn't really know herself.

Sometimes Chris — professionally arbitrating and conciliatory — is herself left with a sharp, shameful impulse to slap Taylor across the face, draw a handprint of flush, an expression of astonishment and acknowledgment of Chris's presence.

But she would never do this, and understands that Taylor will remain unastonished, and probably vaguely contemptuous of Chris for failing to astonish her.

■ ■ ■

RACHEL is having a cookout for the Fourth of July.

"Just her family, a few friends from work — they're okay, I've met them," Daniel tells her. "She'd really like you to come." They're both between appointments, slipping in a late breakfast at The Bagel, cheese omelets, sliced tomatoes. It's an old-timey thing from the early days of their practices, before they had such full schedules. They are rarely able to find the time anymore.

Chris notices from across the booth that his eyebrows are growing in; short, bristly black hairs are sprouting up across the bridge of his nose. She takes this as a sign, akin to a slight weight gain, that he is relaxing into his new relationship, that he has left behind the hard cinder track of dating where his best foot always had to be in forward position.

"Thanks anyway," she tells him, "but I don't think I'm really up to meeting a yardful of new people."

"We're getting our mothers out of the home for the day. They'll be gaga in their wheelchairs. Hers drools; mine talks almost total gibberish. It's terrible."

"Well, that's an inducement."

"I just meant the standards for sparkling conversation won't be all that high."

Chris tries to formulate another, firmer line of excuses.

"Okay," Daniel says, then adds in a freighted way, "Rachel has a sister." The little silence that follows pulls a hundred coal-loaded cars. Chris has to smile.

"Have you seen her, this sister?"

"Hildegarde."

"Oh, come on. It can't be Hildegarde."

"She can't help that. It's a family thing. She got named after a respected aunt, great-aunt, somebody. She goes by Hildy. She's cool. She's a singer."

"A singer." Chris conjures up a hefty diva in a breastplate and horned headdress in the middle of something Wagnerian.

"A jazz singer." Daniel adjusts the fantasy. "She's an interesting person."

"And cute, you were saying."

"I'd say striking."

"Oh boy, I get exhausted just thinking about meeting someone striking and interesting. A performer, too. I'd have to measure up. I'd have to pretend I get out to clubs at night. I'd have to get some decent underwear. Just to gird my loins."

"Think about it," he says, sidestepping her resistance.

Chris nods, but has already decided she won't go.

But then it's Monday, the day before the holiday, and she's coming off a hideous weekend. Bud has fleas and she has spent two days setting off aerosol bombs throughout the house and washing bedspreads and dipping poor Bud, putting him in an herbal flea collar he hates; it makes him smell like Mr. Eucalyptus. This small scourge comes on top of a summer cold that's finally ebbing as it goes into its second week. She needs to stop feeling like a minor-league Job. She's longing to unstoop her shoulders. Years ago when she got the tiny rose and dagger that still resides on her left thigh, there was in the back room of the tattoo parlor a picture of a woman's shaved pubic area with a spray of stars inked across it. When she inquired, the tattoo guy told her the woman had come in late one night, not nearly as drunk as you might think, and said, "I just got me a divorce and I want you to tattoo shooting stars across my pussy." Metaphorically, this is the state of liberation and release Chris would like to achieve.

The new underwear idea is as close as she can get. She goes down from the health club that afternoon to the Victoria's Secret she has always made fun of and buys some underpants that are electric blue and shiny and split at the crotch. She doesn't want anyone to see these — ever — but would like to stand the next day around the grill knowing she has them on underneath her nondescript shorts. A sexual Clark Kent.

She feels giddy and ridiculous. It seems unlikely that a jazz singer named Hildegarde is going to pan out into someone who will be able to catch Chris, break her fall. She can't imagine who *would* fill the bill now, be right in enough ways. Taylor was right. And now apparently, even she was wrong. If Taylor was wrong, anyone else would be wronger yet. This logic seems both crackpot and at the same time unassailable.

Rachel lives in a three-flat in Andersonville with a scrap of a back-yard that has a peculiar garden element to it — George Washington Carver behind-the-laboratory border plots erupting with gnarled rooted growths and vines. A pumpkin here, an eggplant there. An iso-lated cluster of asparagus stalks poking out in yet another otherwise barren patch. There's an ominous, odiferous compost heap alongside the garage.

Chris looks around at the gathering of maybe a dozen people and thinks how many times in how many Chicago summers she has walked into this same setting. The guys in stretched-neck T-shirts and baggy-butt Bermudas, the women in sundresses, the straps sliding off red, freckled shoulders. If the event is gay, the men are a minimal presence or absent altogether, the women wear the Bermudas, roll up the sleeves of their T-shirts.

The grill is always parked on a square of concrete at the foot of the back stairs, always wildly smoking, singeing the bratwursts rolling around on the grate. The background is filled with drift from a ball game on a distant radio, the fanning of a sprinkler in the yard next-door, the rattle and chunk of beers being pulled from the ice chest.

This replication of experience is both wearying and comforting. To-day the weariness gets overwhelmed by gratitude for the familiarity of the scene; she's happy not to have to be entering a jai alai fronton or the first session of a modern dance class in which she has impulsively enrolled. Someplace with drills and rituals she is completely igno-rant about. Nothing here is likely to provide a negative surprise, or require anything more from her than going through a small set of polite social motions.

The aged mothers are on the patchy grass in side-by-side wheel-chairs, seemingly unaware of each other's presence. The guys are magnetized to the Weber, manly grillers. There is a small cluster of women sitting in a rough semicircle of folding chairs out on the lawn, with taco chips and a bowl of Mexican five-layer dip on a low table in front of them. The sister is not among them. She is playing badmin-ton with two small children, a boy and a girl. Chris actually spotted the sister before she noticed the peculiar garden or the smoking grill or the invalid mothers or any of the other guests. What Leigh refers to as "gaydar" is a powerful tool, a dowsing rod to negotiate the ground of a predominantly heterosexual world.

Daniel was accurate in his assessment; she is striking, although not in a way that would translate directly into attractive. Sort of an off-center young Katharine Hepburn. Rachel's fair colleen looks angled off. You'd pick them for sisters, but only if the rest of the lineup were composed of short, rounded Sicilian girls. Like Rachel, she has an odd nose, slightly too large for her face, teeth that expose themselves as a little crooked when she smiles. There's a comic quality to her expression. She is not a woman who would immediately inspire romantic notions.

She does have a strong, confident presence, though — probably, Chris supposes, gained from all those sets in front of tough audi-ences. She's at ease with her small opponents, with being a much worse player than they are. She keeps screwing up, then laughs at herself, which gives her big points in Chris's book.

She has also spotted Chris. The radar works both ways. Chris caught a flicker of recognition a little while back, when the birdie went out of bounds and the sister stood waiting for the kids to retrieve it. It is another half hour, though, before the traffic patterns of the party allow them to arrive casually in each other's presence.

Chris has brought along Bud, who is an extremely amiable visitor. He loves hopping into the car and going to someone's — anyone's — house, and whines at the front door until the host answers the bell, then toddles in grinning like mad, fully expecting that all will be happy to see him, which they invariably are. She thinks he might be losing track of Taylor. He seems jollier, is back chasing squirrels on his walks. At home he's gnawing the rawhide strips he abandoned to corners during the first weeks of Taylor's absence. Chris takes him for a drive weekend mornings now, sometimes up to a small beach she's found in Rogers Park, trying to establish a new, smaller wolf pack.

He stands now next to Chris while she stands next to herself (as she does so much of the time these days) and watches herself flirt — but just lightly, nothing focused or intense — with this likably goofy woman. Who turns out to be serious about her music. Chris now remembers seeing a review of her in *The Reader*. She is able to talk about performing in a way that doesn't make her sound at all like the girls on the pay phones in the locker room of Chris's health club.

Chris isn't nearly as good at this "what I do" line of chat. She always hopes people won't ask her. She has never been able to find quite the right tone about her work. She worries she sounds either too flip — like a TV sitcom shrink with a collection of wacky clients, like Bob Newhart — or, worse, as though she thinks she's Albert Schweitzer. Marie Curie. The Important Helping Professional. But Hildy seems to be interested anyway, and so Chris doesn't feel as though she's messing up, and that it would be okay if she did.

"Do you carry their stories around in a little briefcase in your head all the time, or can you leave them all behind in the office when you shut the door and go home?"

"Briefcase in the head," Chris says.

"Do you get to do them some good?"

"Sometimes. Sometimes I'll even have a stretch where I think I'm doing them all some good, but that doesn't usually last long. Most of the time, I feel I'm batting around five hundred."

"When I write songs, I try to plug into what's underneath our little struggles. A lot of being human seems pretty comic, but I guess there isn't much comedy in your end of things."

"Occasionally," Chris says. "Of course, you try to keep from that point of view. It's not the absolute best response to crack up in a

session. Everyone wants to be taken seriously. Their problems —
even though they'd like to be rid of them — are still part of their identity." She stops. Something has occurred to her. "Did your sister tell
you about my . . . situation?"

Hildy nods. "A little. Are you doing okay?"

"Oh, I don't think so. Probably not. I can't even imagine what okay
would be anymore."

"Hey. You're standing here, having a beer. It's a perfect summer
day. I brought my world-famous potato salad. You can have some
with your bratwurst. You're talking to a new person — me. I mean, if
you took a limited view, that could add up to okay, I'd think."

As she talks, Hildy crouches down to scratch Bud's chest in a
languorous way that has a hypnotic effect on him and draws Chris's
notice to her hands, which are big and great — beat-up, one nail
blackened, the knuckles on the left one scraped and scabbed over.
(She supports her unlucrative artistic pursuits by working for a house
painter.) Chris stares down at them, probably for a little too long. The
flash that comes up is these hands pinning her down to keep her from
moving too much at a critical moment.

She notices Hildy noticing her noticing her hands and decides it's
time to excuse herself. They don't make a plan to get together, don't
exchange phone numbers. Chris goes to get some food, then Hildy
is helping her sister clean up, then Chris gets snagged by Robert
Decker, a very nice guy whom she and Daniel went to school with.
He has taken a corporate turn in recent years and works for McDonald's, testing colors and seating schemes and upholstery prints for
their ability to make people hungry for hamburgers. "Conducive
ambience studies" is what these are called. He talks to her about this
line of work with a straight face; she tries to listen with an equally
serious expression. His annual salary is probably more than hers and
Daniel's combined.

When she can escape him, she looks around but can't see Hildy
and doesn't want to go trailing after her. So she just fades with a quick
goodbye to Daniel, a guest thank-you to Rachel.

In the car, she asks Bud, "So what did you think? She was a good
scratcher, no?"

It wasn't a drumroll meeting, nothing like the night she met Taylor, or even the time Renny showed up with her first FedEx delivery. Both of those times, everything went off inside her as though she was standing in the dollar slots section of Caesar's Palace, the moment rich and ripe and jangling around and through her with the promise of payoff. This moment was quieter, like sitting at a three-card draw table with an already good hand.

She's not sure if she'll ask Daniel for Hildy's number, or if Hildy will take it upon herself to call, or if the two of them will just let things go. It's not exactly Hildy, or this afternoon, or any big imaginings for the immediate future that make Chris turn the radio up a little on the way home, flipping the fingers of her free hand through the sunroof to catch the breeze. It's just that she experiences, for the first time in such a long while, the small stirrings of possibility, of the unknown holding not just grim secrets, but nice surprises.

"You should be getting out," Rosario advises Chris. She has somehow found out about Chris's situation with respect to Taylor, has been coyly alluding to it for several sessions. (She has cop friends; that's the most likely grapevine.) "Meeting new people," she adds, in case she hasn't made her point.

Chris nods noncommittally.

Rosario peers at her, as though Chris is a Magic 8 Ball, floating up an answer. "Ah. Yes?" Rosario leans forward. "Someone nice has come along?"

"Someone maybe nice, yes. It's pretty early on," Chris says, and in the same instant knows it's time to close down the subject.

"My advice is take out a little insurance. If you've found someone special, don't risk her slipping away. Don't trust everything to the fates is what I'm saying."

"I'm not sure I understand."

"There's a very nice product for this part, the beginning. I can get some from my aunts, on the South Side."

"Are we talking animal entrails?"

Rosario waves Chris's suspicions and squeamishness away with a flutter of crimson nails. "This is a high-class product. Stockbrokers use it. Stewardesses. It is very subtle. Easy, too. Just a powder. You make a nice dinner for this girl, right? It has to be something a little strong, like beans with chipotle peppers. You mix a little in — but just on her plate. Then she will come to you like magic." She snaps her fingers to illustrate the surefire effectiveness of this charm.

Chris tries to imagine this adventurous scene. Hildy the jazz singer sitting innocently at her dining room table sipping a glass of cabernet while Chris lingers in the kitchen stirring a love potion into an improbable bean dinner.

"Thanks anyway," Chris says, trying to sound appreciative. "I think I'll just let the dice roll however they will on this one."

Rosario is hurt. "So go ahead. Do it the hard way. You should trust me more, though. You should've told me about your big problem, for instance. I could be a helping hand there. But of course, bringing a person back is a more difficult matter. Not just a little powder for that sort of thing. You would have to make a time commitment. Nine midnights."

Three days later, Chris gets a call from Sikora.

"We've found her vehicle," he says. "The Cherokee. In some woods by a lake."

"In Wisconsin," Chris says. She was right all along.

"Michigan," Sikora corrects her.

"Is this . . . well . . . a good sign?"

"We'll get back to you on that," he tells her.

THE CHEROKEE had been left running, eventually ran out of gas, and then just sat silently through the spring, under a growing cover of the trees where Taylor had parked. The police in the area were able to determine, from some wildflowers crushed beneath the truck's oversize tires, that it was abandoned there in late April or early May, soon after she left home.

Her camera bag was on the back seat, a Michigan road map and an empty bag of mesquite chips on the passenger seat, a half-drunk Coke in the pop-out holder in the dash. It appears she brought nothing else with her, planned no long trip.

The sheriff's office in the rural area is dragging the lake today. Desta has flown out from Vermont, rented a car and driven up alone. Chris couldn't; she couldn't force herself to be there to see whatever they pull out of the silty bottom of the lake.

Until now, she has been going through the motions. Now she's no longer even sure what the motions might be. She is in the middle of her day. She saw clients at eight, nine, then eleven. She's with her two o'clock now, Clarissa Sims, who has backslid a bit. The pale inside of her left arm, which she eventually reveals to Chris, is patterned with tiny dark red dots, minuscule scabs where she has pricked herself with a safety pin.

"I try not to give in to it," she's saying, "but the pressure just builds and there I am again. And then afterward, I feel relieved for a little while. Then I hate myself for being so weak."

"How do you mean exactly, about the pressure building up? Can you describe how that goes?" Chris is trying to stay focused on Clarissa's answer, all the while tuned to the background, to the sporadic trilling of the phone in her back office, set to two rings. Then her voice mail silently sucks up the message. She imagines each one to be the worst; she can feel the worst message coming. If it's not already here, it's on the way, hissing through the air toward her — small and specific, but with terrible momentum, an arrow with a poisoned tip.

When she checks, though, the first call is benign, from Hildegarde, the singer, lead in the lineup of Chris's romantic future. Ordinarily, she would feel a little flutter of relief; she is always relieved when they call first. There's something over the weekend, Hildy says. A performance artist, but funny, not at all pretentious. Maybe Chris would like to go. Her voice sounds nervous. Chris doesn't bother replaying the message to hear *how* nervous, which she would ordinarily do automatically.

The next two spots are occupied by clients. Adele Sidelman canceling the four o'clock appointment for her and her husband. Chris tries to infer from her tone if the cancellation has to do with their fractious marriage, or with their couples therapy, or with a gallery opening.

The second client call is from Nida Louis, who sounds minorly hysterical. Her husband has found some "incriminating evidence." Buzzing latex sex toys flip into Chris's imagination. A tube of K-Y jelly discovered in the nightstand drawer. Randy homemade videos.

There's nothing more in the voice mail, but the next message will be the terrible one. Chris knows this.

She doesn't know how long she has been sitting here, cheating at solitaire, sitting cross-legged at the end of the sofa where her clients

usually sit, across from the chair from which she guides and circum-
scribes what happens in this room. Now, though, nothing is in her
control.

The slow summer dusk is accumulating outside the windows, cut
by an orange glow from the neon sign on the front of the theater
company across the street. Cars struggle through the traffic below,
the immediate world going about its business.

The next time she notices, it is deeply dark in the room. She can't
remember the separate thoughts that have occupied the passing
hours. Or perhaps they have all been the same thought.

The silence in the room is underlaid with theatergoers milling
and chatting in a low buzz across the street. Intermission. The play,
Wittgenstein at Breakfast, is popular in spite of its title. It has been
running forever and draws quite a crowd. Chris imagines another, a
former or future version of herself, free enough of mind to be absorbed into a drama played out on a stage.

The door to the office clicks open, accompanied by a small jingle
of keys. Daniel. He comes in and sits down beside her.

"They found her," he guesses.

"Not yet. I'm trying to prepare myself for when they do."

"Abandoning the car doesn't necessarily mean —" He starts again
from another angle. "I mean Taylor was dramatic. If she had disappearing in mind, she'd do a dramatic job of it. Leave the car running
and walk off leaving us all to wonder."

"Maybe," Chris says. "I keep playing the call in my mind. Sikora
will be wanting the name of Taylor's dentist. She'll have been in that
lake a while. They'll have to make an identification by the teeth.
They'll want her records, to see if they have a match."

Daniel doesn't prompt her to say anything and for a long time, she
doesn't. Then does. "I should have flown up there."

"No," he says.

"Just to be there. And to see it. The lake. To see if it looks the same
as in my dreams."

"You can go another time. Not now."

She wraps her arms around herself. She feels a sudden flush of
cold, blood turning to icy slush as it makes its way through her veins.

"You'll get past this," Daniel says. "If she's dead, or even if she just
stays gone."

Chris glances over at the solitaire layout, moves a red jack onto a black queen, then says, "Oh, I know. That's the saddest part, isn't it? I'll go out with Rachel's sister, or somebody else. We'll see a piece of performance art and laugh about it afterward, find a tiny patch of affinity to start out on. I'll go to bed with her and fall into a chasm, but not a bottomless one. I'll finish with Renny. I'll look at that as progress. I'll have you and Rachel over, fix dinner out of a new cookbook, a dish Taylor never got to try, but that won't occur to me. I'll have a harrowing new client; there'll be a crisis. Or my father will get sick. I'll go a couple of days without thinking about Taylor. Never a week, but when the thoughts come, they'll be less electric. She'll become part of everything that's happened to me; she'll slide out of being part of who I am. That'll be the saddest moment, and I'll miss it when it happens. I'll be snorkeling in the Bahamas, or buying a T-shirt at the Gap. I'll miss it completely."

She looks over at him. "What can we say to each other? Now. I think we shouldn't even try. I don't want to hear what we come up with, what cheap clichés." She stops for a moment. "Poor Taylor. Poor me. The ferocious solitude and isolation of it all. Souls sealed away in separate bubbles. We're reaching out to each other, but fuck us."

He puts an arm awkwardly around Chris and pulls her toward him. She notices that he smells like a lime, a new aftershave.

On the street beyond the windows, the play is letting out. The sound is pure release, a soft, social explosion of chat and laughter as the audience emerges, disassembles into its individual elements, transforms itself into separate people heading for their cars, for coffee, heading toward some version of home.

"Oh, they're going to be impressed with her teeth," Chris says into the soft cotton of Daniel's polo shirt.

He pulls back to look at her.

"The police," she says. "When they get those X rays. Taylor grew up in some early fluoride area. She never had a cavity. Her teeth were perfect. Perfect."

Knowing about Taylor's teeth, their perfection, offers Chris a small comfort, a slight fingertip hold on the sleeve of someone who has taken the air, parted it, and walked through.